POISONED PEDIGREE

Mystery Novels by G. G. Vandagriff

Alex and Briggie Series

Cankered Roots

Of Deadly Descent

Tangled Roots

Other

The Arthurian Omen

POISONED PEDIGREE

A Mystery

G. G. VANDAGRIFF

DESERET
BOOK

SALT LAKE CITY, UTAH

Library of Congress Cataloging-in-Publication Data

Vandagriff, G. G.
  Poisoned pedigree / G.G. Vandagriff.
    p.   cm.
  ISBN 978-1-59038-960-7 (paperbound)
  I. Title.
PS3572.A427P65 2008
813'.54—dc22   2008023173

Printed in the United States of America
Publishers Printing

10   9   8   7   6   5   4   3   2   1

TO

MY SISTER

Buffy Haglund

A GREAT EXAMPLE AND A POSITIVE DELIGHT IN MY LIFE

Acknowledgments

To Alana Tomkins, who waited for every chapter, giving positive advice and encouragement.

To Kathleen Petty, who always gives me the straight scoop.

To Ginny Leavitt, my real-life inspiration for the character of Susan Cox (except that she has more children).

To Anna Stone, for lending me her husband as inspiration for a character and for being an enthusiastic mentor and reader.

To my editor and friend, Suzanne Brady, for her dedication to Alex and Briggie through the years.

To Jana Erickson, for her vision and faith in me.

To my husband, who adores my Briggie.

A Word about Timing

This series was begun in 1993. We have advanced only one year in the characters' lives—to 1994. In those pre-Internet times, genealogical research was done the hard way.

For I the Lord thy God am a jealous God, visiting the

iniquity of the fathers upon the children unto the third and

fourth generation of them that hate me.

Deuteronomy 5:9

Prologue

Southwest Missouri
1857

The big one they called Jake was after him. He had been running so long through the forest that he could hardly draw air into his overtaxed lungs. Fighting for each breath, he heard the coon hounds barking as they chased him through the late autumn trees. If only there were some place to hide! As it was, the crackle of the fallen leaves made his passage under the old oaks seem as loud as shotgun fire.

"Son of Satan!" Jake shouted. He didn't sound winded at all.

Jake's quarry found himself at the bottom of a hill. In the moonlight, he saw his companion starting down the hill to his aid. "Run!" he cried. "They're after us! Get out of here!"

Then, not waiting to see if the man obeyed him, he drew another breath into his exhausted lungs. They felt like they were on fire. Heading for the creek bed, he hoped the hounds would lose his scent if he could just make it to the water.

He hoped Claire was going to be okay. He had no illusions about

1

his fate if he were captured. They lynched people like him in this part of the country.

When the hounds reached him, he was stumbling, his legs and chest burning. They jumped all over him, barking ferociously for their master. Nipping at his frock coat, they encircled him.

Jake was advancing steadily through the underbrush. He squeezed off a shot from his shotgun. "You give me those gold plates and maybe I'll let you go!" Laughing raucously, he shot again.

His hapless victim felt the shot pierce his flesh like a million angry darts, and he fell to the ground. He couldn't move. Jake stood over him, leering, his stringy beard and hair surrounding his puffy red face. Playing with the thick hemp rope in his hands, he said, "Now we're gonna have us some fun."

Chapter One

Trotter's Bridge, Missouri
1994

A large middle-aged woman in a faded pink housedress sat in her rocking chair on the porch. It was spring and her great-grandmother's dogwood was spreading its milky blooms like a mist in the naked forest. Smiling, she rocked her chair and turned the yellowing pages of a scrapbook. The edges nearly crumbled in her hands. It was a record of many things that were forgotten by most people. It also contained what she thought of as her special charge. She was the Keeper.

"Yes," she sighed to herself. "I remember that." Her spotted hands caressed the newspaper clipping rubber-cemented to the page she had turned to. Rhonda Moffit's wedding. It had been such a perfect day. Rhonda had looked like a peach. But, of course, her mother hadn't been there. She never did like Rod McHenry. He, like so many in Trotter's Bridge, was tainted with the bad blood. Tragic that Serena Moffit had died before she could help with her twin grandchildren. They had been left with Rod's mother while Rhonda worked at the

3

chicken factory to support the family. On the facing page was Rod's obituary. He'd died in a bar fight.

Sighing with real sadness, the woman turned the page. Poor Rhonda. Who could've guessed she'd get that horrible disease? What was it? The one they called after the baseball player. Lou Gehrig.

Letting Rhonda go, she set down the scrapbook and picked up an even older one. A fragile religious tract, missing its first page, was stuck in with flour-and-water paste that was giving way. A man's white linen handkerchief, embroidered with the letter C, lay tucked beside it. She wondered sometimes whether she was the only one in living memory who recalled the wickedness that had started this record. Everyone concerned was long dead. Four generations had passed. Would the curse of the bad blood carry into the rising generation? Or would it, like the Bible said, end with the fourth generation? The poison had spread so far, had affected the lives of so many people.

That was the burden of the Keeper. Sooner or later you knew everything there was to know about everybody. And you worried. Some secrets were almost too heavy to bear.

Chapter Two

Kansas City
1994

The audience of ten thousand sat hushed in the humid spring night, straining to hear the fairylike balladeer. The eerie lyrics of "Guinevere" threaded their enchantment through the crowd. To Alex (short for Alexandra) Campbell, it seemed as if the amphitheater had been transported from Kansas City to the wild Cornish coast on an overcast day. There she and Stewart had once seen the remains of a castle, reputedly the birthplace of King Arthur.

Against an image of its jagged ruins, silhouetted by silver clouds and the sound of waves smashing two hundred feet below, Alex pictured Guinevere riding a white horse, bound for a tryst with Lancelot. She was cresting the hill now, reddish hair streaming behind her. Would he come? Would she be discovered by the king's guard?

A worm of discomfort worked in Alex's breast. For a moment she understood Guinevere's decision to abandon all that was familiar in favor of the passion that had overtaken her life.

Alex found she was twisting her hands together in her lap, biting her lip. *I'm impossibly suggestible,* she told herself as she glanced at the ginger-haired man next to her. All of Daniel's attention was fastened on the stage. Used to thinking of him as thoroughly down-to-earth, she was surprised by the look of total absorption on his face. An unexpected arrow of jealousy shot through her. The singer, Kerry McNee, meant something to him. She had given him these seats. She was his patient. And how much more?

Clearly a woman of enormous personal power, the performer was easily capable of swaying an audience as large as this—carrying them away on her voice as though it were some sort of magic carpet. But she was also fragile and vulnerable in a way that would appeal to Daniel.

Why do I care? She was engaged to Charles, for heaven's sake. Or was she turning into one of those women who had to have every man in orbit around her? What an unpleasant character defect! Or was it just that things had never really ended with Daniel? She and the man next to her had a history. She and Charles were just discovering each other—their history was in the making.

Applause exploded in the heavy stillness, taking her by surprise. Daniel had jumped to his feet. "Bravo!" he shouted. "Bravo!"

*   *   *

Alex found the idea of meeting Kerry McNee in person a little daunting. She was waiting with Daniel at a small table in the Italian trattoria the singer preferred when she came home to Kansas City. Its lights dim, its tables covered with heavy white linen, the small restaurant was quiet and intimate.

"Just how well do you know Kerry McNee?" Alex heard herself asking.

Daniel turned to face her, obviously gathering his thoughts from some distance away. "We were in college together. She was my first love." He smiled vaguely.

"Was it reciprocated?" she demanded before she could stop herself.

"Oh, yes." This time his smile was more present to the situation. "And as you've just seen, Kerry doesn't do anything halfway. There were scenes and reconciliations, etcetera. My college years were very turbulent, as you might imagine."

She couldn't. She simply couldn't imagine this side of Daniel. To her he had always represented sense, control, safety. It was Charles who was the romantic.

Clearing her throat, she inquired, "I thought there was something unethical about psychologists being in love with their patients."

He gave a half grin and twisted the stem of his water glass. "All that was over long ago."

Alex wondered. "Did she sing in those days?"

"Kerry's been singing all her life, I think. She's put every ounce of her passion into it. I'm worried she's burning out."

"She didn't sound burned out tonight. She was incredibly intense."

Daniel nodded, his eyes finally focusing on her face. "That's what I mean. She's growing so intense, I don't see how she can possibly sustain it."

"She's really tapped into the New Age phenomenon with all her Celtic stuff. Her CDs are selling in the millions." Alex toyed with her spoon. "Is McNee her real name?"

Green eyes lighting with laughter, Daniel teased, "Good old Alex. Already delving for the roots."

"It's just that she's so obviously Scots-Irish . . ."

"I know. She sings about the 'voices in her blood.'"

"Of course she does."

"Let's just say that I've always known her as McNee."

"But there's some doubt?"

"That's why you've been brought into the case, Alex. I'll let Kerry tell you about it." Abruptly, he sat back, surveying her with an avuncular air. "I only hope that this time you can keep out of trouble."

She was mildly indignant. "You make me sound like one of your incorrigible teenage patients."

He grinned again. "Admit it. Is there anything you like better than a good mystery?"

"All genealogists love mysteries. It's a prerequisite."

"All genealogists don't almost get themselves murdered three times in one year."

Alex shrugged. "As Briggie would say, 'We're not accountants.' Things don't always go according to plan."

"How is your esteemed colleague, by the way?"

"Fit as ever. Spending a lot of time at the ballpark."

"She's been trying to get Dad out to a Royals' game. He's managed to maintain his resistance so far, but I think it's just a matter of time."

"A hardened Cards fan like him?"

"The Cards haven't been the same since Whitey left."

At this point, a surprisingly tiny Kerry McNee made her entrance, her silver-blonde hair shining in the dim light like an aura. The plump maitre d', glowing with goodwill, escorted her to their table. Standing, Daniel kissed her cheek.

"Kerry, meet Alex. She's a fan."

"I sure am," Alex replied. Kerry's powerful persona and her proprietary actions towards Daniel winded Alex unexpectedly. But Daniel deserved some happiness, didn't he? Did she expect him to moon over her forever? Stifling whatever was rising in her, Alex held out her hand.

The singer took it and shook it briefly. She seemed weary. "It's good to meet you, Alex. Daniel has spoken of you."

Sitting down, she opened her menu. "Have you ordered?"

"We waited for you," Daniel told her.

*　　*　　*

"How much do you know about 'The Lady of Shalott'?" Kerry inquired over their cheesecake, fixing Alex with large blue eyes.

"You mean the Tennyson poem?"

"Yes."

Casting her mind back to a freshman English class, Alex tried to recall the lilting text. She'd actually memorized part of it.

> *There she weaves by night and day*
> *A magic web with colours gay.*
> *She has heard a whisper say*
> *A curse is on her if she stay*
> *To look down to Camelot.*

. . . .

The little singer brightened, suddenly animated.

> *And moving through a mirror clear*
> *That hangs before her all the year,*
> *Shadows of the world appear.*
> *There she sees the highway near*
> *Winding down to Camelot.*

. . . .

> *And sometimes through the mirror blue*
> *The knights come riding two and two:*
> *She hath no loyal Knight and true,*
> *The Lady of Shalott.*

Daniel leaned back in his chair and surveyed the two of them. "What's this all about?"

Moving a sheaf of hair off her shoulder, Kerry explained. "The Lady of Shalott lived on this island with a view of the road to Camelot. She was forbidden to look directly into Camelot, so she sat facing a mirror that reflected all its sights. She wove what she saw into a tapestry." Kerry's eyes took on a distant look. "This was all fine until she made the mistake of falling in love with Lancelot. The mirror was no longer good enough. She left her loom and went to look directly into reality. When the mirror cracked, she knew the curse had fallen upon her, so she got into a little boat, where she died just as it drifted into Camelot."

Daniel studied her, an eyebrow raised. Alex could feel the current of intimacy between them. "Lancelot seems to have wrought havoc with a number of ladies. You're the Lady of Shalott, I suppose?"

Forearms on the table, Kerry leaned toward him earnestly, "Isn't it obvious?"

"Kerry, it's only a poem . . ."

"A legend," she corrected. "Legends are powerful things, Daniel. They are woven out of elements that have always existed. That's why they play upon our hearts the way they do. There is something in all of us that recognizes eternal truths."

Startled, Alex heard her own words. She had said almost the same thing to Charles on the phone only yesterday. But she had been talking about the truths of the gospel.

"So what's so eternal about the Lady of Shalott?" he asked.

"The desire to want a life that's forbidden to us. It's like Eve and the apple. Like Romeo and Juliet."

" 'The grass is always greener . . .' "

"Exactly."

"And what is it you want so desperately?" Daniel asked softly.

Alex was growing embarrassed. Three was a crowd.

"A family," Kerry replied wistfully. "A husband. Children."

So was Daniel her Lancelot?

Taking a deep breath, the psychologist settled back in his chair, studying his patient. Then he looked at Alex. "Enter the genealogist."

"I don't understand," Alex said.

The singer turned to her, eyes bright, as though lit by some inner fire. "There's a curse on me, Alex. Just like the Lady of Shalott." Seeming to be satisfied by the look of shock that came over Alex's face, Kerry continued. "There's this woman in the town where I come from. She lives in a little old house in the middle of the forest. You can barely make your way through her books and papers. We call her a Keeper. It's a Scots-Irish thing. There's some sort of relationship between us, but I'm not exactly sure what it is. She told me when I was young that I must never think of marrying. She said there's bad blood in me." Kerry held up her left hand. The little finger wouldn't straighten. "This is the sign of it, apparently. It's an inherited trait that appears sporadically, but the Keeper says it always means that you are descended from those with bad blood. Neither of my parents has crooked fingers."

Alex couldn't keep herself from protesting, "I'm sorry, Kerry, but that's absurd. There is no such thing as bad blood and good blood. Children are born innocent." She leaned forward on her elbows, fixing the singer with her eyes. "Don't be afraid. The old lady is just spinning folk tales. Is she still alive?"

"Yes. She's still in her stone cottage down in the Ozarks. Fitting, isn't it? It's kind of creepy, because you get the idea that she knows everything about you. And you're wrong about the bad blood, I'm afraid. Half the town is cursed with it. There's an enormous amount of crime for a town of six thousand people. Murders, thefts, drug trade. And the McHenrys—that's the family who has the bad blood—

are behind everything. In addition, they all seem to be alcoholics or drug users."

"But you're not, are you?" Alex asked.

"No, I've never used recreational drugs, and I'm not an alcoholic."

"Have you got a criminal record?" Alex pressed.

"No. But it is odd, you know, about the McHenrys. If I have one somewhere in my genealogy, I need to decide for myself whether this whole thing is just bad nurturing or whether there's some basis for concern. Mental illness or something. Daniel will be the first to tell you I'm not altogether stable."

The psychologist leaned back in his chair and smiled. "It's only artistic temperament, Kerry."

"We might find out some things you don't want to know," Alex said.

"I'm willing to take that risk. Daniel says you do genograms. He explained that they're kind of a psychological family tree. I think that's probably what I need to have you do for me."

"You're sure?" Alex pressed her. The last genogram she had done had resulted in a murder.

"I've thought about it for a long time. I know my mother and father both have secrets from me. They won't talk about the past at all."

"That may provide a bit of a challenge," Alex said. "It may take some time."

"That's all right. I need to know. I'm tired of looking in the mirror and seeing only reflections of life. I've always lived through my music, become different characters, had different lives, but it's like the Lady's loom. It isn't enough anymore. I want to have a real life before it's too late. I'm thirty-seven."

Studying the tiny woman with her ethereal wreath of hair and enormous eyes, Alex felt the stirrings of compassion. She knew that desire. She shared it. Feeling Daniel's gaze on her, she turned to meet it.

"Are you game for this, Alex?" he inquired.

"Of course."

"Good!" Kerry said. Raising her wine glass, she announced, "I propose a toast. To uncovering the mystery."

Alex and Daniel echoed her, raising their water and wine glasses respectively.

Watching Kerry and Daniel's eyes meet over the rims of their glasses, Alex reflected that she herself must possess a bit of the Lady of Shalott, too. Otherwise, why would she so suddenly be aware of the emptiness that would be left by Daniel's going out of her life? He was like family to her. She had always taken him for granted, the way you do family members. But it was Charles who had crashed through her walls, who had thawed her frozen heart, had given her the desire to love again. And she had no doubt at all that she loved him. But her feelings for Daniel were part of the person she was, too.

*   *   *

"This is a very strange job," Alex said later as they journeyed in Daniel's BMW towards her apartment in Westport, the multiethnic "old town" of Kansas City.

"She's a passionate little thing," Daniel replied. "What do you think of this Lady of Shalott business?"

"Well, I don't believe in curses on people. But maybe there is a mental illness problem. Does she show any signs at all?"

He sighed. "Artistic people can get carried away. It wouldn't be the first time Kerry has fallen under her own spell."

"But her desire for a family is fairly basic."

"I suppose so."

"You don't seem sure."

"It sounded good at the time. Kerry can make anything sound good. But on sober reflection, knowing her as I do, I can't really picture her giving up her career to raise children."

"Why not? You say she's burning out. Maybe it's time for a change. Are you game to play Lancelot?"

Ignoring her jibe, Daniel pulled up in front of an aged brick apartment house with square, modern sunrooms jutting out from its facade. "The Baltimore, madam."

"Can you come in?"

He turned to face her. "How's Charles?" His expression and his voice were carefully nonchalant.

"What kind of an answer is that?"

Gazing at her steadily, he asked, "Why do you want me to come in?"

Feeling her cheeks grow hot, Alex reached for the door handle. "Never mind," she said coldly.

"Wait, Alex," Daniel stretched out a hand to detain her. "I apologize. I would like to come in."

They walked through the white-tiled lobby of the once-grand apartment building and out the back door. The elevator hadn't worked since anyone could remember. They reached her apartment via the fire escape.

As she unlocked the triple locks, Alex hoped there wasn't any laundry piled on the couch. Had she folded it? She couldn't remember.

Switching on the light, she was relieved to see that the room was in fairly decent order. The two white Bauhaus couches facing each other across the living room were free of debris. The square glass coffee table held only today's paper and Stewart's book on Scotland. Though a bit linty, the imitation oriental rug didn't look too bad, and the junk mail on her cherry wood parson's table was at least neatly stacked.

"I've gotten into Italian sodas," she told him. "Raspberry, lime, chocolate, or blackberry?"

"Lime sounds good," Daniel replied, shrugging out of his blazer and throwing it across the couch. Sitting down, he picked up Stewart's book and began paging through it. He did the same thing every time he came.

Switching on the kitchen light, Alex opened the white enameled cupboard and took down two of her best glasses. Sometimes she thought Daniel was obsessed by her dead husband. He would sit looking at Stewart's photographs as though there were some key hidden there to his personality, to their relationship, to his tragic death. Where she was concerned, Daniel didn't seem able to help being a shrink. He always wondered about Stewart, and she suspected he compared himself to him. But the self-possessed Charles had no such hang-ups, just genuine admiration for her dead husband.

She poured a careful measure of lime syrup into Daniel's glass and a like amount of blackberry syrup into her own. Opening the refrigerator, she removed an unopened bottle of soda water. She had bought it that afternoon. At some level had she known she was going to invite Daniel in tonight?

Placing the sodas on a small, red-lacquered tray, she carried them into the living room and put the tray on the coffee table. Daniel laid down the book. "I can't ever get over how good he was."

Alex sipped her soda and sighed from the heart. She looked at the chrome-framed travel posters that decorated her walls—Stewart's last commission before he had been killed in a terrorist plane crash six years before. It was only in the past few months that she could look at them without anger or overwhelming grief.

Daniel was studying her. She lowered her eyes. "Tell me about

Kerry. As much as you think I need to know. She said you'd fill me in."

"Kerry. Yes." Switching modes, he settled back into the couch. "Well, her father is possibly the leading citizen of Trotter's Bridge. Mayor and would-be gentleman. He inherited a large spread. Used to be sheep, but he switched to cattle. Kerry always had everything she wanted. I went home with her once. I think her mother, who didn't get any real education, has patterned her life after soap operas. That's where Kerry gets her flair for the dramatic. Her mother is a real piece of work, and lives in the Sunset Retirement Home now."

Alex got up and went to the parson's table to retrieve her Guatemalan carryall. Rummaging in it, she finally fished out a manila envelope containing Kerry's birth certificate. This, together with the address of Kerry's mother at a Trotter's Bridge retirement home, was the only material Alex had to begin her search. "I haven't looked at Kerry's birth certificate. Let's see what it has to say." She pulled it out. "She was born in Missouri. Barry County. A year older than me—born in '57. Full name: Kerry Anne McNee. Mother's maiden name is Sylvia Monett. Doesn't sound real, does it? Father is Cameron McNee. They were both thirty years old. Father born in Missouri, mother born in Missouri. The date of the certificate is the same as her birth date, so it doesn't look like she was adopted." Alex tried visualizing the information on a biographical sheet like the one she used for genealogical research. When she had it in place, she said, "Hmm. Does she have any brothers and sisters?"

"No. To her great unhappiness. I know her father wishes he had a son."

"I was just wondering because she was born when they were both thirty. I wonder if there were previous marriages or miscarriages or infant deaths or anything like that."

"Her mother says Kerry was her miracle baby."

"Hmmm," Alex pondered. "Well, unless she wasn't really her father's daughter, which I don't see how this Keeper could know, there doesn't seem to be anything fishy about her birth."

"You know, Alex, that would be much too easy. If you're really serious about this, you're going to have to go down there and meet that Keeper and find out what the story is."

"I'll see if Briggie is available." Brighamina Poulson, Alex's partner in RootSearch, Inc., was far more amenable to work when it wasn't baseball season. "You know," she added, "I'm glad you're going to be taking care of Kerry, Daniel. This could be messy."

He raised an eyebrow, registering irony. "I recall a messy situation about a year ago when you didn't hold that same opinion about me."

"That was different," Alex insisted.

"How?"

She threw up her hands. "You weren't my shrink! But that didn't keep you from trying to protect me, telling me how to live my life. I was just trying my wings. I wanted to prove my independence, prove that I could do hard things on my own."

"And prove your independence, you did." His lips thinned, and the irony disappeared.

It was the old impasse. "Daniel, I didn't want you to think of me as a boo-hooing neurotic."

"Apparently you didn't want me to think of you at all." He stood up. "It's time I was going."

Chapter Three

Alex woke to the sound of a thunderstorm rattling her windows. Glancing at the clock, she saw that it was only six A.M. "Blast!" She would never get back to sleep. Throwing off the covers, she padded into the kitchen, where she fixed an English muffin and put the kettle on for ginger spice tea. When the water boiled, she poured it over the tea ball containing the herbal leaves into the flowered Ainsley china teapot Charles had given her.

She hadn't slept well. This morning she was determined to embark on her new job and keep her mind off affairs of the heart. What she needed was a map of Missouri. Leaving her tea to steep and taking her muffin, she went to her office and unearthed a road map from beneath a pile of books on the floor. She really needed to straighten up in here. An antique beveled mirror stood against the wall awaiting assignment somewhere in the apartment. Charles had bought it at an estate auction in Chicago. Looking into it, she grimaced. The humidity caused her shoulder-length dark hair to explode in a mass of tiny medusa ringlets, and there were shadows under her blue eyes. She was so pale she could see the sprinkling of freckles across her nose. In Charles's Oxford crew T-shirt, which came halfway to her knees, she looked like a gawky twelve-year-old with her long bare legs sticking out. Then there was the background clutter—stacks of books, letters, and genealogy paraphernalia. It seemed that the busier and more creative she got, the less capable she was of keeping her office straight. In fact, it sometimes seemed that the only time her office was neat was when she hadn't worked for weeks.

The map told her Trotter's Bridge was on the northern edge of Barry County in the southwest corner of the state. There wasn't a town over the size of six thousand people in the whole area. Ozarks country. She remembered that Briggie went down there every year for the opening day of trout season. Didn't she have some sort of relative there? Of course, with a large extended Mormon family and nine children of her own, Briggie had some sort of relative almost everywhere. Alex looked at her watch as thunder boomed close by. It was only 6:15. Until seven, Briggie would be "Sweatin' to the Oldies" with Richard Simmons. Determined to get in shape, she held that time inviolate. What could Alex do in the meantime to get started?

When in doubt, make a list. Sticking a pencil behind her ear and a spiral notebook under her arm, she went back into the dining room to eat her breakfast. As soon as she was finished, she started a new page. "Kerry McNee. Who is she?"

She began with a genogram. Putting Kerry's name at the bottom of the page, she added her birth date and the information about her crooked finger and artistic temperament. Adding "miracle baby," she moved on to Kerry's parents. With their names and year of birth, she put down the information Daniel had given her about their personalities plus the information that they wouldn't talk about the past.

Kerry's Genogram

Sylvia Monett
b. 1927 Missouri
dramatic
won't talk about past

Cameron McNee
b. 1927 Missouri
wishes he had a son
won't talk about past
mayor

Kerry McNee
b. 1957
Barry County, Missouri
folk singer, "miracle baby"
genetic defect (little finger) = "bad blood"

Turning to a fresh page, she began her action plan:

1. Meet Kerry's mother. Confront her with story of "bad blood."

2. Find out about the Keeper and visit her. See if she has a family history of Kerry's family. Try to find out what she means by "bad blood."

3. Meet Kerry's father and confront him with the Keeper's story.

4. Ask around. Small towns have long memories.

5. Visit library to look for a county history or a newspaper.

6. Visit courthouse for probate records and whatever early birth and death records may be available.

Question: Why is her mother living alone in the retirement home?

Good. Now to the shower.

By the time she was toweling her hair dry, it was after seven, and the thunderstorm seemed to have moved away. She walked toward the telephone, and then it rang.

"Alex?"

"Charles! What are you doing up so early?"

"Missing you. I thought I might fly down for the weekend."
Charles was presently residing in Chicago.

"Oh. Well, Briggie and I are going out of town, as a matter of fact.
We have a case."

"Where are you going?"

"The Ozarks. They're in the southern part of the state . . ."

"Right. Even an expatriate Englishman has heard of Branson,
believe it or not. Why don't I come with you?"

Alex hesitated.

"Is anything wrong?" he asked.

"No. Of course not. It would be wonderful to see you. It's just
that I thought we might stay with a relative of Briggie's . . ."

"And you're not sure I'd be welcome."

"Well, I don't want to put anyone out or anything."

She heard Charles sigh with frustration. "When will you be back?"

"I'm not sure. I'll phone you, if that's okay. I really do want to see
you, Charles. How's the estate mess?"

"Progressing. We have a court date in September. Hopefully, the
judge will be a Solomon who will divide the value of the property
between your family and mine, and we can finally sell it." Charles
was her third cousin as well as her fiancé.

Wandering over to the mantel, Alex picked up a photograph of
herself and Charles and studied it. She could never get used to his
chiseled good looks—perfect profile, even smile, slightly hooded blue
eyes, blond hair. So different from Daniel with his red hair and
square wrestler's frame.

"Alex?"

"Umm. I was just looking at your picture. It's been too long since
we've seen each other."

She could sense his grin. "Two weeks *is* a long time. And I have
some news for you," he told her.

"What is it?"

"I'll tell you in person, darling. Hurry home."

"Good-bye, Charles."

"I love you, Alex. Keep in touch."

Pressing the End button on her cordless phone, she kept it cradled between her head and shoulder as though it were an extension of Charles. She *did* need to see him. It made everything so much clearer, just talking to him. Their relationship was straightforward, whereas hers with Daniel had always been muddied by so many other thoughts and feelings.

What was his news? Was it by any chance that he was going to be baptized? Though Daniel did not know it, her engagement was only a provisional one. She had been widowed once and had no desire now to be married only "for time." The potential loss was far too great, and she knew she could never go through it again. She wanted to be married for eternity this time, and since her conversion to The Church of Jesus Christ of Latter-day Saints, she knew that could only happen in the temple. To be married there, both she and Charles had to be members in good standing. He had been taking the missionary lessons. And he had read the Book of Mormon before asking her to marry him. She was hopeful.

But, as far as Daniel was concerned, she was irrevocably engaged. He wasn't a Church member or even interested in becoming one.

Sighing, she dialed Briggie's number.

* * *

It always surprised Alex, a native of Chicago, how fast the landscape changed just a few miles out of Kansas City. Suddenly, after only a suburb or two, they were in the midst of gently rolling green pastures and endless sky.

"So what's Trotter's Bridge like?" Alex asked her business partner as her little red CRX sped south on Highway 71.

Briggie ran a hand through her thick white hair until it stood on end while she sipped her orange soda thoughtfully. "It's not one of those graceful Southern towns you read about. It's working class. In its heyday, it was a railroad town."

"What does your nephew's cousin do?"

"He's a doctor. They're still getting used to Mormons down there, but he's got a good practice. He's the only one within fifty miles who will deliver babies."

"Does he have anything to do with the retirement home where Kerry's mother is?"

"Not likely. That's a Baptist outfit, isn't it?"

"That's what Kerry said. Is there really that much anti-Mormon feeling there? I find that difficult to believe in this day and age."

"Remember what it was like at Oxford? Remember the opinion Charles had about Mormons when he first met us? Why should a little town in America be any different?"

"Because it's America. We don't have a state church the way England does."

"It's also Missouri, don't forget. A hundred and fifty years ago Mormons were under an extermination order. It was rescinded only a few years back."

"You're kidding!"

"Nope. Governor Bond rescinded it in 1976."

Alex darted a look at her friend. Arrayed in a blue Kansas City Royals T-shirt and white sweatpants, her spiritual mentor was squinting at the landscape. "This flooding's terrible. Usually that land out there is pasture. Now it looks like one big lake."

"I think you should handle Mrs. McNee," Alex decided. "In fact, maybe it would be better if you went to see her by yourself."

"Does she have you spooked or something?"

"I just think she might relate better to someone in her own genera-tion. Kerry's really anxious about this. I don't think she wanted us to talk to her mother at all."

"It seems to me that we need to be up-front from the beginning. Her daughter's hired us to do a job, Alex. Treat it like a job. If she gets on her high horse and refuses to cooperate, there are ways to get around her."

Good old Briggie.

*　*　*

It was three o'clock by the time they arrived in Trotter's Bridge. Alex noted the squat, unpretentious houses of indigenous honey-colored stone, the bustling town square with its Georgian bank building next to the corrugated aluminum feed store. A restaurant of white-painted cinder block called the Blue Tail Cafe appeared to be the likeliest place to ask for directions to the retirement home. Briggie performed that task and then directed Alex to a wooded area on the edge of town. The Sunset Retirement Home seemed surprisingly pros-perous. Built of red brick with black shutters, it resembled a large apartment house.

The peppy young redhead at the reception desk telephoned Sylvia McNee for them. "Two ladies are here to see you, Mrs. McNee. They're friends of your daughter's. A Mrs. Poulson and a Mrs. Campbell."

Kerry's mother's room was on the ground floor at the end of the main hall. As Briggie knocked on the door, Alex tried once again to plan what she would say. She still didn't have a clue.

Briggie greeted the skeletally thin lady who answered the door. Though she had to be in her late sixties, she had obviously had plastic surgery, and her hair was teased high in a golden chignon. She wore a liberal amount of makeup (including false eyelashes) and a turquoise silk pantsuit. What was this aging glamour queen doing holed up in a retirement home? According to Kerry, her parents weren't divorced.

"We're friends of Kerry's," Briggie was explaining. "She wanted us to drop in and ask you a few questions."

"Questions?" Taken off guard, the woman opened the door wide for them to enter. Alex had expected something to link the woman to Kerry, but there was no photograph anywhere that she could see. The room was cluttered with antiques and mammoth silk flower arrangements. Out of place was an enormous big-screen TV, which was presently showing a soap opera. Walking over to it, Sylvia McNee watched it lingeringly and then, sighing, switched it off and indicated two needlepoint-covered chairs.

They sat down. "I'm Brighamina Poulson. This is my business partner, Alexandra Campbell."

"Partner?" The woman raised her eyebrows, instantly on her guard. "Just what is your business? Are you selling something?"

"We're genealogists," Alex told her, soothing instinctively. "Kerry has come to a difficult decision, and she's hired us to help her. I understand that you may not approve, but she thinks it's time she knew her family history."

"Family history?" Sylvia, in the act of lighting a cigarette, stiffened and looked from one of her guests to the other. "What do you mean?"

Alex drew a long, steadying breath. "Someone called the Keeper told her she has bad blood."

The woman sat straighter in her chair, nostrils flaring, lips tight with anger. "She's descended from the finest blood in the county. Her father's the mayor, her grandfather was the mayor, and her great-grandfather was the town minister. Miss Maddy is crazed."

25

Alex blinked, surprised at the woman's hostility. If what she said was true, why was she angry?

Briggie zeroed in. "What can you tell us about *your* ancestors?"

The woman looked away, and the hand that held the cigarette wasn't quite steady. "Kerry knows everything there is to know. She's never shown the least bit of interest in family. Certainly not in mine. She's her father's daughter."

Alex and Briggie exchanged looks. Here, apparently, was a mystery.

"I have a lot of friends in this town, and if you start prying into my affairs, I'll see that you regret it." The golden-haired woman had developed a tic under her right eye.

"Well," said Briggie, bounding to her feet. "Thank you for your time. We'll be off."

Alex looked at her in surprise. It wasn't like Briggie to be put off so easily. Facing Kerry's mother, Alex said, "You can't deny your daughter the truth about her ancestry."

"Truth!" Sylvia McNee scoffed. "Believe me, Miss High and Mighty. Truth can be dangerous, and if you start poking around you'll live to regret it."

*   *   *

"At least she didn't tell us to be out of town by sundown," Briggie said, as they climbed back into the CRX. "There's always the small town newspaper and plenty of gossips. More than one way to skin a cat."

"Briggie, I'm ashamed of myself. I never even asked Kerry why her parents were living apart."

"We'll find out. We can always call her. It looks as though our next step is to find an account of the marriage in the local paper. It

26

should give details on the bride's family. If her husband was the son of the mayor, I'll bet they did it up fine."

"We found out one thing," Alex said, grinning suddenly as she started up the car.

"What's that?"

"Whatever she has to hide, it's here."

Briggie reflected, and a smile lit her face. "You're absolutely right. She has a lot of friends in this town who'll see that we don't pry, doesn't she?"

"Exactly."

"And unless I miss my guess, she's scared."

*   *   *

The public library was a surprisingly modern stucco and glass building around the corner from the Blue Tail Cafe.

"Do you keep your local newspapers?" Briggie asked at the desk.

The librarian, a round, rosy woman with short brown hair, beamed behind thick-lensed glasses. "We sure do. What year are you interested in?"

"We're interested in coverage of the present mayor's wedding," Briggie said, smiling her most beguiling smile. "We're doing his daughter's family history for her."

"Yes. It's such a shame about the McNees. All on account of a little poker game that got out of hand." The librarian clucked and shook her head.

Briggie and Alex exchanged a look. They'd found a nice little gossip on the first try. "We know Kerry's thirty-seven and that her parents were thirty when she was born," Alex said.

"Yes. It was a second marriage for Sylvia. Everyone knows her first husband was a McHenry. I don't know why we women always think we can reform the bad boys. I heard he died in a car crash. Drunk. He killed the little Rawlins girl."

Briggie was definitely right about small towns, reflected Alex. Was there any significance to the fact that Sylvia's first husband was a McHenry? "Do you happen to remember the year she married Cameron McNee?"

"Same year I was married. 1950. Back in the days of Ike, when the world was right. I'm Betty, by the way."

Briggie introduced them, explaining their business, while Alex did mental arithmetic. Kerry was born in 1957. So that meant her parents had been married seven years. No possibility that she was sired by Sylvia's first husband.

"Do you happen to remember about when in 1950?" Briggie asked.

"June something. I was married the next month. But my Harvey's been gone these six years. Lungs. Refinished furniture, and the lacquer got him."

The widow walked into the open doorway behind her, and they could hear her rummaging on the shelves. Finally, she emerged with a red leather-bound book. "One of these days, we need to get these microfilmed," she said. "They're getting pretty crumbly."

Alex and Briggie carried the large heavy book between them to the nearby table. Spreading it open, they paged through the fragile leaves until they came to June. Alex felt her hands tremble. It was always like this when she was on a case. There was nothing as exciting as looking for clues.

Wednesday, June 28, was the last remaining issue for the month. The society page had been neatly razored out.

Chapter Four

Alex looked at Briggie, who had her hands on her hips in disgust. "Why in the world would anyone do that? They must know we can get the marriage certificate."

"It must be something else," Alex said. "Maybe something about the bride's family." She looked at her list. "Well, the next thing I suggest doing is seeing if this librarian can tell us who this mysterious Keeper is."

Betty was voluble. "Oh, you mean Miss Maddy! She's what I call a character. Have you read *Lord of the Rings?*"

Startled at this non sequitur, Alex nodded.

"Miss Maddy's a regular hobbit. She lives in this tiny cottage that is stuffed to the rafters with books, papers, collections . . . everything you can think of. She's not a chatterbox, but I know personally that she knows all there is to know about the people here, living and dead. The Historical Society wants her to write a history, but she says there are things she knows that no one wants to remember."

"How do we find her?" Briggie asked. "She sounds like just the person we need to see."

"Well, she lives in a stone cottage in the forest. It's a bit difficult . . ." Betty checked the clock behind her on the wall. "If you can wait a few minutes, my evening relief person will be here. I'll show you the way myself. You'll never find it on your own. I'm so excited about your project. I'm a member of the Historical Society myself, and I just love family histories."

*   *   *

The CRX bounced over the rough dirt road as Alex and Briggie followed Betty's battered white pick-up. The forest began to swallow them up. Alex spotted redbud and dogwood through the still-leafless oak trees. "This is like something from another world," she remarked to Briggie. "It's hard to believe there are still places like this."

"Welcome to the Ozarks," her friend said. "It's still mostly wild, just like those French fur-trappers found it."

"When did the Scots-Irish come?"

"Oh, they came early, too. They were kind of ridge-runners. You know, Kentucky, Tennessee, Arkansas. I guess the wild country appealed to them. Reminded them of home. They didn't settle on the plains, where life would have been much easier. Kind of like the Scandanavians all going to Minnesota, where they had harsh winters like home."

The air was so mild that Alex had rolled down the windows.

"What's that smell?" Alex sniffed again. It wasn't the clean, pure spring air she expected. "My gosh, Briggie! It smells like smoke! Too much smoke to come from a chimney. There's a forest fire or something. Get my cell out of my carryall and call 911!"

*   *   *

It wasn't a forest fire, but the porch of the little stone cottage was aflame. Alex flung her car door open and ran around to the back door of the dwelling. Luckily, it was open. *Cluttered* was not adequate to describe the interior of the Keeper's home. Alex moved sideways through cases of food in the kitchen. When she reached the living space, she saw that there was just enough room for a recliner. In the recliner was the Keeper, seemingly dozing. Shaking the plump woman by the shoulder, she tried to awaken her.

Briggie came up behind her. "Look, Alex," she said. "She's been bashed on the head. It looks like someone approached from the rear and surprised her." Briggie began trying to shift the body. "We've got to haul her out of here. We can't wait for the fire crew. It's probably all volunteers. Who knows when they'll get here?"

In the Keeper's lap was a worn leather volume that resembled an old-fashioned scrapbook. Alex grabbed it instinctively, holding it under her left arm as she and Briggie hoisted Miss Maddy. When they had the inert woman's arms around their shoulders, Alex was relieved to see Betty enter the room.

"Can you try to clear a path for us?" she asked. "The smoke's getting bad. We've got to get out."

Surprisingly agile for her age, Betty pushed and shoved boxes out of their way, as Alex and Briggie dragged the woman from her burning home. "I can't stand it that all this is going to burn," Alex said.

"Sylvia McNee," her friend said flatly. "And her friends."

"Thank heavens we got here in time!" Alex said as they stumbled out the rear door with their burden. "Do you realize that if she'd died it would be our fault? *Again?*"

"The good Lord got us here right in time, Alex, so you just concentrate on getting this woman to Jon's office. He'll take good care of her."

Alex remembered that Jon was Briggie's shirttail relative.

Betty agreed. "Dr. Jon is the best doctor we've ever had. I'll take her in the truck. There's no room in your little car."

"Alex," Briggie directed, "you go with her. I'll wait here for the fire crew."

"I'm not leaving you here with that fire blazing away!" Alex told her. "It's going to catch the woods on fire. You're coming with me. We can talk to the firemen later."

* * *

Dr. Jon's office was on the edge of town in what used to be a log cabin. With agility unusual for a woman in her sixties, Briggie bounced out of the car and over to the truck that had just pulled up behind them.

"Go tell Jon what's happened, Alex, while I help Betty."

Obediently, Alex went through the office door, vaguely taking note of the surprisingly cheerful waiting room with yellow walls and daffodils in a vase on the reception desk.

"I'm Alexandra Campbell. We need to see the doctor immediately. Miss Maddy's been hit on the head. She's unconscious," she informed the very young receptionist who had braces and braids.

Startled, the girl inquired, "Do you need help? Where is she?"

At that moment the door opened, and the two older women came through, half-carrying, half-dragging Miss Maddy.

"Here," the girl reacted swiftly, unfolding a portable wheelchair that sat behind her desk. "Just set her down in this."

Briggie and Betty, breathing heavily, managed to get the body of the inert Keeper into the wheelchair. The receptionist disappeared, presumably to find the doctor.

A very large man, whom Alex guessed to be about her age, with woolly brown hair cut close emerged from the short hallway.

32

"Oh, Jon," Briggie greeted him, "this poor woman's been hit on the head. Someone set her house on fire."

Without saying anything, Jon stooped beside Miss Maddy and pulled up an eyelid. Then he took her pulse. His look worried, he used the stethoscope around his neck to listen to her heart.

"Have you any idea how long she's been like this?" he asked.

"I think the fire had just been set, but we didn't see anyone on that dirt road going the other way, so we must have just missed whoever it was."

"I'm going to try a stimulant. Her vitals are bad." He turned to a woman whom Alex hadn't seen enter the reception area. Slim and dark-haired, she reminded Alex instantly of a fairy in a Shakespearean play. Everything about her was tiny. "Beverly, prepare . . ." the rest of the sentence was cut off as he wheeled Miss Maddy into a room and closed the door.

Alex sank onto the oak bench. *Why did this always happen?* Half the time they started poking around in someone's family tree, they provoked violence. She sank her face into her hands and silently prayed for the woman who was losing her house and all her worldly possessions.

It *had* to be Sylvia who was behind this. Hadn't she warned them? What had she done? Come in through the back door and hit Miss Maddy with a tire iron? The fire must have been started to destroy her papers. Try as she might, Alex could not picture Sylvia starting a fire in her turquoise silk pantsuit. What was it she wanted to get rid of, anyway?

It was too late to do any more research today. The courthouse would be closed. Alex stood and began to pace.

Briggie said, "We've stirred up a wasp's nest, all right."

No amount of therapy had been able to rid Alex of the tendency whenever calamity struck to flash back to the time of Stewart's death.

The burning plane falling through the sky, plowing into the ground at Lockerbie, Scotland. Her husband of ten years gone from her life in an instant. Without the gospel, the universe had seemed a random, frightening place. She and Stewart had been living in Scotland in a modest white cottage, leaving it periodically to travel the world with his camera. It had been a ten-year adventure as they flew everywhere from the steamy Amazon to freezing Iceland. She hadn't gone with him this time because she was expecting a baby.

The sudden remembrance stunned her. The baby! She had utterly blocked that little, scarcely formed being from her consciousness. Now, for the first time, remembrance came crashing down upon her like a hammer on an anvil.

She had been heavily drugged when she gave birth prematurely. She was so wrapped up in her grief over Stewart that the loss of the baby must have been too much additional trauma to grasp. Now the pain of it was suddenly there, poignant and real, obliterating every other thought or feeling. Dr. Brace had explained to her in other circumstances that this was the way of post-traumatic stress syndrome. You never knew when grief or pain would reach inside and grab you, as real as though you were actually experiencing the trauma you had resisted feeling at the time it occurred.

Stumbling to her feet, she headed for the door and walked out of the office. Daniel would be full of explanations: she was getting over Stewart, she was in love again, and this enormous loss that she hadn't been able to cope with before had suddenly burst to the fore, claiming all her conscious thought.

Whatever it was, the remembrance was searing. Every detail that had been foggy and unreal at the time stood out in stark reality.

Aimlessly walking around the log cabin to the back, she scarcely saw the blooming lilac but sat on a convenient tree stump, hugging herself. Tears flowed down her cheeks, over her chin, and down her neck. She didn't even have the energy to brush them away.

It had been about three days after Stewart's death. Just long enough for the numbness to wear off. She had been trying to find her own death by hiking in the snowy weather up a narrow canyon. The sharp, damp wind had frozen her face, feet, and fingers. Then she had purposely taken off her jacket, planning to go on until she dropped and froze to death. She hadn't even thought of the baby until the bleeding began. And then she had stumbled to a halt. Unable to believe she could have forgotten Stewart's child, Alex had realized in a panic that she didn't have enough strength to go back. She lay on the snow, feeling birth pains wrack her body. The white, white snow and the red, red blood. *How could she have suppressed it for so long?*

Providence, Stewart's enormous dog, had found her. He had barked, calling the searchers who were out looking for her. But by the time they got her back to the cottage, it was too late for the baby. She had never stood a chance.

Alex realized vaguely that her cell phone was ringing. She answered it absently, her mind in Scotland as she cried the first tears she had ever cried for the child who had died stillborn.

"Uh, hello?"

"Alex, darling, are you all right?" It was Charles. "I just got the most dreadful feeling, like someone walking over my grave."

At his voice, her silent weeping turned to sobs.

"Love, what is it? What's happened?"

She couldn't stay the overwhelming sense of loss, "Oh, Charles, the baby. All of a sudden I remembered the baby. They had me drugged, and I've blocked it, telling myself that it was for the best, but it wasn't."

"You lost a baby?" His voice was gentle.

"Yes. Stewart's. I lost it after the crash. I didn't take care of myself. I didn't eat, didn't sleep. I was hiking in the hills, trying to die. I killed it!"

"Alex, I'm certain you didn't, darling. These things just happen. No one knows why. Why have you suddenly begun thinking about the baby?"

Stifling her sobs, she remembered Miss Maddy. "It's happened again, Charles. An attempted murder. We're just waiting to see if the woman will recover. It's the guilt, you see. If she dies, it's my fault, just like the baby."

"Alex, I don't know what to say. I'm no therapist. Everything in me just wants to be with you to hold you. I've never known you to be so upset. You shouldn't be going through this alone. I'm on the next plane."

She wanted the comfort of Charles's arms so acutely that she ached. "Oh, Charles . . ."

"Surely it must help at least a little bit to know that we can have a family of our own."

"But this poor woman—we hadn't even met her yet."

"Tell me where the devil I fly into."

The question stopped her tears. For the past six years, she had allowed herself to depend only on Briggie. Until a few months ago, at least, when she had resolved certain issues in her life that freed her to trust God. As she had crawled out of the deep hole where she had been metaphorically sulking, she fell suddenly and deeply in love with Charles. She couldn't begin their relationship by pushing him away. But he had never seen her vulnerable. Not like Daniel had.

"Charles . . . I don't really want you to see me like this."

"Love, if we're going to be married, I think this particular issue includes me, don't you?"

"We're in the middle of a stinker of a case. And the only motel I've seen looks like it's out of *Psycho*."

"I'll manage. What's the name of this place?"

"Trotter's Bridge," she said grudgingly. "The closest airport is

Springfield, about fifty miles away. I'm sure you won't be able to get a flight until tomorrow."

"Then I'll be there in the morning. Where are you staying?"

"With a distant relative of Briggie's, on his farm. He's the local doctor. And since tomorrow's Saturday, we won't be able to go down to the courthouse. I don't know what we're going to be doing."

"Is there somewhere we can meet at, say, noon?"

"There's a greasy spoon called the Blue Tail Cafe. It'll ruin your gourmet palate for good, I think."

"I'll risk it. See you soon. Hang on, darling. Remember how much I love you."

Alex took a deep breath when she hung up. Even Briggie didn't know about the baby. She must trust Charles more than she realized. Wanting him to believe she was strong and capable, she had resisted telling him anything about her disastrous past, except how she was widowed.

At that moment, her friend came around the corner of the log cabin.

"Alex, the police are here. Betty called them."

She wiped her tears as well as she could with her hands.

"Now, what's the matter?" Briggie asked with the gruffness that disguised her tender emotions.

Alex reflected, not for the first time, that she didn't know what would have become of her if Briggie hadn't turned up in their little village on Loch Fyne looking for her Campbell ancestors.

"How's Miss Maddy?"

"Jon's still working on her. That little nurse of his says she's finally coming around. They were afraid she was in a coma. He's given her a stimulant, and for a little while she opened her eyes. He says she's out of immediate danger, but he's calling for an ambulance to take her over to Aurora, the closest hospital."

* * *

Alex was certain that the uniformed policeman who awaited them was below regulation height. He was far shorter than her five foot seven. He was even shorter than Briggie. His eyes were deeply recessed, and his head nearly shaved bald with only a stubble of red hair.

Turning to her, he said, "Your friend here has been tellin' me about your findin' Miss Maddy. How'd you happen to go out there, a stranger like you?"

Oh, dear. Alex knew instinctively that this was going to be difficult. With all the patience she could summon, she told him about Kerry's commission, omitting the part about the bad blood because it sounded so fanciful.

"Miss Maddy knew about Kerry's family tree, you see."

"Why didn't you spare yourself the trouble and just go see Sylvia McNee? She's Kerry's mother."

Alex exchanged a look with Briggie. "We tried. She wouldn't help us."

"She threatened us," Briggie said stoutly. "Told us she had friends in this town that would keep us from meddling."

The policeman shifted on his feet uneasily. "You know she's the mayor's wife."

"Someone started that fire, Sergeant," Briggie insisted. "Someone didn't want us talking to Miss Maddy. If we hadn't come along, she'd be dead."

"You think Sylvia McNee would do something like that?" the little officer asked, his incredulity plain. "Who're you to come in here and accuse our mayor's wife of attempted homicide? Why should I believe you? I've known Mrs. McNee all my life. A real lady."

He looked Alex up and down, and she was very conscious of her jeans and Hard Rock Cafe T-shirt. Snapping his notebook closed, he said, "I hope you haven't come here to make trouble. We're not real fond of strangers in this town."

"I'm related to the doctor," Briggie said. "Known him since he was a nipper. He can tell you that we're not troublemakers."

The sergeant swiveled to survey Briggie with his little deep-set eyes.

For the first time, Betty spoke up. "Conrad, you're forgetting me. I was there. These ladies saved Miss Maddy's life! You wouldn't have wanted her to die, would you?"

"You're right, Miss Betty," he said with a small sigh. Some of the self-righteousness went out of him. "You saw it all?"

"Yes. And I brought Miss Maddy into town in my truck."

His eyes darted between the three of them. "There's plenty o' dirt in this town that folks would rather you let lie," he said. "You know that, Miss Betty."

"So you're not going to investigate this?" Alex asked.

"No evidence," he said shortly. "Except that the fire crew tells me the fire was set with gasoline."

"It was done to keep Miss Maddy from speaking to us, Sergeant," Briggie repeated. "When she wakes up, she may be able to tell us who hit her, you know. Will you accept that as evidence?"

The policeman looked down at his feet and shuffled a bit.

Betty protested. "I'm sure Sylvia never would have done such a thing! I think we'll find she wasn't involved at all."

Briggie insisted, "Someone didn't want Miss Maddy to talk, and who else could it be? She's the only one who knows we're here."

Betty and the sergeant exchanged a worried look. Suddenly tired after her emotional storm, Alex couldn't deal with this right now. "Let's just wait and see what Miss Maddy has to say."

Chapter Five

As they drove through the forest on another dirt road, Briggie sat fuming in the passenger seat. "Typical small-town prejudice. We're the strangers, so we don't know what we're talking about! The sainted Sylvia couldn't have soiled her lily white hands by attempting murder!"

Alex said wearily, "Tell me about Dr. Jon. He seems nice. What's his last name?"

"Cox. He has a regular little haven out here a ways. Eighty acres. He has eight kids, and the older ones help with the farm. His brother lives on the property, too. Will Cox. He's a teacher. Has six kids. It's kind of ideal, really. The kids call it Farmville."

"What brought them here, of all places?"

"Jon went to the University of Missouri medical school and did his residency in Springfield. He found out they didn't have a doctor here. He's the kind of soul who wants to make a difference. So he bought a farm and moved his family here. He and Will are almost twins, born a year apart. They're real close. So Will followed him.

There's a tiny branch of the Church here, and Jon is the branch president."

"How many people are in the branch?"

"Only about twenty-five. There's a cheese-processing plant here in town that's a subsidiary of a company headquartered in Logan, Utah. They rotate executives through here. So it's just the two Cox families and whatever families are working at the cheese factory. They meet in the old opera hall. On the third floor. Last time I was here, part of the ceiling came down. Once a bird flew through the open window. It's an experience."

"So the missionaries haven't had any luck?"

"It's been years since they've had any missionaries here. The last ones were treated real poorly, Jon tells me."

Alex turned in where the mailbox was lettered "Cox." As she started down the driveway, her cell phone rang again.

"Hello?"

"Alex, it's Daniel. I just wanted to let you know that Kerry and I are coming down for the weekend to stay with Kerry's father. Have you made any progress yet?"

"Well, we almost managed to get Kerry's Keeper killed. We're still not sure if she's going to recover. It's pretty bad. Her house and all her records were burned." Alex recounted the episode briefly.

"Good grief! Any ideas who did it?"

"Well, Kerry's mother threatened us when we went to see her. Then we went by the library, and the librarian took us out to the Keeper's house. We found it on fire. Sylvia McNee would have just had time."

"So," Daniel sighed, "we're at it again."

"Doesn't Kerry have to perform this weekend?" Alex asked, dreading the arrival of the singer for a reason she couldn't name.

"No, she's finished her spring tour. She always ends with Kansas City. What's Briggie's cousin's nephew's name?"

"It's her nephew's cousin. Dr. Jon, they call him. Dr. Jon Cox. And we've just pulled up to his house, so I'll talk to you tomorrow." Alex firmly pressed the End key and stopped the car.

The house was a surprise. It was a gorgeous rambling brick Georgian with white columns. On a rise in the distance she could see Will Cox's residence, more modest, with ranch-red siding and white trim. Lilacs were in full bloom on either side of Jon Cox's enclosed porch, and the front lawn was immaculate. Iris of every color lined the walkway, obviously someone's pride and joy. What a change from the grime of Trotter's Bridge!

A little girl with kinky brown hair exploding from her pony tail came running towards them. As she smiled, Alex could see she was missing her front teeth.

"Zina!" Briggie crowed, getting out of the car and enfolding the overalled girl in a hug. "How're your chickens?"

"Jutht fine, Aunt Briggie. They have chickth. And we have a new baby colt and kittenth!"

"Has the tooth fairy made a visit lately?"

"Yethterday! I got a whole dollar!"

Zina must be about six years old, Alex calculated. Her own baby would be six now.

But it was worse than that. Susan Cox came out on the steps to greet them, a newborn in her arms. Tears started to Alex's eyes. A baby. A live, healthy baby. Guilt smote her, followed by a hunger she had never felt before. She had never thought she was mother material. Even when she was married to Stewart.

She sat in the car a moment, gathering strength. If Stewart hadn't been killed, she would have stood on their porch in just that way with his daughter in her arms. She had even named her: Megan. But

Megan was in the little cemetery overlooking Loch Fyne. Alex had visited her grave only once. She had felt empty and cold, unable to believe that the product of her's and Stewart's love was lying there in the ground. Listlessly, she'd wandered away. *It's for the best, it must be for the best,* she had kept telling herself. *Everyone says so.*

How was she going to get out of this car? Oblivious, Briggie was embracing Susan and admiring the newborn and following them into the house.

Zina came shyly up to the car and looked at Alex. "Aren't you going to thtay here, too?"

Alex wiped her eyes hastily. "Yes."

"Why are you crying? Are you thad?"

Alex nodded as another swell of tears brimmed over.

"Come and thee my kittenth, then. No one can be thad when they look at kittenth."

Smiling at the concerned little girl, Alex obediently opened the door to the car and followed the child across the driveway to the big red barn. Frolicking inside the barn door on their bed of straw were six kittens, varying in color from marmalade to black and white.

Zina picked up the marmalade. "Thith ith my favorite. It'th a boy, and I call him Tigger."

"Ah," Alex said. "Like Winnie the Pooh."

"Yeth."

"Have you named the others?" Alex asked, thinking of a particular cat of whom she had become very fond in a case last winter. Tuppence now lived in Roger's Park, Illinois.

"No. Not yet. Would you like to name one? What'th your name?"

"I'm Alex." She picked up an elegant little white kitten whose paws were like neat black slippers. "I'd like to name this one Dashiell."

"Whoth that?"

"A famous detective story writer. Do you know what a detective story is?"

Zina shook her head.

"It's about someone who solves mysteries," Alex told her.

"Whatth a mythtery?"

Alex cast about for some explanation. "Like if someone were to steal something that belonged to you, and you didn't know who it was. That would be a mystery."

The girl looked doubtful. "Okay."

"He's very handsome," Alex said. "Thank you for showing me your kittens. But maybe it's time I went to meet your mother and your brothers and sisters."

*　　*　　*

It wasn't as bad as she thought it would be. The baby had been put down for the night when Alex made her entrance. Susan was very welcoming, and there was the smell of fresh-baked whole wheat bread. Four loaves sat on the counter. Alex suddenly realized she was terribly hungry.

"Jon doesn't like fancy food," Susan confided. Her luxurious auburn hair was pulled back in a clip. Lightly freckled, her face featured a pair of large, confiding brown eyes. "We live on hamburger casseroles of one sort or another. It's our own beef." She stooped to pull something from the oven. "Tonight it's enchiladas. But don't expect anything vaguely Mexican. With eight children under twelve years old, we go for tame, not spicey."

"What can you tell us about the bad blood in Trotter's Bridge?" Briggie asked as she laid the table.

"Oh, that old tale!" Susan laughed without humor. "You know as well as I do that there's no such thing as bad blood. But this family called the McHenrys are a bad bunch. There's no doubt about it. It makes me nervous sometimes, because they really are a criminal element. Everyone knows it, but they're such a big, dangerous clan no one dares arrest them. They have a lot of trouble with drugs and alcohol, too."

"No insanity or anything?"

"Not unless you count old Isaac. He runs the shoe repair. Occasionally, he goes on a rant no one can understand. He calls it speaking in tongues."

Alex saw the basket of napkins on the counter and began folding them. "What do you know about Miss Maddy? She believes in the bad blood for some reason. How did it start? It must be some sort of genealogical phenomenon."

"Well, since you can't inherit criminal tendencies, I really don't know. Sometimes I think it's because they've never had a chance. From the time a McHenry is born, he's expected to turn out badly. Jon and Will spend a lot of time trying to rehabilitate them. They've managed to set up a chapter of AA, but nothing they do seems to help. It's like they're determined to destroy themselves, like they have no control."

At that moment, the back door opened and a bevy of youngsters descended upon them.

"Wash up," Susan commanded. "Then come meet our company."

Alex, an only child in a far from happy home, had never been around so many children at once, except in school. She wondered how on earth Susan maintained her serene demeanor. She heard loud splashing, shouting, and giggling coming from what she supposed must be the mudroom.

Eventually, the youngsters returned to the kitchen. They could have been stair steps. Half of them had red hair, and the other half had the brown frizz she had observed in Zina. How was Alex ever going to tell them apart?

Zina, looking very self important, introduced her to her brothers and sisters. "Thith ith Alekth. She named one of the kittenth Dashiell. He findth thingth that thomebody thteals."

Susan laughed. "I always feel like Captain von Trapp when I have to introduce my brood. The three boys are Matthew, Mark, and Luke, in order. You've met Zina. The other three girls are Sandra, Alana, and Rondi. The baby is Suzanne. We call her Z because she's such a good sleeper."

A girl who was older than Zina and wearing a carrot-red bob stepped forward. "The boys call me Alana Banana, but I usually go by Abee. You can call me that, if you like."

The oldest girl, whose hair was worn in two auburn braids, said, "Please don't ever call me Sandy. I'm Sandra, and I'm going to be a famous artist."

The boys showed little interest in anything but wrestling one another to the ground. Rondi was hardly more than a baby, toddling around in bare feet.

"Boys," Susan said without raising her voice, "if you want dinner, you need to sit at the table."

"Where's Dad?" the eldest, who had to be Matthew, asked.

"He's at the hospital. Miss Maddy is sick."

"Oh, not Miss Maddy!" Abee's forehead wrinkled with concern. "Is she gonna die?"

Briggie answered, "I think she's out of danger now."

*　　*　　*

When Jon arrived home, he informed Briggie and Alex that Miss Maddy was sleeping peacefully in the hospital. "She came around briefly. I tried to question her, but she was very confused. She has a congestive heart condition, so she's very lucky to be alive after such an ordeal. I imagine she'll have more to say when she wakes up tomorrow."

"Is there a guard on her room?" Alex asked.

Jon heaved a sigh. "The whole police department is in denial. They're treating it like an accident. No one wants to believe someone tried to kill Miss Maddy."

Briggie said, "How far is it to Aurora, Jon? It's just up Highway 60, isn't it?"

"Why?" the doctor asked.

"I'm going to take my toothbrush and spend the night by her bed. We put her in danger. The least we can do is keep her safe."

"Are you sure that's necessary?"

Briggie nodded shortly. "Very sure. Someone doesn't want her to talk to us."

"Do you want me to come, Briggs?" Alex asked.

"Maybe Jon can bring you when he makes his early-morning rounds. You can take over."

"Then you'll need to meet Charles at the Blue Tail Cafe at noon. He's flying in. Oh, and I didn't get a chance to tell you. Daniel and Kerry are coming. They're staying at Kerry's dad's."

"Good grief, Alex. All we need now is Richard, and the cast will be complete." She referred to Daniel's father, a normally respectable estate lawyer, who loved to elbow his way into their cases. Especially when murder was involved.

"Don't even think it, Briggie." Her friend and Richard were not a reliable pair. They were known to get into scrapes no law-abiding lawyer should ever find himself in. Then Alex suddenly remembered something. "If she wakes up, tell Miss Maddy that we saved her scrapbook. I have it in the car."

"Good," Briggie said. "I'll have a look through it while I'm keeping watch."

*   *   *

After family prayer and scripture study, during which Rondi danced free-form in the middle of the room, Alex made her way up into the bedroom that had been assigned to her, under the eaves. In her prayers that night, she remembered Miss Maddy.

As she climbed under the quilt (of course Susan would have handmade quilts), Alex thought about what it would be like to be a member of this family. It soothed her soul greatly to know that such families still existed.

The memory of the tiny blue body she had given birth to three months prematurely assailed her again and refused to leave. She hadn't even held her. The nurse had just taken her off somewhere, anxious to get her out of Alex's sight. If she had been born in the States, would it have been different? Would they have been able to revive her and keep her alive? She was an individual—Megan Campbell. A real person who had died. Would Megan have had Stewart's intense black eyes under those translucent lids? Would she have had his artistic talent? Turning over on her stomach, she felt the grief pounding in her chest as she let the pillow absorb her tears. She must get hold of herself and quit acting like such a drama queen.

Her cell phone rang. It was Briggie.

"Alex, a kid just tried to get in here. Real scraggly looking. You know the type—about a week's growth of beard, razored jeans, an earring."

Rousing herself, she tried to take in this information. "What did you do?"

"I asked him his business. He got real flustered and ran out."

"It's a good thing you're there, Briggs. Did he have a weapon or anything?"

"No. But he could have been planning to suffocate her. That's what I'd do if I were him. Everyone would just think she died in her sleep. Do you have a cold or something?"

"My nose is stuffy. Keep your eyes peeled, Briggs. I'll see you in the morning."

"Another thing," Briggie forestalled her. "This scrapbook. You'll never guess what's stuck in the front."

"What?"

"A tract. It's got to be an old Mormon missionary tract. Part of one, anyway. It must be a hundred and fifty years old."

Chapter Six

Alex was stunned. "Mormon missionaries? For heaven's sake, what do they have to do with anything?"

"Parley P. Pratt was martyred real near here sometime in the late 1850s."

"I sure wish Miss Maddy would wake up," Alex said.

*　　*　　*

Zina awakened Alex the following morning close to dawn. "Daddy thaid to get you up tho you can have breakfatht before you have to go to the hothpital," she said gently.

"Thank you, Zina." Alex stretched. *Charles was coming today!* Her angst of the night before lightened at the thought.

Of course, the perfect Susan had whole wheat waffles for her with some of last year's defrosted blueberries and fresh whipped cream over the top. Alex wondered if she ever lost her temper or simply stayed in bed. She noticed a copy of *Les Miserables* sitting on the table with a bookmark halfway through the book. When did the woman have time to read?

Jon noticed her glance. "I read to Susan while she cooks. It's the least I can do," he said with a laugh.

"You know, Jon, you're a very lucky man," Alex said.

"I never let him forget it," Susan said.

Alex told Jon about the intruder in Miss Maddy's room the night before.

He sighed. "Sounds like one of the McHenry clan. All the other kids in town make sure they look as clean-cut as possible, so everyone knows they don't have the bad blood. They refer to the McHenrys as trailer trash."

"It's really that bad?"

"Yup. They keep themselves real segregated."

"I wonder what he wanted with Miss Maddy, then. Briggie said he was only a kid. Oh! And she said something else that was interesting. You know what she found in Miss Maddy's scrapbook?"

"I can't imagine."

"A hundred-and-fifty-year-old Mormon missionary tract!"

"Well, I'll be . . . I wonder where in the world she got it?"

"It must be important to be in her scrapbook."

Jon paused in his eating. "That's intriguing. I think I'll put a call through to the Church Historical Department Monday morning. Find out if they ever had any missionaries through here."

*   *   *

Miss Maddy was awake and indignant when Alex arrived. Briggie was looking frazzled, most unusual for her.

"Dr. Jon? Who is this woman? Why am I here? Why did she have my book? She says someone tried to kill me! No one would want to kill me! She's crazy!"

"Now, now, Miss Maddy," Jon calmed her. "You had a little trouble out at your place yesterday."

"What kind of trouble?"

"These two ladies here were on their way to see you with Miss Betty from the library. Before they could get there, someone hit you over the head and set fire to your cottage. Alex and Briggie here saved your life and your book."

Miss Maddy was holding her scrapbook close to her ample bosom. "It's private," she said mulishly. Then Jon's words seemed to penetrate. "My house? My house is gone? And all my books and papers? Oh, glory, Dr. Jon. Who would want to do that? My great-grandfather built that house! And all my records . . ." The woman began to weep, not uncontrollably but with quiet dignity.

"We saved your scrapbook . . ." Alex said.

"Only one of many. Oh, and I had the family trees of everyone who's lived in this town."

She appeared truly heartbroken, and Alex tried to imagine what it would be like to lose your life's work and all the work of the former Keepers.

Briggie said, "If you're like me, you've probably got a lot of it committed to memory."

The Keeper nodded.

"Then I guess that'll be your life's work right there to reconstruct as much as you can."

The woman looked at Briggie thoughtfully. "Who did you say you were?"

"A genealogist hired to do Kerry McNee's family tree."

The Keeper's face closed up as though she had just locked her brain.

"Let me have a look at you, Miss Maddy," Jon said. "I need to check your heart."

The woman put the scrapbook down on the hospital tray, shooting Briggie a warning glance. Jon used his stethoscope. Apparently, he was satisfied.

"I think I can discharge you. You have a concussion, but according to the X-ray, the bleeding has stopped. I'd like you to come on over to my house for a couple of days so we can keep an eye on you, pack you in ice, and so on. Someone tried to sneak in here last night, so I don't think you're safe here."

"Who?" the lady demanded.

"A kid. Sounds like he was from the McHenry clan. Scruffy."

She looked down and began pleating the sheet. "Probably Rick. Been helpin' him with his readin'. Must have been worried about me. He wouldn't do me no harm."

"Then why did he run away when he saw Briggie?"

"Spooks easy. Doesn't want any of his friends to know he's tryin' to get on in the world. Thinks they'll laugh."

Jon pulled himself up to his full height of what looked like six foot six. "Miss Maddy, we need to know who hit you. Was anyone visiting you?"

Miss Maddy's eyes flashed. "Why would anyone want to murder me? Just tell me that!" Her face, which reminded Alex of a plump scone with raisins for eyes, flushed. She was obviously full of pluck.

Briggie spoke up. "Someone didn't want you talking to us, Miss Maddy. Like I said, we're here to do Kerry McNee's genealogy. We went to Mrs. McNee first, and she wouldn't have anything to do with us. She threatened us. So Betty at the library took us to see you. Kerry told us about you. You're called the Keeper, aren't you?"

"So little Kerry's looking into her past, huh? Hired you to do it?"

"Yes. And she's here now. She's staying with her father. Would you like to see her to confirm what we've told you?"

"I b'lieve I would, if you don't mind. I b'lieve I would."

"Well," said Jon, "first things first. I've got the rest of my rounds to make. Then I'll spring you out of here, Miss Maddy and take you around to the police. They want to question you. After that, I'll take you home to my place, where we can take care of you. We need to decide whereabouts you're going to land. Did you carry fire insurance?"

"Course not. I'll probably move in with Sally, my sister up t' Mount Vernon. Her husband's in construction. He'll lend me a hand with my place. I know those stones couldn't have burnt."

*   *   *

Alex asked Jon for directions to the McNee home. She was anxious to meet Kerry's father. With directions from Jon, Briggie and Alex headed back to Trotter's Bridge. Briggie insisted on doing this errand before she took a nap.

"I don't think that Miss Maddy's going to tell us anything, Briggs," Alex said. "Our only hope is that she will decide to talk to Kerry."

They drove a while in silence. Then Alex said, "It has occurred to you, I suppose, that if the Keeper's in danger, we are, too?"

"We'll be safe enough out at Jon's," Briggie said, waving a hand dismissively.

"If she does talk to Kerry, our job will be over."

Briggie shifted her bulk and eyed Alex sternly. "Not until we find out who attacked Miss Maddy. There's something strange going on in this town."

"Briggs, just because the police are incompetent doesn't mean we need to take over their job."

"That doesn't even sound like you, Alex! Just because you've gone and gotten yourself engaged doesn't mean the world has stopped spinning. We owe it to Miss Maddy. Something stinks around here."

"Could it be the chicken factory?" Alex asked.

The McNee residence was in "The Estates," a small tract of well-built houses next to the municipal park. As they pulled into the drive-way, Alex recognized Daniel's BMW. She prayed that every trace of her crying jag was gone. She didn't want Daniel walking around in her mind.

A thickset man with a bushy gray mustache answered the door. A drinker, Alex thought, seeing his red-veined nose. He looked like a hard-riding rancher from an old B movie.

"Hello," Alex said. "We're Kerry's friends, Alex Campbell and Brighamina Poulson."

At once, he became jovial. "Ah, yes, she told me about you. Tracing her family tree, are you?" Holding out a large hand he said, "Mayor Cameron McNee. Kerry's in the living room with her young man, getting caught up with Mike. Come along."

He opened the door wide, and Alex saw sky blue carpet and a gilded mirror hanging in the entryway. She detected Sylvia's taste. Why wasn't she living here anymore?

The living room where Kerry, Daniel, and the unknown Mike sat was crammed full of heavy Victorian antiques and two Tiffany lamps. Daniel rose as they walked in. Mike, obviously in the middle of a con-versation with Kerry, didn't even notice them. The mayor left them to it and disappeared down the hall. Alex was sorry to see him go.

"Hello, Briggie! Alex! Join the party." Daniel greeted them with unusual enthusiasm. "Kerry, look who's here! Mike, these are Kerry's genealogists."

The man whom Alex would have described as medium every-thing stood up and gave them a wide, bright smile. Moving towards them, he stuck out his hand. "Mike! Mike Wentworth! I hear you're from Kansas City! I grew up in a suburb, Overland Park."

Overland Park was the wealthy part of town, over on the Kansas side, where Daniel and his father lived. Alex wondered at his connection with Kerry if they hadn't grown up together.

Daniel was scrutinizing her face. Could he see the puffy eyelids?

She smiled brightly. "What do you do in Trotter's Bridge, Mike?"

"I'm an attorney, but I'm running for state senator for this district. I've got the primary coming up in a couple of months."

That explained his outgoing ways. A politician. Instinctively, Alex distrusted him. With his brown hair, brown eyes, medium height and weight, the only thing that distinguished him were his tortoiseshell glasses. The last person she had known who wore tortoiseshell glasses had been a killer.

Briggie was telling Kerry, "We've really stirred things up."

The singer replied, "Yes, Daniel told me. I can't imagine who would do such a thing. Is Miss Maddy going to be all right?"

"She was released from the hospital this morning. She is going to stay with us out at Dr. Jon's place. She wants to see you before she'll tell us anything."

Alex asked, "Do you have any idea why the McHenrys wouldn't want us doing your genealogy? I understand they are the ones with the bad blood."

Kerry looked down. "My mother's first husband was a McHenry. But I don't see what that has to do with anything. I'm definitely my father's daughter. And his lineage is solid. That much I know."

"Well, Miss Maddy obviously knows something, or she wouldn't have told you you have bad blood," Alex insisted. "She's not talking, however, so if you have any ideas you'd better tell us, because I don't want to endanger that poor woman."

Kerry looked helplessly at Daniel, who nodded at her. Then she said, "My mother has always been real sensitive about her family, the Monetts. I never knew my grandparents because she didn't want anything to do with them."

"Where did they live?" Briggie asked.

"In Mount Vernon. Just twenty minutes from here."

"It would have helped if you'd told us that before," Alex said.

Kerry sat up a little straighter, almost bristling. "I'm sorry. I'm just sensitive about my mother. Remember, Alex, I told you at the restaurant that I was worried about how she'd react to all this."

"Well, she's pretty angry right now. At us." Alex said.

"I'm really sorry. I'm devastated about Miss Maddy. Maybe I had better call this whole thing off."

"Not on your life!" Briggie said. "You've upset the anthill. Don't you think we owe it to Miss Maddy to get this straightened out and find out why her life is in danger?"

"We've faced sticky situations in the past, as Daniel can tell you," Alex added. "Now, unless there's anything else you can tell us, we'd better go. Briggie was up all night and needs her sleep."

Kerry's eyebrows rose, and her mouth hardened in an ugly manner. "No, I can't think of anything. Mike, do you know where Dr. Jon lives?"

He nodded.

"Can you take Daniel and me out there to see Miss Maddy this afternoon?"

"Of course."

Daniel said, "It looks like Briggie wasn't the only one up late. You're pale, Alex. Is anything else wrong?"

"Not a thing. And Charles is coming today," Alex said, deliberately holding up her fiancé as a shield.

Daniel raised his eyebrows. "Do I get to meet him?"

"You really want to?" The last time a meeting seemed imminent, Daniel had gone to extreme measures to avoid it.

"I do. When's he arriving?"

"Shortly."

"Why don't I take the two of you out to dinner, along with Briggie and Kerry?"

Briggie had a soft spot for Daniel and was not altogether thrilled with Alex's engagement. She piped up, "Just give me a few hours' sleep, and I'll be rarin' to go. There's a German restaurant on the way to Mount Vernon that's not half bad."

"Too bad Dad's not here," he said with a twinkle in his eye.

Briggie replied, "Actually, we're not speaking."

This was news to Alex. "Why not, for heaven's sake?"

"He was real rude to me."

Daniel laughed. "Don't take it personally, Briggie! Haven't you figured out he's rude to everyone he really likes?"

"Well, it's time someone taught him a lesson. He's going to apologize to me, or I'm not going to speak to him. And that's that."

"Well, then, Mike, will you be Briggie's date? We'd love to have you join us."

"Are you sure?"

Alex was touched by Mike's pathetic eagerness. Maybe she had been wrong about him. Maybe he was a completely nice person.

"I'll ask Charles about dinner and call you on your cell," Alex told Daniel.

*　　*　　*

By the time Alex and Briggie arrived back at Jon and Susan's, Miss Maddy was ensconced on the living room couch surrounded by children. She was teaching them cat's cradle with a ball of yarn.

After her friend went up to bed, Alex sat down in the living room. Zina crawled into her lap. "Wanna go vithit the kittenth?"

"Maybe in a minute. Right now I need to talk to Miss Maddy."

The Keeper looked up, a wariness in her eyes.

"You know, Miss Maddy, you could save us a lot of time if you would just tell us where Kerry's bad blood comes from. Is it her mother's family? The Monetts?"

"I'm called the Keeper for a reason. I keep things to myself."

"Why? What's the point?"

"When I'm sure of the fifth generation, I'll make everything known. I'm kind of—what do you call it? A trustee."

Fifth generation? What was she talking about? "For whom?" Alex asked.

"For the good Lord."

Alex thought of the tract. Should she mention it?

"My daddy workth for the Lord," Zina told her.

"Your daddy is a good man, even if he *is* a Mormon."

Rondi moved off Miss Maddy's lap and began to dance. Sandra said in a superior voice, "I'm a Mormon, too."

Alex hoped her face was straight. So the Keeper didn't know the tract was from the Mormons?

"Why don't you go to our church, Miss Maddy?" Sandra pressed her.

"I get along just fine. I have my own b'liefs."

Trying to figure out a way to get the Keeper alone, Alex suddenly remembered Charles and looked at her watch. It was almost noon. "I have to go meet my fiancé, Miss Maddy. I'll see you later."

Chapter Seven

The Blue Tail Cafe might have been the Ritz, the way Charles was sitting there so elegantly in the cracked plastic booth. Alex stood in the doorway and just looked. He was wearing his yellow cashmere polo neck sweater and gray flannel slacks. The whole scene could have been a modern Rembrandt, as light from some obscure source fell on his blond head, making it gleam in the dimness of the room.

Charles must have sensed her presence, for he stood and smiled the glorious smile that warmed his countenance. She hesitated, still a little unable to believe in his love for her. Finally, feeling the slightest bit foolish, she walked over to him, stood on tiptoe and kissed his cheek.

"You do liven this place up, darling," he said. "I thought you'd never come."

"Have you been waiting long?"

"Forever," he said, moving back so he could look into her face. "Still miz?"

"Not now that you're here."

She slid into the booth, and he joined her. Too excited now to eat anything, she ordered a root beer float. More optimistic about the food, Charles requested a Reuben sandwich.

Alex's mind took a leap out of the present moment. "Have you ever read *North and South* by Elizabeth Gaskell?"

Used to Alex's leaps in conversation, he replied, "Extraordinary piece of literature. Seriously overlooked by moderns. Has the charm of Austen and the social conscience of Dickens but better than both. However, why in the world would you bring her up at our long-awaited reunion?"

"Her heroine, Margaret Hale, was such a marvelous character— so obdurate, so truly good—healing the schisms in that industrial town with her high principles and love. *She* was lovable. I've tried and failed to be like her. What in the world have *I* ever done to make you love me, Charles?"

His face split into a broad grin. "My dear, you've cracked open this crusty old bachelor and given him a new world!" Leaning on his elbows across the table, he pinned her with a look. "Your eyes mesmerized me from the beginning. I told you—Jeanne Moreau eyes— bravery and vulnerability, tragedy and strength." Taking her hands, he continued, "I had to find what lay behind them." Now he looked around him. "So what happens? I find myself investigating an outlandish new religion and embarking on an expedition to this infant country. Voilà! I'm reborn! Margaret Hale you may not be, but Alexandra Campbell is the woman *I* love."

Alex felt a little unsettled by all of this. He knew nothing of her weaknesses, of her fight to overcome panic attacks and deep depressions. He saw her as a heroine because she had saved him from a life in prison by unmasking the real murderer.

He added, "You've become a magnet to my soul. I don't feel

complete without you, Alex. You've got part of me, and you're not giving it back."

Alex relaxed against the booth. That, she could live with. "Oh . . ."

"And, of course, you come attached at the hip to Briggie, so I am ensured a life of continued excitement."

Chuckling, she said, "It was a job, but I persuaded her to leave her deer rifle behind this time. Now, I wish we had it. This place is really wild, Charles. It's barely civilized."

"That sounds interesting."

Their orders appeared, and Alex gave him an account of the case thus far. "By the way," she added, "how would you fancy dinner with Daniel, Kerry, Briggie, and Mike?"

"Who the devil is Mike?"

"One of the characters of the piece. He intrigues me because he is completely ordinary. Not a single distinguishing characteristic. He's running for state senator. Some connection to Kerry—I'm not sure what. He'd be the murderer for sure in Agatha Christie."

"We'd better keep an eye on him, then. And, of course, I'm game to meet my competition, Dr. Daniel Grinnell." He rubbed his upper lip with his index finger, studying her.

"We're engaged, Charles," she said playfully. "Remember? Daniel is no longer an issue. But don't let anything slip about Megan, because I don't want him to psychoanalyze me."

"Megan?"

"The baby. That was her name."

"Oh." He sat up straight and looked at her seriously. "Tell me, Alex, I'm a little vague. Can we have Megan sealed to us?"

"Wait a minute," she said, stunned by his question. "Back up. We're going to be sealed?"

"Eventually, I hope. I've set a baptismal date."

Forgetting her surroundings, Miss Maddy, and Kerry McNee's bad blood, she opened her eyes wide and said, "You're going to be baptized? You're sure? You're not just doing it for me?"

His eyes gleamed. "This isn't the time or place to tell you about it, darling, but I've had my confirmation that the Book of Mormon is just what it purports to be."

She hugged herself in delight. "Oh, Charles!" She looked around her at the worn black linoleum, the dirty windows, the cinder block walls, and held out her arms as though she would embrace them. "I will love the Blue Tail Cafe forever."

"My dear," he said, eyes twinkling, "I don't believe I've ever seen you so thrilled. Whatever am I going to do for an encore?"

"Marry me forever, in the temple," Alex said, tearing up unexpectedly. "Oh, Charles . . . when?"

"Whenever you want."

*   *   *

After checking Charles into the Park Plaza, a string of rooms that had recently been sprayed for bugs, judging from the insect corpses that littered the sidewalk, Alex drove with her fiancé out to Farmville. There they found Susan quilting by Z's cradle, and Jon and the children cavorting with the new colt, but no Miss Maddy.

Following introductions, Alex asked, "What happened to Miss Maddy?"

"I don't really know. I was trying to get Z down when she asked to use the phone. After I had finished nursing, I went to check on her, and she wasn't anywhere to be found. She must be coming back, though. She left that scrapbook of hers in her bedroom. Jon is going to be cross. She was supposed to be lying down with ice on her head."

Feeling vaguely uneasy, she asked if Kerry and Daniel had come yet.

"No. They telephoned, and I told them she'd gone."

"That's too bad. I was counting on her telling Kerry where her bad blood came from. Oh, well." Alex twined a curl around her finger. "I guess I'd better call Daniel and confirm about tonight. We're having dinner out, Susan, so you needn't worry about us."

"Is that fresh bread I smell? I didn't know anyone in the world baked bread anymore," Charles said in wonder. "Would you be willing to teach me?"

As Susan looked at him in surprise, Alex said, "Oh, Charles, that would be heaven! I can't imagine anything more wonderful than waking up to the smell of bread baking."

He tickled her lightly under the chin. "Well, I can see we'll have to work on your imagination a little."

Susan giggled, and Alex blushed. "I'm going to call Daniel. Maybe you'd like to learn to quilt, too."

Daniel answered his cell on the first ring.

"Charles and I would be happy to dine with you this evening, doctor," she said, feeling playful.

"You sound unusually chipper," he remarked.

"Does Kerry know this German place?"

"Yes. I suppose it's up to us to bring Mike."

"You sound unusually grumpy."

"He never gives it a rest. He's always running for office," Daniel said.

"We'll bring Briggs. Seven o'clock?"

"That sounds good," Daniel answered, gloomier than before.

Poor Daniel. Was Mike posing a threat to the reignition of his romance with Kerry? Alex had been surprised that he hadn't seemed heartbroken when he learned of her engagement. Maybe he hadn't believed it would pan out, or perhaps he'd always had Kerry on the back burner?

Zina introduced "Charlth" to her precious kittens. "Thith ith Tigger, and thith ith Dashiell. Alekth named him. Do you want to take him home with you, Alekth?"

"What do you say, Charles? Do you think we need a cat around the place?"

Charles knelt down and held Dashiell so they were eye to eye. "Looks like an honest fellow. Don't think he'd break the furniture."

Jon came walking into the stable. "Ah! The fiancé! You must be Charles."

Settling the kitten on his shoulder, Charles rose, hand outstretched, "Charles Lamb. Your wife is going to teach me to bake bread."

"Jon Cox, father to this brood and husband to the finest woman on earth."

"Amen," said Alex.

Charles raised an eyebrow. "Is that an implied slight of my lady, here?"

"If he thought I were the finest woman on earth, it would be a bit problematic, Charles." Turning to Jon, she said, "Did Miss Maddy make her statement to the police?"

"With a little prompting."

"Speaking of which, did you see her leave?" Alex asked.

"Leave?" Jon echoed.

"She's gone," Alex told him. "She phoned someone, and now she's gone."

*   *   *

Miss Maddy hadn't returned by the time Briggie came downstairs. "My stars," she said, white hair standing on end. "I don't know when I've slept so hard."

"You needed it," Alex told her. "Look who's here!"

Charles kissed Briggie lightly on the cheek. She looked flustered, as she always did when he saluted her in this manner.

"And guess what!" Alex added. "He's getting baptized, Briggie!"

Her friend's seamy face shone with a sunny smile. "Well, glory be. I never thought this day would come! Congratulations, son. I'm real happy for you."

"Briggie . . . oh, never mind." She had been about to ask her if Megan could be sealed to them, but she remembered in time that her friend had no knowledge of her baby.

"Where are you all going to live?" Briggie asked.

Charles and Alex looked at one another and laughed. "Everywhere!" they chorused.

As Alex put on her black dress slacks and turquoise silk shirt, she realized that she had never, ever been this happy in her entire life. It was impossible to imagine how wonderful it would be to live with Charles every day—to laugh, to work, and even to pray together. And in addition to all that he was a gourmet cook.

Briggie, dressed in clean cherry-colored sweats, met them downstairs, and they took their leave of Jon and Susan. Alex, in her happiness, was only mildly concerned about the still-missing Miss Maddy.

*   *   *

The minute they walked into Biermann's, Alex knew why she had been uneasy at Kerry's appearance. The woman took one look at Charles and smiled a "come hither" smile. She was draped in gauzy sea-foam green with a delicate Celtic cross at her neck. Her pale gold hair stood out from her head like a cloud. She said, "Charles Lamb, you do get around."

Alex's happiness fled in an instant.

"Kerry, is it?" Alex's fiancé said with an edge.

66

"Don't tell me you've forgotten." There was a coy lilt to her voice. "It was so lovely! Two golden weeks. I never visit London or Great Britain, for that matter, without thinking of you." She sipped her cider in the awed silence. "But what are you doing *here* of all places? This is the absolute end of the earth!"

Charles's voice was cold. "You've hired my fiancée to do your family history, apparently. I was missing her."

The band struck up a polka, but Briggie, Alex, and Charles stood like statues. Kerry made a face. "Fiancée? You do surprise me, Charles. I'll sing later on, I think. Better than this dreary polka band. You always liked my singing, didn't you, darling?"

"See here, Kerry," Daniel said uncomfortably, "the guy's engaged. Switch off the act."

"But you don't understand! Charles is a bit of a legend. The most attractive man in Britain. And now, to see him caged! It will be on the front page of the *Times*. Fortunately, I wasn't looking for marriage, or he would have broken my heart. And now, *regardez!* It would appear that he's been caught by an ordinary woman—no goddess or sprite. Alex must have some magic that isn't readily apparent, don't you think? There's certainly no accounting for tastes, is there?"

Alex's temper blazed inside until explosion was imminent. Turning, she walked straight out of the restaurant to her car, got in, and slammed the door. "The most attractive man in Britain!" How could she ever have thought such a man could love her—ordinary Alex with all her emotional baggage? Of course Charles had a past. Who didn't these days? But confronted with it in the form of Kerry, she doubted very much if she could live with it. Pounding the steering wheel, she was too angry for tears. Two weeks? Had they had a two-week affair?

She drove aimlessly, but part of her mind must have been guiding her, for she found herself on the road to Miss Maddy's place. No one would expect to find her there.

What could Charles possibly see in her after the charms of someone like Kerry? And she was sure there were dozens more women of fame and beauty. Wasn't that what had kept her from falling at his feet in the first place? The knowledge that he could have any woman he wanted? She was just a challenge, with her moral standards that couldn't be seduced away. Was she ready to run into Charles's old flames around every corner? How could she contemplate an eternal marriage with such a faithless man? She simply couldn't. What she felt must be infatuation. It was a wild, out-of-control feeling, not the steady regard she had built for Stewart nor the companionship she had felt for Daniel. If she just didn't *see* Charles anymore, perhaps her feelings would die a natural death. Perhaps, after all, Daniel was more her speed.

But it had been such a glorious, wonderful dream, complete with the proverbial roses, stardust, and temple spires. There had been Oxford in the summer, punting on the Isis. And children. Little blond boys like Charles dressed in gray flannel school uniforms.

She only slowly became aware that although it was a long spring twilight, the woods appeared dark and almost threatening. Pulling up at last to the charred ruin, she got out of her car. What did she expect to find?

Certainly not Miss Maddy lying among the rubble, clearly dead.

Chapter Eight

The world spun around her. Dead. The killer had made sure this time with a solid blow to the head. Sitting down on an overturned stone that had once been a part of the woman's home, she shook as she tried to take it in. How had Miss Maddy arrived here? With someone she trusted, obviously. Who had she called from the Coxes'?

Alex felt numb all over, but she managed to pull her cell phone out of her purse and dial 911.

*   *   *

The short officer designated as Sergeant Griggs showed up with his partner, Corbett, another redhead who looked like he played football for the local high school, complete with a chaw of tobacco in his cheek.

"*Now* do you believe someone wanted Miss Maddy dead, sergeant?" Alex asked.

"How did you come to be here, Mrs. Campbell?"

"I was worried about her. She disappeared from Dr. Jon's after lunch, and no one knew where she went."

The sergeant chewed his lip. "Well, we don't have no forensics or nothin' like that, so I'll have to call the sheriff. He'll want to interview you about this genealogy hunt you was on."

"Would you like me to wait here, or can I go in to the police station? It's getting kind of cold."

"If you could just wait to see the sheriff, I'm sure he'll have questions."

*   *   *

It was immediately obvious that Sheriff Thomas was *not* a Trotter's Bridge man. A large specimen, nearly twice the size of Sergeant Griggs, he combed back his oily black hair with his hand. On his arm was tattooed *Semper Fi.* A marine! Alex silently rejoiced.

"Get a man out to pick up Mrs. McNee pronto, sergeant, like you should have done in the first place."

"But she wouldn't have had the strength . . ."

"Ever heard of hiring someone to do your dirty work? Mrs. McNee wouldn't want to get her purdy hands all dirty, would she?"

The police station was like something from an old Andy Griffith movie. Clapboard with most of the paint peeled off to reveal the wood, a rickety screen door, a worn wooden floor, and a counter laminated in forest green. Alex took a wooden chair that sat unevenly on the floor and folded her arms across her chest.

She loathed and detested Kerry McNee with every part of her being. She obviously had buckets of bad blood in her. And poor old Miss Maddy with her hidden knowledge had died because of her.

If it weren't for Miss Maddy and Alex's responsibility for her death, she'd pack up and go home this instant, leaving Briggie to return with Daniel. She was embarrassed to face Daniel ever again, and Briggie's strictures on the subject of Charles would be too over-whelming to handle right now.

She was dictating her statement when they brought in Sylvia McNee. She had obviously been drinking, and her coiffure was lop-sided. She was dressed in a satin bathrobe, carrying the ever-present cigarette. "I'll speak to my husband, you little worm," she told the ser-geant. "Just how long do you think you'll have your job?"

Then she sighted Alex. "You! What business did you have com-ing here? We ought to put walls around this town to keep outsiders outside. They only bring trouble and disgrace!"

The sheriff stood and took the woman by the elbow. "Now, madam, come with me. We need to have a serious talk."

Alex was free to go home. She hoped they could pin the murder on Sylvia because she wanted to get out of Trotter's Bridge and never come back.

*   *   *

Thankfully the Cox children had gone to bed. They kept early hours with their farm chores. Susan was quilting through a big hoop that occupied her lap. Alex couldn't bring herself to tell her about Miss Maddy.

"Jon's out on an emergency, I'm afraid," Susan said.

Knowing well where the doctor probably was, Alex just mur-mured good night, went upstairs, and climbed into her nightshirt. Then she pulled it off and threw it in the wastepaper basket. It was Charles's. At the bottom of her bag was a pair of workout sweats. She put them on and was brushing her teeth when Briggie returned.

"Well, the party didn't go with much of a swing after you took your dolly dishes and went home," she said. "I thought you had better manners."

"What would you have done?" Alex demanded.

"I'd have stayed and showed that self-centered harlot how a real lady behaves."

Alex plunked herself down on the bed. "Well, I don't care how much bad blood she has in her veins, I'm through with her case. The only thing that's keeping me here is Miss Maddy. She was murdered sometime today."

"What?" Briggie's little agate brown eyes grew wide.

"I found her. She was hit in the head out at her place."

"My stars!"

"The sheriff doesn't believe in *noblesse oblige.* He's brought Sylvia in for questioning. Hopefully they'll get her for it quick, and we can hightail it out of town."

"You're probably hungry," said the ever-practical Briggie. "I'll bet Susan has some whole wheat bread and honey. That's just what you need. I'll go down and get it. If you want to get your mind off your troubles, you might have a look through Miss Maddy's scrapbook. It's on her bed in the next room over."

Alex retrieved the scrapbook, and shunning mental images of Charles, his hooded blue eyes sending her messages of desire, she tried to concentrate on it. She had come down to earth with a thump and was the ordinary Alex once more. But the pain in her heart was a physical thing nothing could talk her out of.

In spite of this, the Mormon tract intrigued her. It was about four inches by seven, and its contents stated there was a prophet on the earth once more. Following was an account of the First Vision, the golden plates, the restoration of the priesthood, and the organization of the Church. She read the small print carefully. At the end was a scrawled name: Elder James E. Call.

The yellowing handkerchief had a monogram, quite an extravagance for the times. A C was embroidered in navy blue.

What had happened to Elder Call? Had he had a companion? What was the tract doing in Miss Maddy's book? Turning the page, she saw a clipping from the Joplin newspaper. They had driven through Joplin on their way down. It was about thirty miles away. The paper carried an account of one Jake McHenry being scalped and butchered by Indians. Apparently, he was the only one. His companions had fled, leaving him to be slaughtered.

Following this were clippings from Springfield, Fayetteville, and Joplin papers about the gang of outlaws marauding the area. They were the sons of Jake McHenry, turned angry at the desertion of their father by his friends. Apparently, they rustled cattle, set barns afire, and even raped women. A large reward was offered for their arrest. They camped in the forest like Indians, moving frequently, always one step ahead of the law.

Well, thought Alex. That was certainly a beginning account of the bad blood. Murder and slaughter, arson and rape.

But what did the missionary tract and the handkerchief have to do with Jake McHenry and his horrible demise? Miss Maddy had talked of generations. What had she meant? Was it some biblical reference? And what was Sylvia Monett's role in all of this? What was she afraid of? Had she really killed Miss Maddy?

Briggie arrived with her toast, liberally covered with honey and a glass of fresh milk.

Alex barely noticed her arrival. Taking the toast without looking at it, she crunched it, chewed, and swallowed, licking the honey off her lips.

"So what d'you think of the baby booties?" Briggie asked.

"I haven't gotten that far." Alex turned the page, and there were two pairs of baby booties, one blue and one pink, secured with metal brads that pierced the paper. They were delicately made for very tiny feet.

"I can't imagine them belonging to any of these McHenry hooligans," Briggie said. "Maybe they belonged to one of Miss Maddy's ancestors."

"That's the only thing that makes any sense . . ." One of Stewart's cousins had crocheted a complete layette for Megan in soft green wool. She had forgotten it until this moment. It had magically disappeared after Megan had been born blue and cold.

Alex was on the verge of breaking down and telling Briggie about Megan when they heard gravel against the window. Her heart sprang, and then she quelled it. It could only be Charles, and how could she face him tonight?

But she was wrong. It was Daniel. She especially didn't want to see him.

"Go down and see what he wants, will you, Briggs? I'm not in the mood for psychoanalysis."

"What makes you think I am?" her friend grumbled. "You know it's you he wants to see."

Alex reluctantly got to her feet and went downstairs in her sweats, her hair standing out in a mop of black curls. Images of Megan still haunted her, and only slowly did the events of the evening return. Kerry and Charles. Miss Maddy's dead body. She felt as though she had been on a roller coaster all day.

As she walked softly to where her visitor stood beneath the window, she said, "What are you doing here?"

"I just thought you might want to talk about things," he said solemnly, looking her in the eye. "It just about killed me to see the light go out of your eyes tonight."

Alex turned her face away. There were too many things to talk about. "Where did they go?"

"What makes you think they went anywhere? Kerry's home at her father's, and Charles disappeared immediately after you did. I have no idea where he went. He's a man of the world, Alex. I imagine he found your reaction a bit childish." The words were said with a grimness she could hear without even looking into his face.

"If I married him, we'd be running into his old girlfriends whichever way we turned," she said bitterly. "He's too good-looking. I've always thought so."

"A Lothario, just like I imagined. Think of him fat and bald. Would you still love him?"

Charles would be one of those men who aged gracefully. She knew the question wouldn't arise. Shrugging her shoulders, she put her hands deep in the pockets of her sweats and said, "I don't want to talk about him. There's been a murder."

Daniel sighed. "Who?"

"Miss Maddy. Somehow she got out to her cottage, and someone killed her with a handy rock. If it hadn't been for Kerry, she'd still be alive."

"The woman must really have known something dangerous to someone. But what? I mean, do you really believe in all this bad blood stuff?"

"No. Not really. But we found some things in the scrapbook from the middle of the last century that seem to explain what Miss Maddy meant. We're missing too much, though. The pieces don't all fit together."

"Well, then," Daniel said. "Keep your mouth shut. If the murderer knows you've got that scrapbook, you'll be the next victim."

It must have been the accumulation of shocks the day held that numbed Alex to his words. She went on speaking. "There were baby booties. Little pink and blue baby booties. They were for some poor children who were part of this great big mess."

As though it were the most natural thing in the world, Daniel gathered her in his arms and said softly, "Do baby booties have some significance for you, Alex?"

She settled her head on Daniel's chest. "I'd leave tomorrow if I knew who killed Miss Maddy. I feel I'm to blame for that, but I never want to see Kerry again."

"Leaving Kerry out of it for a moment, you must realize that it's dangerous for you to poke around. People tote guns around here instead of briefcases."

Just then headlights coming up the road blinded them. Finally, Alex recognized Jon's truck. She sprang away from Daniel, embarrassed.

To her surprise, not only did Jon alight from the car but Charles as well. Ignoring Daniel, her fiancé came to her instantly. "Alex! What possessed you to go out there to that place alone at night? The murderer could have been there! Jon seems to think you just missed him. Miss Maddy hadn't been dead long." His voice was full of scarcely controlled anger.

It was as though the confrontation at Biermann's had never happened.

"Jon? You were called to look at the body?" Alex asked.

"I have to do an autopsy, but it looks like someone just picked up a rock and hit her in the back of the head. Shortly before you found her."

Alex put her arms about herself, suddenly cold. She had never thought that the murderer might be lingering nearby. Her mind and heart had been otherwise occupied.

"How do you come to be here?" Charles questioned Daniel.

"I thought Alex might need some moral support."

"You knew about the murder?" Charles asked with some surprise.

"Not until Alex told me."

Charles pondered this answer and ultimately figured out what Daniel was referring to. He spoke to Alex in his most distant, superior voice. "I suppose that little contretemps with Kerry cast me in the role of Don Juan and you decided to find comfort elsewhere?"

Alex didn't know how to respond. His hauteur was wounding, and her heart, soft with sorrow, felt it deeply. She straightened and without a word went into the house.

When she got to her bedroom, she was shaking. Charles must have come looking for her here, so he'd been with Jon when he got the call to go examine the body. How could she go from ecstatic to miserable in such a short time?

She had been riding for a fall. Briggie had been right to worry.

Then she shook herself. She must concentrate on the really important horror of the night. Miss Maddy was *dead*. All because of her prying and poking. Had Miss Maddy called Sylvia McNee of all people to come pick her up? It seemed unlikely. Kerry's mother hadn't struck her as the type who would ferry nosy old women about. Or do anyone a favor but herself. The sheriff had probably discovered by now that she had an alibi. But Alex hoped being arrested had made her dang good and angry at her daughter, who seemed to fear her.

Briggie came into her room. "What did Daniel want?"

"To offer comfort and support, like he always does." She pounded her bed with both fists. "I'm sorry, Briggs. I'm not good company. I have to think this through somehow."

"I realize this is real hard, kiddo. But don't you think you ought to give Charles a chance? If the Lord can forgive him, maybe you can, too."

"There are feelings to be worked through, Briggie. Forgiveness isn't an automatic thing. At least for me it's not. I'm not like you."

"My Ned was no saint," her friend said.

Alex was shocked out of her preoccupation. "What do you mean, Briggie? He didn't run around on you, did he?"

"No, I'd probably have shot him if he had. But he was what we used to call a matinee idol. Looked like Clark Gable, only taller. Before we were married, that man was honey to bees. I was like you. I wasn't having any of it. Besides that, he was RLDS."

"Ned? *RLDS?*" Alex felt as though she'd been slugged. She'd always thought Briggie had the ideal Latter-day Saint marriage.

"Oh, goodness, child, don't look at me like that! I cured him of it, of course. And once he'd caught me, he settled down real nice. Don't forget our nine children." Briggie had a wicked glint in her eye, and Alex was startled into laughter.

"Now, you go to sleep and leave all this up to the good Lord. You haven't been forgettin' to pray, have you?"

"Briggs, don't nag. Of course I haven't."

That night she said a very long prayer laying out her concerns and asking for the Lord's help in making the most important decision of her life.

Chapter Nine

Next morning Alex found it difficult to concentrate on the fact that it was the Sabbath. She pulled out her periwinkle blue sheath dress and the gold watch (now on a neck chain) that had been her grandfather's. Though it was spring, the air was sultry, as though a storm were about to descend, so she shunned stockings for bare legs and high-heeled sandals. She brushed her unruly hair and rubber-banded it high on her head into a pony-tail, tied with a matching ribbon. "What you see is what you get," she said to her reflection. She had no patience for makeup this morning.

When she got downstairs, she found Susan flipping pancakes. She was alone. "Jon's getting the children dressed," she said. "Pull up a chair."

"I couldn't eat a thing," Alex told her.

"Not even with fresh strawberries?"

"From your garden, I suppose."

"Yes. The children picked them yesterday."

Alex said, "That sounds good, actually." What were the chances she and Charles could ever enjoy such an idyllic existence, raising a family in tandem, enjoying the solitude of their own little paradise where nothing from the past could trouble them?

"I'm afraid I don't feel my best this morning," Susan confided. "I couldn't sleep until Jon gave me a sedative. It's my fault about Miss Maddy. Jon brought her here for safety. I should have kept a better eye on her."

"You had the baby to see to. No. The fault's mine," Alex said. "I'm the one who came poking and prying. I hope they've got Kerry's mother locked away."

Briggie came down shortly, dressed in her all-purpose navy polyester suit and lace-up black shoes. "Morning, merry sunshine," she greeted Alex. "Morning, Susan! Oh, strawberry pancakes! I'd have made this trip just for those!"

"Hopefully, we'll be going back to Kansas City this morning after church," Alex said.

"Don't you think the police will need more than a threat to link Miss Maddy's death to Sylvia?" Briggie said. "I'll bet you a sundae the mayor sprang her last night and she's back at the retirement home."

A weight descended on Alex. She hadn't counted on that.

Her partner patted her hand. "Today's a day of rest. Tomorrow we'll go up to Mount Vernon and see what we can find on the Monett family."

"Why are the mayor and Sylvia living apart? Have you any idea?" Alex asked Susan.

Susan chuckled. "It's a town legend. Sylvia got caught playing high stakes poker. She gambled away the house. Fortunately, Mayor McNee was able to buy it back, but he sent her to the retirement home as punishment. Said she had no right to live in her house if it meant that little to her. They're not divorced. They still go everywhere together."

Jon came downstairs dressed in a suit and tie, followed by seven of his eight children in their Sunday best. Susan handed him a paper lunch bag and kissed his cheek. "Thanks for dressing the kids, honey. We'll see you at church."

He pinched her cheek. "You have help this morning, so maybe there's a ghost of a chance you'll be on time."

"Oh, go to your meetings," she said, shooing him out.

Seeing the loving ease that existed between Susan and Jon made Alex feel as though she had glimpsed something almost sacred. She had never seen any kind of LDS marriage up close before. But somehow she couldn't see herself and Charles with eight children on a farm with her quilting and him making bread.

No. They would probably live a very sophisticated life. She caught herself. Alex had no intention of marrying a man who used women and discarded them. She had to hold on to her anger or her heart would come apart.

Zina was examining her watch. "Whatth thith?" she asked.

"My grandfather's watch," she answered, springing it open to show the little girl. "He gave it to me when I was about your age."

"Itth pretty," Zina said, sitting down at the long kitchen table with her brothers and sisters.

Briggie said, "I'll get the children fed, Susan. You go get dressed and see to the baby."

The boys began beating on the table with their forks. "We want pancakes! We want pancakes!"

Sandra looked down her nose at them. "You're so uncivilized. Can't you see we have company?"

Briggie took the plate of pancakes out of the oven where they had been kept warm and began dishing them up. It was then that Charles walked in.

Alex drew a sharp breath. In this humble kitchen, among all the little Coxes, he looked absolutely gorgeous in his navy blazer, Christ Church college tie, and gray trousers. How could she resist him? But she stiffened as he kissed her cheek.

"Jon invited me to breakfast," he said. "Have I missed him?"

Briggie said, "He's the head honcho at the little branch of the Church they have down here, so he has meetings. Susan's tending to the baby. Sit down, and I'll give you some strawberry pancakes. Alex, would you mind giving me a hand?"

Ten-year-old Alana asked, "Are you a movie star?"

Charles turned to her. "What's your name?"

"You can call me Abee."

Thus, another woman bites the dust, Alex observed sourly.

Church in the white brick opera hall, complete with chipped gargoyles, was an amazing experience. A narrow flight of dusty stairs led to the third floor, where folding chairs were set in rows facing a makeshift podium. The large windows were open wide to provide cross-ventilation on this humid spring morning. As she took her seat, Alex heard a cardinal chatter while he groomed himself on a branch of pink magnolias.

As the service progressed, she marveled at the contrast between this little bit of Trotter's Bridge and the tragic death of Miss Maddy. Alex seemed now to be in another universe, the dusty old floorboards notwithstanding. God is in his heaven, but all is not right with the world, she told herself.

Oblivious to her withdrawal, Charles sat at her side, cuddling Abee with his other arm. "I can't say I've ever been in a church quite like this. It's rather thrilling. Like the Wild West."

Abee giggled.

Jon presided, recognizing Miss Maddy's unfortunate death and asking everyone to pray that she might find peace in the next life. He even mentioned that among her treasured possessions was a missionary tract, bestowed on someone in her family nearly 150 years before.

He proposed that as she had no living family, the branch should give her a fine LDS funeral later in the week. Since everything she owned had been lost in the fire, Jon asked if members could be generous with donations toward her burial costs.

All of this brought some peace to Alex, but she was still determined to find Miss Maddy's murderer. Briggie sat next to her, imparting her usual measure of strength.

The truth about the murder is in Kerry McNee's genealogy. The thought startled her. *Revelation.* The Lord was sending her revelation.

Bowing her head during the sacrament, Alex acknowledged the Lord's help, thanking him, and then, holding her breath, asked if she should marry Charles. The answer came in another whisper—*Live the gospel.*

Pondering on that, she remembered how the Lord had healed her in the past. Her heart had been very contrite at the time—an unusual occurrence. She must not let her pride stand in the way of the Lord's will. If she were humble enough, he would make that will known unto her in his own due time. If she was going to live the gospel, she knew she should endeavor to have "the mind of Christ." That was one of Briggie's favorite scriptures from Corinthians. Her friend had imparted to Alex a great love of the apostle Paul, knowing that humility seemed to be the hardest part of the gospel for her. She suddenly wondered how the erudite, handsome Charles scored in this area. How could he possibly be humble? Maybe one of the greatest tests on this earth was to be handsome, intelligent, and well-off. What could such a person think he needed Christ for?

* * *

"I was thinking," Briggie said on the way back to Dr. Jon's, "it wouldn't hurt to do a little cemetery crawl. Maybe it would help us to make some sense out of Miss Maddy's scrapbook."

Alex told her hesitantly about her prompting concerning Kerry's genealogy.

"That makes sense," her friend said, "Remember, Kerry told you they were related in some way. So, if we do Miss Maddy's genealogy, maybe it will lead us somewhere."

"We'll have to ask Jon for her last name. Do you realize we don't even know it?"

Over dinner, which consisted of a huge pot roast that had been cooking during church, carrots, potatoes, whole wheat rolls, and strawberry shortcake, Briggie announced their intentions. Charles said, "I say, that sounds jolly. Do you do this sort of thing often?"

"You'll have to spray for ticks and chiggers," Susan warned. "I've got a closet full of stuff. There's nothing worse than chiggers."

"Another unique American experience," Charles commented. "Anything with the name of chigger wouldn't dare show its face in England."

Abee giggled. "Chiggers don't have faces. But don't worry, Charles, I'll spray you myself, so you won't get bit. Mom, can I go? Please?"

It ended that the cemetery expedition included Zina, Abee, Charles, Alex, and Briggie, who carried the scrapbook under her arm. The cemetery was on a beautiful green hill facing west. As they entered through a surprisingly lovely arbor of roses, Alex forged ahead on her own, striding towards the top of the hill, drawn by something she couldn't name. Megan's cemetery had been a somber place behind a gray stone village kirk. How she wished her daughter could have been buried in a place this beautiful! Tears came to her eyes, swept away by the stiff wind that had come up. The sun suddenly darkened, and she realized that black clouds were moving in.

As she reached the crest of the hill, she stepped on a flat stone lettered with words that were nearly worn away. Unrolling the parchment she used for rubbings, Alex placed it over the stone and, with a stick of drawing charcoal, made a rubbing. The printing was faint and inexpertly carved. After some study, she made out the words "Missionary Call Point."

"Hey, guys," she called. "Come look at this!"

The little girls were beside her in no time, Charles and Briggie climbing behind them.

"Briggie, what was the name of the missionary on that tract in the scrapbook?"

Her friend opened the book gingerly and inspected the tract. "It was Elder Call. What have you got there?"

Alex displayed the rubbing. "What do you think it means?"

"Let's have a look around here at the headstones. Maybe they'll give us a clue."

The limestone headstones were worn and difficult to read.

"What're we looking for, Alekth?" asked Zina, who was doing somersaults.

"We're trying to solve a mystery. We need to see if we can read the writing on any of these stones."

"Ohh, look!" Zina exclaimed. "I think thith hath pretty flowerth on it."

It was the grave plot closest to the stone. Alex knelt and tried to make it out. It was a lengthy inscription. Carefully, she made a rubbing of it.

Briggie exclaimed, "Over here, Alex!"

Charles said, "I think I've got something here, too."

"Wait just a second. This could be really important," Alex told them.

The writing was small, so she had to brush over it very lightly with the charcoal. Slowly, a name appeared "Claire Prestcott." After that the dates: 1837–1867. Then a scripture: " OD HAS ELIVERE E AND I O PUT Y TRUS N HIM AN E W LL DE IVER ME."

"Briggie! Come here! I think this is a scripture from the Book of Mormon. It's my favorite scripture in Alma 36!"

Charles strolled over to her with Briggie and laid a casual arm across Alex's shoulders. "Extraordinary," he said. "What is the full text?"

Alex, proud of the one scripture she had memorized, said, "Parts of it have been left out, but basically it says "God has delivered me, and I do put my trust in him and he will deliver me."

"So, that tract bore some fruit," Briggie said. "This Claire may be the first Keeper. That may be why the tract is in the scrapbook."

"Elder Call," Alex said. "He must have baptized her."

"Come along and look at what I've discovered," Charles invited. A large, old oak tree shaded the graves in an unkempt section of the cemetery. On it was a deep carving, partially legible. Reading it, Alex gasped.

Briggie said, "Well, that explains a thing or two."

"What does it say?" asked Abee, holding Charles's hand to her smooth little cheek.

Charles intoned, "I imagine the full text is something like this: 'On this tree Elder Samuels was lynched by Jake McHenry in 1857.'"

"Oh, goodness," said Abee. "Is that very bad? What is lynched?"

"Good grief! What went on here?" Alex asked. "This *is* getting more like the Wild West by the moment. He must have been Elder Call's companion!"

Briggie spoke to Abee. "It means hanged, honey. But don't worry about it. They don't lynch people any more." Then she appeared to be deliberating. "You know, that's right around the time Parley P. Pratt was martyred, and that happened, if I'm not mistaken, less than fifty miles from here."

Alex's mind was racing. "The C on the handkerchief, Briggie. I'll bet you a sundae that Claire monogrammed it. I'll bet she was in love with Elder Call and he skedaddled after the lynching, maybe even promising he'd return."

"And she knew her Bible. There's that scripture in Deuteronomy. That the 'sins of the fathers will be visited on the children down to the third and fourth generation of those who hate me.' I'll bet her scrapbook is a record of all the bad things that happened to the McHenrys."

"So all the Keepers have kept records of everything that happened to the descendants of this Jake McHenry," Alex concluded. "But somehow the fact that Claire was a Mormon didn't carry down. Maybe she was afraid to tell anyone after the lynching."

"Which brings me to my little discovery," Briggie said. "Over here in the tall grass."

Then, catching sight of Zina cartwheeling through the cemetery, she called, "Zina, you're going to be eaten alive by chiggers!"

"They don't like me," Zina replied. "I don't have the right kind of blood."

Alex's ankles were already starting to itch. "Lucky you, you little monkey."

Briggie took them to a stone that had been erected a long ways from the tree. The engraving on it was deep, as though it had been carved under the influence of strong emotion. "Jake McHenry. 1830–1860. Scalped by savages and murdered."

"Well," said Charles, "a neat little picture is emerging, isn't it?"

"Thanks to the scrapbook," Alex said.

"You know," Briggie said, "I don't know why I didn't think of it before, but I have a Call line in my family tree. Pretty far back, but they have a big family organization. I wonder if they know anything about this."

"Can you get in touch with them?" asked Alex.

"I'll have to get Richard to go to my house and unearth the file from my study. He can read me the contact info over the phone."

Alex sighed. "Here we go. It just needs Richard sticking his nose in. I thought you weren't speaking."

"One thing you need to learn, Alex, is that at times it's best to bury your pride."

At that moment, distant thunder cracked, and the storm that had been threatening all day began to pour down upon them. Running down the hill, they made for their cars as quickly as possible.

"Abee, Zina, you go with your Aunt Briggie. I'm taking Alex," Charles said.

Alex's mind quickly swerved from the puzzle teasing her brain to the weightier matters of her heart. With an impending feeling of dread, she got into Charles's rented Lexus SUV.

The windows steamed quickly as the rain poured and the muddy dirt road grew slick beneath their tires.

"We haven't ever had a chance to talk about the baby, Alex," he said in a deliberate voice. "That's the whole reason I came down here. Can you talk about it? Was the cemetery difficult for you?"

Looking over at his profile, she stiffened. Hadn't he realized that when she walked out of the restaurant the night before, she was furious with him, full of doubts, ready to call the whole thing off? Daniel had understood immediately. Daniel had come to the house . . .

She said nothing. She couldn't trust herself.

"Alex?" Looking over at her set face, he pulled the car to the side of the road and stopped. Rain fell like a heavy curtain around the car, closing them in. There was no running away this time, no escape.

Shrinking against her door, she said, "I don't want to talk about Megan."

"Is it because of the Coxes and their happy family? Are you thinking about how old Megan would be and whether she would be like Zina or Abee? That's what I've been thinking—how much I'd like a little girl."

Lashing out like a cornered animal, Alex said finally, "How can you know me so little? How can you be so completely off the mark?"

Charles's face was quizzical. "What do you mean? Why are you angry?"

"How can I believe that you are even capable of love, Charles? You had a two-week fling with Kerry. She's gorgeous and talented. How many women like her have there been? Am I going to keep running into them for the rest of my life? I don't think I can handle that, Charles."

His face was earnest. "Kerry McNee is a self-centered diva. Most beautiful women are. It's very boring, actually." He reached over to take her hand. "Alex, I suppose you are thinking right now that I'm a playboy—that I have seduced every woman from Scotland to Cornwall."

"Something like that," she said.

"How can you have so little faith in me? Could a man like that accept the gospel of Jesus Christ? Could you really fall in love with a man like that?"

"Kerry sounded as though you were a living legend."

"She meant to wound you. In real fact, I squired Kerry around for a couple of weeks, but I never slept with her. You are forgetting Philippa."

89

"What about her?" Alex asked, feeling her heart soften. Could he really be telling her the truth?

"I loved her. I wouldn't have done anything unworthy of that love. I'm not claiming to have been a monk. I am forty-six and a red-blooded male. But I always hated myself afterwards, because I knew I wasn't in love."

"You said you fell in love with me because of my eyes. That doesn't seem enough to build an eternal commitment on. Lots of women have beautiful eyes, for Pete's sake."

He reached a hand up and smoothed her cheek. "The eyes are the windows to the soul, remember. You have been different from the very beginning. And you have brought me the gospel." He tilted her chin so she looked directly at him. "I have always thought I was a worthless sort of person. Philippa brought out the very best in me. And, of course, ours was a platonic relationship because she was my first cousin. When she was killed, I thought I'd lost my best self, but you have given me an even greater gift. A chance to be completely reborn."

She bowed her head.

"I've never loved anyone but Philippa before, Alex. You know that. Besides, I'm not the only one who has a past. There's Stewart. And, more importantly, I think, there's Daniel."

"I've never slept with Daniel," she said.

"Can you deny that there is a great deal of feeling there? That you don't still love him? I saw you in his arms just last night."

"Daniel and I have been through a lot together. He knows me at my worst and still loves me. I'm not sure you really know me, Charles. If you did, you'd understand why I fought so hard against this relationship, why I have such a difficult time with your past."

His face hardened. "If the Lord can forgive me, Alex, don't you think you can? As for Daniel, there are different levels of intimacy. I

90

think what you have with him is more intimate even than a sexual liaison. I'm trying to find my way into your confidence, trying to earn your trust. But I'm wondering if I'll ever have it as long as Dr. Grinnell is around."

"Daniel came after me last night because he knew how devastated I was. You didn't."

"I did. But you weren't at Jon's. I waited, and then we got the call about the murder. When I returned, you were pouring your heart out to Daniel."

It was true.

"Are you always going to hold me at arm's length, Alex? I thought with this business of your daughter, there was finally a crack in the wall. I thought you were going to trust me. Who do you really love, Alex? Daniel or me?"

She squirmed. "I feel so differently about each of you that it's hard to tell," she finally admitted.

He slammed his car into gear. "Well, darling, I suggest you figure it out."

They drove to the Coxes' in silence. What had she done?

"I'm sorry," she said. But she knew with the noise of the rain and the swish of the wipers that he didn't hear her.

Chapter Ten

Alex was right about Richard. When she got home, Briggie told her that he was not only going to find her Call file but would drive it down personally tomorrow. Semiretired, he was declaring the next week a much-needed vacation.

"Where's he going to stay?" Alex asked helplessly.

"He's arranging all that with Daniel. I imagine Kerry's father will put him up."

"So, all is forgiven between you?"

"It was only a little tiff. He apologized."

Alex thought about the chasm she had just chiseled between herself and Charles. Her heart, which had been so light over the last months, was heavy. She had to divert herself or she would give in to emotions she didn't want to examine.

"Let's have another look at the scrapbook, Briggs."

They spread it out on her friend's bed. First, there was the missionary tract and the handkerchief with the carefully embroidered C. Elder Call's. Then there were all the newspaper clippings about various McHenrys and their raucous doings. From the dates on the articles, the perpetrators appeared to be contemporaries of Jake McHenry, so they were probably his brothers or cousins.

The next page held the baby booties. Assuming it was Claire Prestcott's scrapbook and that she was the original Keeper, it looked as if she had made the booties for a child she hoped to have. She must have expected Elder Call to return.

Alex thought about the flat rock next to Claire's headstone. "I'll bet he went west," she said to Briggie. "I'll bet they said good-bye at that stone in the cemetery, and I'll bet she stood there watching for his return."

"Hopefully, he's part of my Call crew, and they'll have some idea what happened to him."

"From what Miss Maddy said, this scrapbook must be a record of what she thought of as the curse on the McHenrys. So, somehow, Kerry is tied into all these people."

They turned a page and found an account of a barn burning and cattle rustling by Clive McHenry, who was sentenced to five years in prison, leaving behind his infant son Bo and his common-law wife Betsy. He was noted as the son of the "infamous Jake McHenry," who had been scalped by the Indians. Briggie opened her research notebook and began a descendancy chart.

"Okay," Alex said. "That's three generations. The date on this is 1872, so Bo must have been born about that time."

"What we need is a nice juicy county history. Traveling historians used to come through towns like this and write them up and have them bound and then sell them to everyone in the county. Happened back in the 1880s and then again in the 1930s," Briggie said.

"You know what I think?" Alex said, forcing her mind to concentrate. "I think these McHenrys intermarried with the Monetts over in . . . Where did Miss Betty say they were from?"

McHenry Descendancy Chart
("Bad Blood")

Jake McHenry
1830–1860
(scalped and butchered by Indians)
lynched LDS missionary

Clive McHenry ———— Betsy
imprisoned for barn burning
and cattle rustling

Bo McHenry
b. circa 1872

"Mount Vernon," Briggie said. "So you think Kerry's 'bad blood' comes from her mother's side?"

"She gambled away their house. That sounds like a McHenry thing to do. And she's really touchy about her family history. I'll bet it was a secret marriage or something. We need to concentrate on her genealogy, I think."

"You may be right." Briggie was paging through the scrapbook. "Hmm. Here's a page out of a family Bible, looks like."

Alex focused on the crabbed writing. "There's Claire, born 1837. She never married."

"Yes. But her sister did. Look. Patience married Robert McGovern in 1851. She died in 1852, but it looks like she gave birth to a daughter, Mary. Patience probably died in childbirth. I'll bet Claire raised her and that Mary was the next Keeper."

"Yes. And Mary married Pierre Delacroix and had two daughters, Nancy and Sarah. You'd better start another descendancy chart, Briggs."

"Look. It gives Nancy's marriage to William Colby, but it doesn't

Prestcott Descendancy Chart

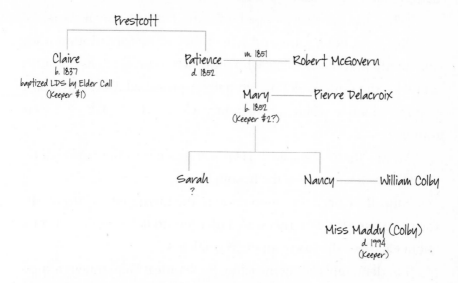

Prestcott

Claire
b. 1837
baptized LDS by Elder Call
(Keeper #1)

Patience —— m. 1851 —— Robert McGovern
d. 1852

Mary —————— Pierre Delacroix
b. 1852
(Keeper #2?)

Sarah   Nancy —————— William Colby
?

Miss Maddy (Colby)
d. 1994
(Keeper)

say what happened to Sarah. Miss Maddy's name was Colby, Jon says, so that's her family line."

"And there's no death date for Sarah?" Alex squinted at the page.

"No. That's odd, isn't it? There are death dates for everyone else."

"Maybe she was stillborn," Alex suggested with a twinge.

Paging through the rest of the scrapbook, they found only newspaper accounts of the various misdeeds of sundry McHenrys, all apparently cousins and brothers of Bo's. Briggie noted them all down but could only guess at relationships. There were Sam and Andrew, Bo's brothers by different mothers, and there were Tom and Sean, who appeared to be his cousins.

The scrapbook ended with that generation.

"Well," said Briggie, closing the scrapbook reluctantly, "I'd say Miss Maddy must have had another scrapbook that burned. This was probably Nancy Colby's, or even her mother, Mary Delacroix's."

"I think we should approach it from the other end. We're doing a genogram, after all. Let's look into Sylvia Monett's lineage."

"You realize that after what happened to Miss Maddy, it could be dangerous," Briggie said.

"When has that ever stopped us?" Alex felt suddenly reckless.

They went downstairs and joined the family for scripture study and family prayer. Matthew, who promised to be as tall as his father and with the same kinky brown hair, approached Alex. "Abee says you found a tree where a missionary was lynched." His eyes were round.

"What's that?" Jon asked. He'd just made it to the family devotional from his rounds at the hospital.

"Must have been the companion of the missionary who gave the tract to Miss Maddy's ancestor. Elder Samuels." Briggie told him about Charles's discovery on the big oak tree.

"I'm definitely calling the Church Historical Department tomorrow. If they don't already have this information, they should."

"That's why Miss Maddy thought the McHenrys were cursed," Alex said.

"Have you given that information to your client?" Jon asked.

"Good grief, no," said Briggie. "And we'd better get a move on if we're going to. Daniel and Kerry are leaving at six tomorrow morning. I'd plum forgot."

Alex cringed inwardly at the thought of seeing both Daniel and Kerry, but she got her car keys and said good night to Jon and Susan, who looked worn out.

Kerry, Daniel, and Mike were playing cards with her parents when Alex and Briggie arrived. Mrs. Sylvia McNee, dressed in a copper caftan, narrowed her eyes at them as Daniel, Mike, and the mayor stood. Cameron McNee looked rumpled, and his eyes were bleary, as though he had been imbibing. But he seemed lively enough to perform a jig, winking at Alex and Briggie.

"What are you doing here?" Sylvia demanded.

"I'm sorry to interrupt your card game, but we came to speak with Kerry."

Sylvia threw down her cards. "Whatever you have to say, you can say in front of me, you meddlers. Do you realize that because of you, I was arrested?"

"It was because of your own threat, Mrs. McNee," Alex said.

Kerry, though she had stated that she didn't want her mother to be upset, now seemed unmoved by her reaction. "What have you done with the divine Charles? Don't you know he is in serious consideration for my Lancelot?"

"I'm sure he'll be pleased to know that," Alex said levelly. "Perhaps you can tell him. He's staying at the Plaza."

"What?" exploded Kerry. "That bug-infested hole? He must come to us immediately!"

"Would you like to hear our report, or not?" Briggie intervened.

"Have you found my cursed blood?"

"We've found the source, but with Miss Maddy dead, we haven't been able to find how you tie in, yet."

"Kerry, I forbid you to go ahead with this. You're to go back to Kansas City and put it all out of your mind," Sylvia warned. "Miss Maddy was nuts."

"No, Mother. I think my interests lie here. I have nothing waiting for me in Kansas City but an empty house and a long vacation. Daniel has decided to stay on for his own reasons, and Father has no objections. I'm thirty-seven and richer than you'll ever be, so you can stop giving the orders."

"Do you think Miss Maddy's death was an accident?" Sylvia demanded. "Don't you realize that you're stirring up the river and the cottonmouths are going to come after the lot of you?"

Kerry placed her hand over Daniel's. "I have my knight in shining armor, Mother."

"And we can take care of ourselves," Briggie said.

"So, what's your story?" the mayor spoke for the first time.

Briggie pulled out her descendancy charts and placed them on the card table. "Miss Maddy was a real believer in the Bible. There's a scripture in Deuteronomy that must have gotten in her head like a bee in her bonnet. It's about a curse upon the children, down to the third and fourth generation, for their fathers' wickedness."

"Everyone knows the McHenrys are full-out wicked," said Mike, speaking for the first time. "So maybe what she believed is true. But what did their ancestor do that was so bad?"

"You really don't know?" Alex asked.

Mike said no.

The singer shook her head of golden hair. She appeared to have Daniel wrapped around her little finger, as well. Why else was he staying? And yet, in front of him she could speak of Charles as her Lancelot! Alex suddenly wished there were such a thing as bad blood.

"Oddly enough, it started with a Mormon missionary," she said. "Briggie and I are Mormons, and Charles is about to be baptized."

Kerry raised a brow. "Really? Charles? I find that very hard to believe. He's far too sybaritic to go for a life of tee-totaling chastity."

Alex resented this corroboration of her own doubts. She was about to make a crushing remark when Briggie intervened. "We don't take slurs on our religion kindly, Ms. McNee. Are you some kind of bigot?"

Kerry looked startled.

"This town was full of bigots in 1859." Briggie stood foursquare in her cherry red sweats, and Alex had no trouble discerning her pioneer heritage. "One of our apostles was martyred not far from here. And one of our missionaries was lynched by Jake McHenry right here in this town. Jake was later scalped by Indians. Bigots usually get what they deserve. What goes around comes around."

"Whatever Jake McHenry did, you know perfectly well there's no such thing as bad blood," Daniel said.

Briggie continued. "On this descendancy chart I've listed all his descendants that we could find in Miss Maddy's record. Unfortunately, her most recent records must have perished in the fire. We only go down three generations, so far. I'm afraid that even though I agree with you, Daniel, they were a lawless and wicked bunch."

"So far?" The mayor said. "How can you continue, if her records were burned?"

"We root diggers have a few tricks up our sleeves. We're receiving reinforcements tomorrow. Daniel, I suppose you know your father's coming down?" Briggie remarked.

He looked startled, and Alex realized this was the first he'd heard of it. "I thought you weren't speaking to him."

"They made up," Alex said. "He's bringing some documents Briggie has that we hope will help."

"Great! That's all we need—Dad running around, laying down the law."

Alex smiled at the picture of the dignified, white-maned Richard Grinnell running around Trotter's Bridge, barking commands at Daniel over his shoulder as he was wont to do.

"Now, Daniel," Briggie said. "You just don't know how to manage him. I'll see that he stays under control."

"That hasn't exactly worked in the past," Alex said. "More like the two of you get completely *out* of control. You're not a good influence on each other."

Briggie looked offended. Daniel rose and tossed the cards he was still holding onto the table. Looking at Alex, he said, "We need to talk. Now that the rain has stopped, shall we go for a little walk over by the park?"

Alex knew she should say no, but after her conversation with

Charles, she needed time with Daniel to attempt to sort out her feelings.

"That sounds like a good idea. Briggie, you take the car." She tossed her the keys. "Daniel can run me back."

"And I," announced Kerry, "am going to take Daddy's car and drive over to that pit where Charles is staying and bring him back here. Michael, you can keep Mother and Daddy company playing three-handed gin or something."

Daniel and Charles staying in the same house! Alex must have looked alarmed.

Kerry said, "Don't worry. I'm not going to steal anything that doesn't want to be stolen."

Fuming, Alex took formal leave of Mike and the McNees, who merely nodded, and followed Daniel back through the gleaming, modern kitchen out the back door.

For a few moments they didn't say anything but just walked along wet streets, with water still gushing down the gutters. It was the only place in Trotter's Bridge she had seen sidewalks, she realized. The rain still dripped from the willows with their new spring growth, and the reflection of the street lamps shone on the black pavement.

"Is Charles really being baptized?" Daniel inquired.

"Why are you so surprised?"

He was clearly uncomfortable. "Alex, I realize you're engaged. I don't want you to think I'm trying to sway you in any way, but I must tell you, after the account Kerry gave me of their affair, I find it just as hard as she does to see him as a Mormon."

"What did she tell you?"

"Well, you know she's rather a drama queen, but apparently he whisked her away to Switzerland for a week's skiing and then to France where they did a wine tour of the Loire Valley. She claimed he was the most passionate man she had ever known, even though he

100

was an Englishman. She also told me that she was forced to put an end to his pursuit of her, because she had engagements in America she would not cancel, though he tried to cajole her into it."

Alex felt her heart thumping so loud she could hardly think. Did she trust Charles? Did she really trust his version of events?

"She lied," she told Daniel finally. "I don't know why, unless it was to make you jealous, but she made that up completely."

What had she seen in Charles's eyes? When he had asked why, if God forgave him, she could not, she had read real hurt. Was it his ego? Or was it his spirit?

"I don't think I would dismiss it that easily, if I were you. She was pretty convincing."

"I love Charles. I wouldn't have fallen in love with a man like that."

"I know you don't realize it, Alex, but I have actually been studying your religion for the last couple of months. So has Dad, believe it or not."

She stopped dead. "Why?"

"When you returned to Kansas City after that last visit with your mother, and I saw how you were healed—I mean really healed from all those years of your mother's alcoholism and abuse and abandonment—I knew, as a psychologist, that there must be a higher power and that you had accessed it. I was curious."

"And what do you think?"

"I'm intrigued. I find that all the doctrines make a lot of sense, but I have trouble accepting the story of Joseph Smith. And I can't see someone as sophisticated as Charles taking it seriously for a minute."

She turned on him. "You met Charles and talked to him for what? Five minutes? How can you think you know him?"

"Well, there's Kerry's story . . ."

"Haven't you had an affair with Kerry? Yours lasted four years, from what you've said. Why should I listen to you?"

"Alex." He put his hands on her shoulders. "I just don't want to see you get hurt."

"You think Charles is a cad," she accused with heat.

"I think he's a player."

"Take me home!" she commanded. "Now!"

Chapter Eleven

When Alex stalked into the Coxes' after her ride with Daniel, Briggie and Jon were talking in the living room. Jon said Susan had gone to bed.

"Whoa!" Briggie said. "I know that look! Has Daniel been tweaking your tail?"

Alex collapsed into a chair. "Jon? Will you level with me? What do you think of Charles?"

The doctor grinned. "He's seriously out of place in Trotter's Bridge but loving every minute of it. For an Englishman, he's extremely laid back."

"He says he wants to be baptized. But he's led the bachelor life for at least twenty-six years. He's an Oxford don and a theater critic for the *Times.* Can you really see him as a Mormon?"

"Why did you join the Church, Alex? You seem fairly sophisticated yourself."

"Briggie scooped me up in Scotland after my husband died and

103

loved me into it. I've only been a member since a year ago last December."

"What do you mean, loved you into it? Did you join for Briggie's sake?"

Alex thought back to her conversion. The year of therapy for her post-tramatic stress, Briggie's big white house in Independence, Missouri, which they had shared, the young missionaries with their cowlicks and Southern accents, the feeling of peace and belonging that she had never had. "I think I loved the gospel because it was like a homecoming. It all seemed familiar. But I had a lot to learn after my baptism. I never really learned to trust God until last winter."

"Well," Jon hesitated, "to be frank, I think Charles is capable of accepting the gospel. Everyone is. But they must access the power of Christ's atonement to help them change their hearts. Charles is steeped in centuries of British tradition in addition to his twenty-six years of bachelorhood. What does he think of Joseph Smith?"

"We've never discussed it, believe it or not. His conversion is based on the Book of Mormon. He loves Alma the Elder, and he compares himself to both him and Alma the Younger. He believes the Book of Mormon is scripture, so he must believe in Joseph Smith."

"That's good. Why don't you spend some time reading the third chapter of Mosiah and see what King Benjamin taught about putting off the natural man? It's not going to be easy for Charles, but King Benjamin tells how it can be done."

Briggie spoke up. "Why all these doubts all of a sudden, Alex?"

"Daniel," she said. "He thinks Charles is just a player. And, much as I hate to say it, Daniel's usually right."

Briggie came over and sat next to her on the couch and gave her a rare hug. "If I loved you into the church, what makes you think you can't love Charles into it? It's true, isn't it?"

Alex relaxed against Briggie's arm. "Yes. I guess what it all really comes down to is that I have a hard time believing Charles could love me and an even harder time believing he can change."

Jon stood up. "I can tell you from spending an evening in frantic search of you that he is a man in love, Alex. Men manifest love in a desire to protect and defend. To make their woman's world safe."

Alex reflected on this. Unfortunately, it was a characteristic shared by Daniel and Charles.

*   *   *

Monday dawned bright and clear, the humidity washed away by the storm. After studying King Benjamin, Alex had slept deeply and well. She knew just what she was going to discuss with Charles when next she saw him.

"Well! Ready to tackle the Monett line today, Alex?" Briggie entered her room, dressed in her Royals T-shirt and royal blue sweatpants.

"When's Richard coming?"

"He's driving down. I expect him about noon, so we have the morning to ourselves."

"I wonder where Charles is."

"He called this morning. I told him what we were doing and sent him back to that cemetery. We didn't finish looking at it."

"Briggie! I wanted to see him!"

"Plenty of time for that later. You've gotten distracted from the case, Alex. It's not like you."

"It's not every day I'm trying to decide my eternal future! Sheesh!"

"Just live the gospel, honey, and your answer will come. I'll be downstairs. Don't forget your morning prayers."

Mount Vernon had a whole different feel than Trotter's Bridge. It was the county seat of Lawrence County and had a tall brick court-house, surrounded by professional buildings. Before they started hunting, Briggie demanded that they visit the Ben Franklin Five and Dime. It was a wonderful old-fashioned store with candy in jars and bolts and bolts of quilting fabric.

"I always come in here when I'm down this way and buy some fabric for Leann."

Leann was Briggie's youngest daughter. "She's expecting in June, and if I were a proper grandmother, I'd make a baby quilt. But I haven't the patience. I'll send her the fabric. She loves to quilt."

While Briggie was searching among the calico bolts, Alex bought some licorice and stared out the window at the bustling square. So this was where Sylvia had grown up. It seemed much more like what she expected a nice little Southern town to be.

"There, I think that'll do it," Briggie said, placing a dozen or so "fat quarters" of fabric on the checkout counter.

When they left the store, they climbed the steps to the imposing courthouse. Alex's tumultuous feelings calmed. From all the time she had spent doing genealogy, courthouses were familiar territory.

The recorder of deeds had them fill out a form with their request for Sylvia's marriage certificate. While they were waiting for it, Alex sat on a bench eating her licorice.

The certificate showed Sylvia's parents, just as they had hoped: Miriam Gardner and Gordon Monett. Birthplaces were both Missouri. Sylvia was married June 28, 1950.

"This is Lawrence County," Briggie said. "Trotter's Bridge is in Barry County. Let's go to the local library and see if we can get some gossip about the Gardners and the Monetts and maybe find one of those nifty county histories. With any luck, the families will be mentioned."

The library was a comfortable building near the square and

looked as though it had been a late 1930s WPA project. Briggie went straight to the desk.

"We're genealogists who have been hired to research the Monett and Gardner families. Can you tell us if there is any family history material here that we could use?"

The librarian was not at all like the comfortable Miss Betty. She was very tall and angular. Her gray hair was worn in a French braid down her back.

"Oh, my, yes! They're two of our finest families! Miriam Gardner founded our Library Guild way back when. And her husband, Gordon, was a judge."

This did not sound promising to Alex. No scandal here. She took a stab in the dark. "Did you ever know Sylvia? I realize she's a lot older than you . . ."

Halfway through her speech, the librarian began to look as though something had a bad smell. "She's ten years older than me and went to settle in Barry County, praise the Lord. What a time she gave her parents! She always thought she was too good for this town after she worked in Washington, D.C., towards the end of the war. Dyed her hair platinum and wore bloodred lipstick and nail polish. Had her skimpy little clothes made by some poor creature her mother was trying to pull out of the gutter. Then, of course, she *had* to get married to one of those wild McHenry boys. Like to broke her mother's heart. She'd raised her daughter for better things. But Sylvia was faster than a speeding bullet."

"You mean, she got pregnant?" Alex asked, startled at this flood of vituperative information.

The librarian licked her lips. "I shouldn't be talking this way. It's shameful."

Briggie said warmly, "But we're genealogists. These are the things we need to know. Do you happen to know when she got pregnant?"

"Soon after she got home from Washington. Once she married that McHenry, she wasn't received in the county. So I don't know much after that."

Another child? Could this be what Sylvia was trying to hide? Did Kerry not know she had a half sibling? He or she would be more than ten years older. One of the bad-blood McHenrys?

As Alex recalled, Sylvia's first husband had died in a drunken car wreck. She must have been a real beauty for Cameron McNee, son of the mayor of Trotter's Bridge, to take her on with that kind of baggage. Before she could forget any of the information, Alex took out the beginnings of Kerry's genogram from her carryall and updated it with this new information about Sylvia and her parents.

Maybe Miss Betty would know what had become of Sylvia's child. So far this investigation had been pretty irregular—a mysterious

Kerry's Genogram

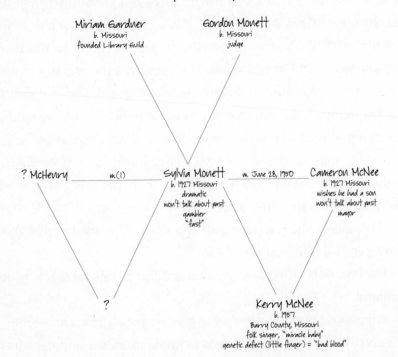

Miriam Gardner
b. Missouri
founded Library Guild

Gordon Monett
b. Missouri
judge

? McHenry — m.(1) — Sylvia Monett
b. 1927 Missouri
dramatic
won't talk about past
gambler
"fast"

m. June 28, 1950

Cameron McNee
b. 1927 Missouri
wishes he had a son
won't talk about past
mayor

?

Kerry McNee
b. 1957
Barry County, Missouri
folk singer, "miracle baby"
genetic defect (little finger) = "bad blood"

scrapbook, cryptic tombstones, carved trees, and rumor. She looked at her watch. Richard would be here soon. If they drove fast, they might just have time to collar the Trotter's Bridge librarian.

"Thanks so much, ma'am," Alex told the helpful woman.

*   *   *

"A baby?" Miss Betty asked in answer to Alex's inquiry. "I never heard talk of any baby . . ." She wrinkled her brow. "There was no child around when she married the mayor. But I was new to town then. I'd just gotten married and moved here that year. The only thing I ever heard about her was her wild first marriage. Let's see, who would know?"

While Betty thought, Briggie moved away and began browsing shelves.

"Well, there's old Gladys McIntire out t' the retirement home. She's thick as molasses with Sylvia."

"She wouldn't be likely to tell her secrets, then," Alex mused.

Betty blushed a little. "Is this real important?"

"Well," Alex said, "I think it must be. Sylvia doesn't want us poking around for some reason. Maybe this is it. And there's the whole business with Miss Maddy, who surely must have known about her child. She kept scrapbooks of everything to do with the McHenrys."

"Well," Betty simpered slightly, "I do play bridge on Tuesdays with Gladys and several other friends. That's my day off. We've played bridge together for years. I might just be able to edge the conversation around to Sylvia's first marriage."

"Here's the county history, Alex," Briggie said, carrying a large leather-bound tome. "Let's have a look at the index. Did you bring the descendancy chart?"

"Yes." Finding a table in a nook by the window, Alex sat down with Briggie, acknowledging the spurt of adrenaline that always accompanied a find.

"Hmm," said Briggie. "Robert McGovern—that's Patience's husband, remember? Claire's sister?"

Her friend flipped to the page indicated.

Robert McGovern was one of the founders of Trotter's Bridge. Originally from Dumfries, Scotland, he had a 180-acre sheep farm on the county road in the 6th precinct. He married Patience Prestcott, who died giving birth to their only child, Mary. Patience McGovern's sister, Claire, had a small stone cottage in the forest near McGovern's farm. She raised Mary McGovern from babyhood.

There followed details about Robert McGovern's career as a founding father, which Briggie skimmed. Then she came to the next pertinent bit.

Mary McGovern was taught midwifery by her Aunt Claire Prestcott and continued in this capacity even after her marriage to Pierre Delacroix, a wealthy fur trader. The couple had two daughters, Sarah and Nancy.

A long, elaborate ancestry of Delacroix was given, together with all the achievements (among them the opera hall) he had undertaken for the city of Trotter's Bridge. ("He probably commissioned this book, I'll bet you a sundae!" Briggie said.)

Sarah grew to become the wife of the town's Presbyterian minister, Ernest McNee, in 1888. Reverend McNee was a new immigrant from Scotland, having been ordained in Edinburgh, where he was a graduate of the Divinity School. The town was very fortunate to have such a distinguished minister who was so well educated.

There followed a long catalog of his achievements, which included a campaign to educate the farm children beyond the age of twelve. Apparently, he held school in his home during the evenings after farm work was done. His wife, Sarah Delacroix McNee, fed the young boys. The couple had only one son, Cameron, born in 1889. At the time of publication, young Cameron stood to inherit his grandfather Delacroix's fortune as well as the original McGovern farm.

"Well, then!" Briggie said. "That joins up with the material that Sylvia gave us about Kerry's McNee ancestry. But there must be a misrepresentation somewhere, because none of these people has anything to do with the McHenrys." She frowned. "Even if Sylvia did have a baby by a McHenry, that doesn't have any effect on Kerry's blood."

"But why is Sylvia so anxious and upset about our investigation?" Alex asked, as she drew in the new information on her genogram.

"There must be something she's afraid of our finding out."

Prestcott Descendancy Chart

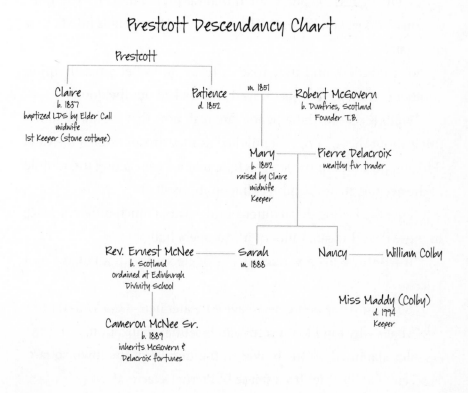

"Well, there's a lot of sources we haven't checked out yet. Land records and probate can tell us a lot. Plus, in the early days of the county, they *did* keep birth and death records here, not in Jeff City. Hopefully, Miss Betty will come through for us on the name of the child and what happened to him or her."

Alex looked at her watch. It was noon. "When and where are you meeting Richard?"

"He's going to meet us for lunch at the Blue Tail Cafe at noon."

"It's noon now, Briggie. Can't we check this book out?"

"You forget, we're not residents. Richard can wait a few minutes while I just check up on the McHenrys. I'm interested to see if the lynching is in here."

There was no mention of the McHenrys whatsoever.

"Well! I guess no one wanted that family around. They're non-persons," Briggie exclaimed. "Have you got those details filled in on the chart?"

Alex nodded, and they rose to leave. Miss Betty was helping another patron, so they just waved and walked out the door.

"Well, I feel like these people are real, now that we know something about them," Briggie remarked as they drove towards the cafe, dodging potholes in the street. Huge maples grew along the middle of the avenue, their roots breaking up the asphalt.

"I get the feeling that Trotter's Bridge was a much different place in those days. I mean, think of it! An opera hall?"

"It would've been vaudeville," Briggie said with a laugh. "Not Puccini."

"But, still. They don't even have a theater here. Or a Wal-Mart."

"That's why Jon likes it so much. Essential civilization."

Alex slammed on the brakes in the middle of the town square. "Look at that, Briggie! It's a statue of Pierre Delacroix!"

"Well, now," her friend said. "It looks like Kerry came from way uptown, doesn't it?"

* * *

Richard was pacing the parking lot of the Blue Tail Cafe, one hand clutching a file and the fingers of the other running through his beautiful white mane. He was dressed like a lumberjack. Alex laughed. "Richard actually purchased some Levi's and a flannel shirt!"

"He looks downright human," Briggie added. "Except that the Levi's are new. He should've bought stone-washed."

"He's irritated. Try not to inflame him, Briggie. Note the hiking boots. I'll swear they're from L. L. Bean."

Her friend only laughed, and Alex nearly groaned at the twinkle in her eye.

"Hello, Mr. Hot Shot!" Briggie greeted her friend and adversary.

"It's about time, Brighamina! This place is most unsavory. You don't actually propose that we eat here, do you?"

"It's either here or the local KFC."

Richard shuddered, and opened the door for them. "Alex, you're looking well."

"Thank you, kind sir. And you? How have you been?"

"I've been better. The Cards aren't starting out the season too well."

"Did you find my Call file, Richard?" Briggie asked as they sat down on the cracked vinyl seats of the cafe.

"After a hunt. You really need someone to take you in hand, Brighamina! That so-called office of yours is a disaster. The Call file was in the last drawer of your filing cabinet all the way at the back."

Her friend grinned. "I know. I should have told you. Did you gorge yourself on my Hershey's kisses?"

He looked sheepish. Then he said gruffly, "The alphabet. A. B. C. You've heard of it?"

They all ordered chicken noodle soup from a sullen waitress as wide as the Mississippi. In a moment, she was back, plunking a bread basket and three glasses of water on the table.

Briggie was pawing her way through the file. Finally, she pulled out a yellow stapled document. "This is an index of all the Call names before 1900 and the person who is researching that name together with the contact info."

"James Call," Alex reminded her.

"There are about a zillion James Calls. I wish we had his birth or death date. Dang. I'm going to have to phone at least eight people to try to find him."

"Be my guest, Brighamina," Richard said, holding out his cell phone. "Who is James Call?"

"A missionary whose companion was lynched in this fair town back in the 1850s. We want to know what became of him. We think he baptized someone who's related to our client. It's not real important, but we're trying to get the whole picture."

Briggie began dialing. Before the soup arrived, she had struck gold.

Chapter Twelve

It looks like our James Call left on his mission from St. George," Briggie informed them after returning Richard's phone. "He was the son of a cotton farmer. Came across the plains when he was just a kid. Brigham Young sent his father, James Sr., down to St. George. They called it Dixie, Alex, because it was the farmers' mission to grow cotton for the Saints."

"Well, what happened to him?"

"No one knows. The last letter they had from him told about baptizing Claire. I guess she was his first baptism. He said he was going back after his release to marry her."

"The fellow could have been lynched, too," Richard remarked.

"No. Otherwise there would have been no baby booties," Briggie told him.

"Baby booties?" Richard looked resigned, as he always did, at Briggie's seeming non sequiturs.

"There were two pairs of hand-knitted baby booties in the scrapbook, one pink and one blue. I think Claire was planning her layette.

She fully expected to marry him. I think the lynching spooked him and he took off."

"Why did no one ever hear from him again?" Alex asked.

"Probably felt like a coward," Briggie surmised. "I'm going to comb through all this stuff tonight before I go to bed. There may be a random piece of unconnected information that would fit smack-dab in the middle of our puzzle."

They had finished their soup and were enjoying surprisingly good blackberry cobbler.

"Tell me about the case so far, Brighamina."

Briggie spent twenty minutes giving him the "lowdown" and showing him the descendancy charts and genograms they had begun.

"This Kerry McNee. What's she like?" Richard wanted to know.

Alex maintained her silence.

Briggie shrugged. "Pretty full of herself. She's trying to steal Charles away from Alex. Seems they met when she was singing in England."

"Why would she let the word of a crazy old woman keep her from marrying?"

Alex reflected on this for a moment and then said, "She believes in legends, and curses, and all that sort of thing. She collects stories and writes songs about them. From what we've been able to reconstruct, she probably should be the next Keeper." Alex sighed. "Then there's her little finger. It's crooked. According to the Keeper who died, that meant she had McHenry blood. It's a genetic fluke in their family."

"I think she's been too selfish to get married, and now she's getting old and realizes her career won't last forever. She's probably one of those women who see children as accessories to herself," Briggie differed. "What is that word? Narci . . . something."

"Narcissist," Alex said, surprised that Briggie had taken Kerry's measure so quickly. Reflecting on her own age and the loss of Megan, she played with her cobbler, suddenly unable to eat. Would she ever marry again? Why had Charles not called her cell phone? Was he still disgusted with her? Then, for no particular reason except her own fears, she began to wonder if he was with Kerry.

"Yoo-hoo! Alex! Where did you go?" Briggie called, waving her hand in front of Alex's face.

"But you must know Kerry McNee!" Alex exclaimed suddenly. "She was Daniel's girlfriend all through college."

"That Kerry?" Richard put a hand to his forehead, ran it down his face, and shook his head. "He's gotten mixed up with her again? What is it about the boy that makes him pick the bad apples? Glory! You should have known his wife. If there ever was a narcissist, it was Caroline! Look what she did, running off with her tennis pro and leaving Daniel to raise Marigny!" He leveled his gaze at Alex. "The only good taste in women he has ever shown was falling in love with you, Alex. I thought things were settled between you, and then along comes Superman."

Alex felt herself color. "Things aren't irrevocably decided between me and Charles, you know."

"Don't get me wrong, Alex. If I were a woman and had to choose, I would make the same decision," Richard said with a sigh. "Daniel's never lived up to his potential. Now, if he had gone into the firm . . ."

Perturbed as usual by Richard's dismissal of Daniel, Alex said, "Daniel is an excellent psychotherapist and a wonderful human being. This thing with Charles just sneaked up on me. And, to tell you the truth, Richard, I'm not entirely sure of myself. I may never marry again."

To her surprise, Richard nodded in understanding. "When you're young, it's easy to make that leap. The older you get and the more you see of the world, you realize what a risk it is."

"That's why you need the good Lord to be third party to your marriage," Briggie said in her usual down-to-earth manner. "If you and your spouse put the Lord first, where he belongs, then you end up going in the same direction and you meet each other in the same place."

Richard looked uncomfortable. "So what's the next step, ladies?"

"I suppose we ought to talk to Kerry and see if she has ever heard that she had a half-sibling," Briggie said.

"That's not the kind of thing you can spring on someone, Briggie," Alex said as her friend reached for Richard's cell phone. "We need to talk to her in person, in spite of the fact that I never want to see her again."

"I'm just calling to make sure she's home." Briggie called information for Cameron McNee's number. "Besides," she added as she waited to be connected, "we need to finagle an invitation for Richard so he doesn't have to stay at that unspeakable motel."

Kerry was home and anxious to see them.

When they pulled into the McNees' long driveway, Alex was powerfully relieved to see that Charles's Lexus was not there. Kerry and Daniel were looking through their college yearbook in the living room. Mayor McNee, who welcomed them cordially, was puffing on a pipe and sipping from a glass of what looked like scotch or bourbon.

"Hi, Mr. Grinnell!" Kerry greeted them. "Remember me?"

"I certainly do," Richard remarked blandly. "I certainly do."

She smiled and became kittenish, patting the seat on the couch next to her. "Now, why don't you have a seat here next to me, and I'll get you a drink? Briggie? Alex? What would you like?"

"Just plain soda water," Richard requested.

"Do you have orange crush?" Briggie inquired.

"Nothing for me, thanks," Alex said.

"No orange crush, Briggie. Do you like ginger ale?"

"That'll be fine."

They seated themselves—Richard, in spite of Kerry's invitation, on a love seat facing his son, Briggie next to him, and Alex in a straight-backed chair.

"Well, son, what have we got here? Why aren't you at work today?"

Poor Daniel took on the harassed look he always wore in the presence of his father. "I don't have to account to you for my movements, sir."

The room was silent until Kerry returned with the drinks. "You said you wanted to talk to me about something?"

Alex nodded at Briggie to begin.

"We're hoping you can help us," Briggie said, seemingly oblivious to Mayor McNee's presence. "Have you ever heard that you have a half sibling?"

Kerry sat up straight. "A what?"

"A half sibling. We don't know if it is a brother or a sister."

The mayor suddenly began to choke. Coughing violently, he sat doubled up in his chair. What they could see of his face was bright red.

Kerry ran to him. "Daddy, Daddy! Hold on, I'll get some water!"

Daniel said, "I don't think she wants to hear this right now. Maybe you guys had better leave."

Cameron McNee waved his hand at Daniel to silence him. He downed the water Kerry brought and managed to quit coughing.

"It was nothing," he said, looking up at his daughter. "I don't know how they found out, but it was a slipup when I was a teenager. A girl from Aurora. Dad settled some money on her, and she moved south, where no one knew her. New Orleans. She had a little girl there, but then she married, and we lost touch."

Alex looked at Briggie and saw her wooden expression. She hoped her own was unreadable. *What was this?*

Kerry turned on them, as though defending her father. "How in the world did you find out about that?"

Deciding it was not the time to tell her about her mother's first marriage, Alex said, "You have a lot of gossips in this town. We didn't go looking for that information. People just like to talk."

"Well, you stick to your job, you hear? I won't have you upsetting my daddy!"

Alex stood, "I'd quit this minute if I didn't think it was my duty to find out who murdered Miss Maddy."

"We've raised our rates to fifty dollars an hour," Briggie said stiffly, getting to her feet. "Apiece."

*　　*　　*

"Was that all an act?" Alex asked Richard as he climbed into his black Suburban.

"Brighamina has never been known for her diplomacy," he said, strapping himself in. "Now where?"

"I mean that tale Cameron McNee spun."

"I think he panicked. It didn't even occur to him you could be talking about his wife's past. I'd say that young woman comes by her narcissism naturally. Now where?"

"I guess back to Dr. Jon's farm," Alex said. "Maybe you can have Miss Maddy's room."

*　　*　　*

The Georgian house was a welcome sight to Alex, especially when she saw Charles's Lexus. As she alighted from the car, Zina came running towards them. "Charlth ith playing with Dashiell! He liketh him. I didn't know you were going to get married! That meanth Dashiell can live with both of you!"

So, according to Charles, the marriage was still on. While Briggie and Richard went inside, Alex went to where her fiancé was playing with the kittens inside the barn. "Well, what do you think?" she asked, glad that this encounter was in front of Zina. "Will Dashiell make a good addition to RootSearch, Inc.?"

Charles looked up, squinting against the sun. "He seems to have extraordinary taste, anyway. He likes me, for one thing."

She knelt down next to him and kissed his cheek. "Who wouldn't like you?"

Standing, he pulled her to her feet. "Dr. Daniel Grinnell for one."

"What does that matter?" she said carelessly. Daniel's championing of Kerry had done little to endear him to her. And could she help it if the mere sight of Charles made her heart skip? If his physical presence dissolved all her doubts?

Charles's eyes grew warm. He pulled her to his side and kissed her forehead. "You've decided between us, then?"

Zina had taken Tigger out of the barn and was showing him the new colt in the corral.

Alex knew she couldn't put off the conversation. "I couldn't sleep last night. Daniel told me you are a player."

Now his eyes hardened. "And because he is a psychologist you believed him, right?" He dropped his arm. "What in the world can I do to prove to you that my feelings are new, different? Don't you realize that when I come out of the baptismal font all my pitiful past will be washed away?"

Alex looked at the kittens gamboling together, the essence of innocence. "But you will still remember. What if I don't measure up, Charles?"

"Measure up?"

"I'm not very experienced. There's only been one man in my life."

"Alex, you are reducing love to one dimension. Physical attraction is important, I give you that. But we already know we have that. And for me, at least, there is so much more. There is a spiritual dimension I've never felt. The knowledge that what we are going to build is eternal. That God will be part of our marriage. There will, God willing, be children. And they will be made out of us. Out of our love."

Alex's eyes filled, and she lowered her head and sniffed.

Zina reentered and threw her arms around Charles. "I think you're going to make Abee cry."

"Why?" asked Charles, startled.

"Because she wantth you to wait and marry her, not Alekth."

"When Abee grows up, she'll have all sorts of chaps who will want to marry her. You, too, Zina."

"You think so?" the little girl's brow furrowed in earnestness.

"Right now, your business is to look after your animals and learn to be a good mom like your mom. Do you know, she's the best mom I've ever seen?"

"Charles," Alex protested. "You have a wonderful mother."

"But she couldn't teach me the gospel," he replied. "Zina's mom teaches her about Jesus every day."

When they entered the house a few moments later, Briggie was talking nineteen to the dozen to Susan who was nursing the baby, her shoulder draped with a quilt. Richard was sitting back, amused, as he frequently was when Briggie was about.

"Alex! I think I've found something!" her friend crowed, holding up a piece of paper.

"What?"

"There is a Call that could never be accounted for."

"What do you mean?"

"Well, there was this little note in my file. Apparently, during the gold rush years in Colorado, there was a miner who got trapped in a cave-in. He was badly hurt and asked for some Mormon elders to be found to administer to him. By the time they got there, he could hardly speak. He said his name was "Trader Call." They blessed him to die peacefully and the last word on his lips was 'Claire.'"

"Oh, my gosh! Briggie, it must have been Elder Call! But why 'Trader?'"

"Allowing for the American accent, it's possible that the word was *traitor*," Charles remarked. "Mightn't he have thought he was a traitor to leave the mission after his companion was lynched?"

"That makes a certain amount of sense," Briggie said.

"Where did you get that piece of paper, for heaven's sake?" Alex asked.

"It was a letter sent to a prominent Call in Utah by the elders who blessed and buried him. The family didn't know what else to do. At the last Call reunion, someone made copies for everyone and distributed them, in case we might be able to figure out who he was."

Alex thought a moment. "Does the letter give the death date?"

"It's 1858, the year after the lynching."

"So he was probably trying to make his fortune to go back and marry Claire."

"Yes. Alex—now we can do their sealing!" Briggie exclaimed.

"By proxy?" she asked.

"Yes. We'll save it until you go to the temple, and you can stand as proxy for Claire."

Alex sat down and pondered this. "That's wonderful, Briggie. What a healing thing the gospel is."

Susan interceded. "This is great, what you're doing. Maybe someday this whole town will be healed somehow."

"Well," Charles said, sitting down on the couch next to Alex, "I found out a few more facts about the McHenrys at the cemetery today."

Briggie scrambled for her descendancy chart. "Shoot."

Taking a small pad out of his hip pocket, Charles said, "From what I could tell, Jake McHenry had three boys: Tom, Clive, and Andrew. They were all buried around him. The cemetery is filled with their children, but only one really caught my eye."

"Why is that?" Briggie asked.

"Because he was murdered. It said so on his tombstone. Bo McHenry, b. 1872, murdered 1888."

"Just like his grandfather," Alex remarked. "I wonder what a sixteen-year-old kid did to get murdered?"

"Well, someone was upset enough about it to put it on his marker," Briggie said. "I wonder if we'll ever know. He was mentioned in Miss Maddy's scrapbook, but it didn't say he was murdered. Probably it's in her other scrapbook. The one that got burned."

Charles asked, "How did the two of you do in your investigations today?"

Alex filled him in on the unknown child of Sylvia and the daughter of Cameron born in New Orleans.

"Didn't it occur to you that that daughter was tidily disposed of?" remarked Richard at last. "Maybe too tidily?"

Briggie pulled out her *Handybook for Genealogists*. Looking up Louisiana, she read a bit. "The state has recorded births since 1914, but that's not likely to do us any good, since we don't know the mother's name."

"This town is so full of gossips, someone will tell us," Alex said.

"Ladies, you're too trusting. What makes you think he was telling the truth?" Richard asked. "I've had experience with lying witnesses on the stand. I give you one hundred to one odds he was lying."

Charles said, "That makes him dangerous."

"It's a good thing I brought Brighamina's deer rifle then," Richard remarked. "I thought, the way she operates, it might come in handy."

Alex choked with laughter.

Chapter Thirteen

Susan put baby Z in her cradle and said she had to go see to dinner. Alex offered to help. Charles followed her.

"I'm going to make a couple of shepherd's pies," Susan said. "I really don't know what either of you can do."

"We can peel potatoes," Alex offered. "Charles is very handy in the kitchen. It's one of the many reasons . . ."

"Yes?" Charles prompted.

Susan giggled. "You're lucky. Jon's all thumbs when it comes to anything to do with cooking."

"You know, for someone with eight kids, you have an awfully quiet house," Alex remarked hastily.

"It's the farm. They have a lot of chores in taking care of the garden and the animals. Plus there's the pond to swim in, and their cousins up the road. They have a fort somewhere I'm not allowed to visit. Zina is the only one who hangs around home much. She's my little helper."

"I could eat her up," Alex said with a grin. "She's just precious."

When Jon came home, he was bursting with news. He had called the Church Historical Department, and after half a day they had returned his call. Two missionaries, Elder James Call and Elder Lloyd Samuels, had been sent to the Central States Mission in 1857. Church headquarters had received notification from Elder James Call of Claire Prestcott's baptism and confirmation, but that's the last that was heard of James Call, Lloyd Samuels, or Claire Prestcott.

"They were very interested to hear of the lynching. They're going to coordinate with the Family History Library to try to find any other descendants of Elder Samuel's parents. Now we just have to account for Elder Call."

"I think Briggie's done that," Alex told him. "She's very pleased with herself."

After dinner and scripture study, Jon suggested that they have a tug of war for family home evening. Alex and Charles were assigned to Matthew's team, along with Luke, Abee, and little Rondi. Briggie insisted on being assigned to a team, and Richard, with a look at his brand-new Levi's, also made a halfhearted request to be included.

Alex hadn't felt so carefree in a long time. They played best two out of three. Charles really got into the spirit of the thing. "Come on, Rondi! Stand on my feet, put your hands on mine, and pull!"

Despite the fact that they were pitted against the tall and strong Dr. Jon, Alex and Charles's team won.

"It's nice to know my crew muscles haven't atrophied completely," Charles said with a laugh. "It's been nearly a year since I've been rowing."

"How do you know it wasn't Rondi who made the difference?" Alex asked.

"You ought to take Alex out on the river," Susan said. "We have a canoe."

At that moment, Daniel's BMW pulled up. Kerry climbed out

without assistance, and Daniel was right behind her. She walked straight up to Alex. "I'm sorry to interrupt, but can I speak with you a moment in private?" Alex's bubble of well-being burst.

Walking around to the back of the house, they found a bench on the porch. "I know you must think I'm an awful stinker after that scene at Daddy's," Kerry began. "The fact is, all that business of the 'Lady of Shalott' was just an excuse. I've known for years that there are family secrets. It makes me see red. I don't know why they can't trust me and tell me the truth. I know Daddy was lying to you. I want to know why. And I want to know why my mother is so dead set against all of this, as well. I don't think there should be secrets in families."

Alex found herself unexpectedly agreeing with Kerry. Family secrets had all but destroyed her own family. "Then that scene you created was just for show?"

"Yes. I'm really anxious over Miss Maddy's death. I don't want you or Charles or Briggie to get hurt. The fact that someone close to me evidently had her murdered or even murdered her themselves is really frightening. What is it they don't want to come to light?"

Alex responded. "One thing we have found out is that your mother was married before and had a child. We have no idea what happened to him or her. That's what Briggie was talking about today. We were completely surprised by your father's 'confession.'"

"I knew about Mother's first marriage. But a child? That's news to me. And Daddy has something to hide, but I don't know what."

"So does your mother."

"What will you do?"

Alex shrugged. "Something will turn up. Briggie always thinks of a strategy. The only problem is, it always turns out to be completely outrageous. She has an extremely fertile imagination."

"And a deer rifle, Daniel says." Kerry's face was perfectly serious.

"Yes. And she doesn't hesitate to use it when necessary. Having Daniel's father here is a complication," she confided. "They make rather a reckless combination."

"Richard?" Kerry arched her brows in disbelief.

"You would be surprised." Could this be the same person who had lied so fluently to Daniel? She seemed genuinely sincere. But she had seemed genuinely angry a while before. "So you really want us to go ahead with it?"

"Please. I'm sorry about the scene at Daddy's. With Miss Maddy's death, well, I just don't want him to think I'm interested."

"That makes sense. We'll try to be discreet."

Pleating her dress with her long, slim fingers, the singer said, "I really ought to warn you about Charles, if you won't take it wrong."

"Warn me about what?"

"He has a very short attention span. Once he's sure of you, he'll be on to greener pastures."

Alex gritted her teeth. "I might as well tell you, I don't believe your story of a two-week fling with Charles. He denies it, and I believe him."

"I have no idea what you're talking about," Kerry said, her brow furrowing in puzzlement.

"Daniel told me all about it."

"What did he say?"

"I'm sorry, but I don't want to discuss it." Could it really be possible that Daniel had lied? Fabricated the whole thing? She wouldn't believe it.

Kerry looked at her, and Alex read sincerity in her eyes. "I just wanted to warn you. Charles is very good-looking, of course, but of the two, I think Daniel would make a far better husband."

Alex stood up. "Then why don't you marry him?"

The other woman smiled wryly. "For some reason, he's terribly stuck on you."

"We've been friends for a long time," Alex said. "I'm very grateful to Daniel. He's helped me through some sticky times."

"He's good at that."

They stood. A shot rang out. Kerry crumpled onto the porch. Throwing herself over Kerry, Alex screamed. Another shot was fired, and then Charles, Daniel, and Dr. Jon were rounding the corner of the house.

"Help! Someone in the woods just shot Kerry!"

Chapter Fourteen

D r. Jon and Daniel went immediately to Kerry. Charles gathered Alex in his arms. "Darling, it could have been you!"

"It's her shoulder," Jon pronounced. Producing a bandana handkerchief from the back pocket of his blue jeans, he asked Daniel to apply pressure to the wound, while he called the sheriff. "There's no such thing as an ambulance out here, so we'll have to take her into my office."

At that moment, a plump figure in royal blue sweats rounded the house, deer rifle aimed towards the woods. "You skedaddle, you coward!" She fired a warning shot into the air.

Richard followed, his face red with exertion. "Brighamina! Come back here! You might get shot, too, confound it!"

But there were no more shots. Alex was shaking in Charles's arms, burrowing her head in his shoulder. "She had just finished telling me her father was lying this afternoon when he confessed to having an illegitimate daughter. She said both her parents had things to hide, and she wants to know what they are."

In spite of the circumstances, Alex felt Charles's strength burn into her like a warm fire on a cold night. His hands caressed her hair as he kissed her temple. "I suppose it's useless trying to get you to go back to Kansas City and give this up?"

Pulling away a little so she could look into his face, she asked, "Don't you care about who shot Kerry?"

"Not as much as I want you to live to see our wedding day."

"One of the children could have been around," Alex said. "We're endangering Jon's family by staying here."

"I'm glad you can see a little sense. You'll just have to join me at the roach motel."

Alex gave a little shiver. "Briggie!" she called out. "We need to pack our things and move out of here."

Briggie came up to her, panting. "Are you all right Alex?"

"Perfectly," she answered, watching Jon scoop Kerry up in his long arms. "Jon's taking her to his office to get the bullet out. Just in case that shot was meant for me, we can't afford to stay here and put Jon's family at risk."

"I agree," Briggie said.

Richard came up behind her. "Brighamina, I think you and Alex ought to go back to Kansas City. That woman doesn't want her family history done anyway. This is not a civilized place. I don't like the idea of your being in danger."

"Kerry does want her family history done," Alex said. "She knows there's a secret. I don't blame her for wanting to know. We're going to pack up, though, and find another place to stay. We don't want to put Jon's kids in any danger."

Briggie said, "I think we might want to go down to Cassville. That's the county seat of Barry County, and it has all the records. It also has a touristy motel. Good fishing nearby."

Richard had the cell phone to his ear and was calling information for the number of Cameron McNee. Once he was connected, his face relaxed. "Mayor McNee? Your daughter has been shot."

Even Alex, still in Charles's arms, could hear the burst of profanity at the other end of the line.

"Fortunately, it was out here at Dr. Cox's. He's taking her into town to his office. Do you have any idea who would want to shoot her? It was someone in the woods west of the pasture. Must've had a rifle."

There was silence on the other end, then a few curt words, and the mayor terminated the conversation.

"What'd he say?" Briggie asked.

"He's going to get the sheriff."

"Well, at least we know it wasn't her father," Alex said with a shudder. Charles clutched her more tightly.

It was full dark by the time they'd answered all the sheriff's questions. The daughter of the mayor apparently merited more of his attention than Miss Maddy had. Alex and Briggie hurriedly packed up their things.

As they came downstairs, Zina was looking for them, her eyes sad. "Are you coming back?"

"Right now there's someone out there with a gun, sweetie," Alex said. "We'll be back once we know it's safe. You'll take care of Dashiell, won't you?"

"The very betht care," the little girl promised.

Charles loaded their suitcases into Alex's CRX, after getting directions from Briggie to the touristy motel in Cassville. Then he drove off to collect his own baggage from the Plaza. Richard awaited commands from Briggie.

"You might as well come down, too, Richard, unless you have to get back to the city."

"Not with someone on the loose who's got a rifle. I can't be sure what mischief you're going to get up to. Just give me directions. I've never been in this part of the state."

After sending Richard off, Alex and Briggie hugged Susan, thanking her. "We'll be in touch," Briggie promised.

The motel in Cassville consisted of several small stone cottages, about fifty yards apart, strung along the side of Highway 37. From the outside they looked pretty grim. However, when Alex opened the door, she was surprised to see a neat little dwelling with woven rugs on the oak floors and a tidy stone fireplace stacked with logs. There was a small kitchenette and, through a narrow door, a room with two quilt-covered twin beds.

"Actually, this place has good memories for me," Briggie said with a happy little smile. "Ned and I came here for our honeymoon the opening day of trout season."

"I've got to tell you, I already like it a whole lot more than Trotter's Bridge. Except I miss Jon's family."

"We'll invite them down for a picnic at the river, once we've gotten to the bottom of this."

"Who would want to shoot Kerry?" Alex asked.

"You know," her friend said, "I don't think they really cared if they got you or Kerry as long as they frightened us off."

"Well, let's hope they think they've done that. I don't want anyone lurking around Farmville."

Someone knocked. Briggie answered the door. "Come in, Charles, Richard. We need to have a counsel of war."

Sitting around the tiny kitchen table, they all turned to Briggie. "What next, Briggs? Probate records?" Alex asked.

"The only ones crazy enough to pull that stunt with the rifle are these here McHenrys," she said. "I think it's time we got them sorted out. Even if they died intestate, there will be probate records. They should clue us in to who belongs to which family."

"Land records, too," said Alex.

"If this were a typical English village, everyone would know those things off the top of their heads," Charles said.

"This isn't even a typical American town," Alex said. "I feel like I've gone back in time a hundred years. I sure hope Kerry is all right."

"Jon seemed certain she was going to make a full recovery. He said she'd probably be wearing a sling for a while," Charles said.

Alex felt guilty that she hadn't asked Jon about Kerry's condition. All she had been able to think of was how wonderful it felt to be held so tenderly in Charles's arms.

*   *   *

Tuesday morning evidenced a southern Missouri spring rain—hard and unrelenting.

"This'll about finish the lilacs, I'm afraid," Briggie said. "I'm always sad when they're gone."

"Did you and Ned have lilacs for your honeymoon?" Alex asked curiously. Briggie rarely made references to her husband, who had died fifteen years ago of a sudden stroke. He was only in his fifties at the time.

"Oh, yes," her friend said, her eyes lighting with some memory. "We brought huge bunches of them into our cottage. The manager gave us mason jars for vases. The smell of lilacs always does remind me of my Ned."

Putting up their umbrellas, they ventured outside to pound on Richard and Charles's doors. Both proved to be in Richard's cabin and looked distinctly guilty when Alex and Briggie showed up.

"What're you dudes up to?" Briggie demanded. "No good?"

"We were just discussing where to go for breakfast," Charles said innocently.

Briggie gave a knowing laugh. "Yeah, and I'm a Card's fan."

Alex drank in the sight of Charles in a black turtleneck and matching trousers. He looked as if he'd come straight from the pages of *GQ*. She was wearing jeans, boots, and a sapphire T-shirt and didn't feel that she matched him in any respect. If she married him, would she have to buy all new clothes and dress like a model? Since being forced to leave home at age eighteen, she had paid very little attention to her clothes. All Stewart had ever worn were blue jeans and flannel shirts. She wondered, once again, what Charles could possibly see in her. Then she stood a little taller. Why couldn't she just internalize what he'd said? Why couldn't she just believe him? It wasn't his fault that he was the most gorgeous man on the planet. What would it be like to walk around looking like that? To have females falling all over themselves because of your looks, never knowing or even caring what was really inside?

"Alex?" Charles said. "You look as though you've had an epiphany."

"I believe I have. I want an omelet with hash browns."

Over breakfast, Briggie consulted her *Handybook*. "Uh-oh," she said. "Fire."

Alex drank her fresh-squeezed orange juice. "The courthouse burned?" she asked.

"Yup. In 1872. Fortunately, though, it looks like they still have the probate records."

At that moment, Charles's cell phone rang. He threw a quick glance at Alex when he heard who was on the line. "I really don't see that that's necessary. Jon told me she's not in any danger."

He listened a bit longer. "Look, we've got our hands full down here, and the only way I'm coming is if I can bring Alex with me. I don't think she's going to want to . . ."

"What is it?" Alex asked.

He covered the phone. "It's Daniel. He claims Kerry is feverish, and she is asking for me, for heaven's sake." Charles's eyes were pleading with her for understanding.

"You're right. I don't want to go. But you go," she said, feeling noble. "There are three of us."

He went back to the phone. "Where are you? At Kerry's dad's?"

Listening again, he cast up his eyes. "There's three of them. I really don't think they need your help, Grinnell." Before Daniel could reply, he pressed the End button.

Richard looked at Charles keenly. "You're going?"

"Your son made me feel the worst kind of worm."

Daniel's father drank from his coffee cup, still assessing Charles over the rim. "You want to steer clear of that woman," he said finally. "She's trouble."

"I can handle her," Charles reassured him. Kissing Alex lightly on the cheek, he threw some bills on the table and stood up. "Happy hunting."

The office of the probate court on the second floor of the noble gray courthouse was stuffy. While the clerk searched for what they wanted, Alex looked out the window at the trees that were leafing out in their spring green. She tried to keep her mind on the hunt, but the idea of Charles watching over Kerry's sickbed made her feel deeply uneasy. She still didn't know who was lying about that all-important two weeks.

"Okay," Briggie said finally. "The first McHenry they've got records on is Clive, back in 1880. Here they are."

At that point, Daniel walked in. "Hi, Alex. Briggie. Dad. What's going on?"

Richard had pulled out his half glasses and was scanning the document with professional acumen. Estate law was his specialty. He ignored his son. "It looks like he left his property to his surviving sons, Sam and Andrew. May I see that descendancy chart, Brighamina?"

Briggie handed it to him mutely. Then she looked up at Daniel and smiled. "Welcome. We're just trying to figure out who the modern-day descendants are in this clan that we think is behind Kerry's shooting."

"Look's like this Bo's line died out when he was murdered," Richard said. "Anyway, if he had any descendants, they weren't mentioned in his father's will. He was murdered when he was only sixteen, so it's unlikely."

Alex moved her wooden chair to make room for Daniel and the chair he was bringing to the table. "This is like the old days," he said with satisfaction.

"How's Kerry?" she asked.

"Little bit of a fever. I'm sure she'll be fine." He took the will from his father and read it through with relish. "Want me to go see what I can find on Sam and Andrew?"

"This is ridiculous," said Alex. "It doesn't take four people to do this. The rain has stopped. I'm going for a walk."

But she didn't go for a walk. Almost automatically, she headed directly for her car, climbed in, started it, and headed for Trotter's Bridge. Daniel had turned up a little too opportunely. Had he gotten Charles out of the way on purpose? How could she suspect him of such a thing? But she couldn't help wondering whether the account of Charles's "affair" was of Daniel's or Kerry's making.

Daniel was the man she had always depended upon because of his honesty. It truly irritated her at times that he was so overprotective of her psyche. And he always thought he knew what she was thinking. The fact that he was usually right was another irritation. But she had never suspected him of being dishonest.

When she arrived at the McNees' home, she saw Charles's Lexus parked in the driveway. Rapping the brass door knocker, she wondered what she expected to find. It was absolutely crazy to be running after Charles like this.

But when the mayor showed her into the family room, she found her fiancé in a chair drawn up to the side of the couch, holding Kerry's hand. The one with the crooked finger.

Chapter Fifteen

lex stood in the doorway, stunned. Kerry's face was flushed with fever, her eyes closed.

"The doc says her shoulder's infected," Cameron McNee told her. "I could've told him it would happen. Her skin's real sensitive. Even if she just scraped her knee, it would get infected."

Charles turned to see who had entered the room. When he saw that it was Alex, he merely put an unoccupied finger to his lips. "Sssh. I finally got her to sleep."

"Is it really necessary for you to hold her hand?" Alex asked and then immediately wished it unsaid. Her voice had been shrill, sarcastic. When had she turned into such a shrew?

A look of annoyance flashed from Charles's eyes. "Alex, she's really ill."

"I'm sorry," she said, but she felt his impatience slice through her. To avoid angering him further, she turned and left the room.

Mike was just entering it. "I heard Kerry was shot," he said in a low voice, his forehead corrugated with concern.

Alex stood wondering, not for the first time, what Mike Wentworth's relationship was with Kerry. He took off his glasses and used the sleeve of his suit coat to wipe the perspiration from his forehead. Full of self-loathing, she absently noticed his little finger. It was crooked, exactly like Kerry's.

She raised a finger to her lips. "She's sleeping," Alex whispered. Then she saw herself out the front door.

Driving back to Cassville, her feelings were scathing. Was she going to spend her whole life being jealous? She didn't like this feeling at all.

A memory assailed her. She was in Vienna. She and Stewart were atop the huge Ferris wheel in the Prater by the Danube. It was a warm spring day, just like this. All of Vienna was below them, wearing the splendor that had reigned over much of the continent for a millennium. But Stewart's black eyes were studying her face. "When are you going to believe that I love you, Alex? What in the world will it take for me to prove it?"

Poor Stewart. She had been so crippled during their marriage with fears of abandonment.

But now she knew the reason behind her parents' sending her away to Paris when she was eighteen. She knew they had been trying to protect her.

Last winter, she had genuinely forgiven her mother, her only remaining parent. Alex reflected on that experience now. It was a new understanding of the Atonement that had made it possible. She had allowed Jesus Christ to be the mediator between herself and her mother and had laid all her grief on his shoulders. Now she and her mother were discovering a new and loving relationship, one without blame. They had recovered their early closeness, before alcohol had taken her mother away from her.

That forgiveness had greatly helped her healing process. Almost immediately she had fallen deeply in love with Charles, for the walls protecting her heart had disappeared.

Why was she trying to put them up again? Knowledge of the Atonement had helped her in the past. Could it help her now? She could never go forward into a marriage if she remained crippled with doubt and suspicion, no matter how much she loved Charles. Suddenly frightened of the strength of that love and of what it was turning her into, she wondered if marriage would be fair to either of them.

Perhaps it would be better, after all, to settle for the steady affection she had for Daniel. But now she was even suspecting him of lying to her. What was happening to the self-controlled Alex who never let her feelings rule her heart?

It wasn't until she pulled up in front of the courthouse that she remembered Mike's crooked finger. If the Keeper knew what she was talking about, Mike had McHenry blood in his veins, too.

This revelation jerked her mind back into gear. What did she know about the lawyer's parentage? Did he know that he was part McHenry? He was running for statewide office. Would the community vote for him if they knew?

Then she screeched to a halt. Mike had grown up in Overland Park, Kansas. A long way from the inbred Barry County troublemakers.

So why had he come here? Then, as her mind made connections with the various aspects of this thought, a brainwave startled her. *If he was part McHenry and wanted to keep it secret, wouldn't that give him a perfect motive for murdering Miss Maddy?*

Perhaps she should give her troubled love life a rest and take a little trip up to Topeka to find Mike's birth certificate. First, she needed to find out how old he was, however. His smooth olive complexion gave no clue.

A cardinal flew past, calling its mate. Alex rolled down her window and felt the balminess of the spring day. She took a deep breath, feeling as though she had just barely pulled herself out of the Slough of Despond.

At that moment, a large, flashy red pickup drove slowly by. The man sitting on the passenger side wore a cowboy hat, which he lifted slightly as he spat tobacco juice out the open window. His leathery face wore a leer. Then the driver of the truck gunned it, spinning its tires in the gravel of the parking lot and leaving in a cloud of white dust.

She didn't know why exactly, but she was absolutely certain she had just been saluted by a McHenry and that he knew exactly who she was and what she was doing here.

The trio in the courthouse had been working hard. They proudly exhibited the product of their labors.

McHenry Descendancy Chart
("Bad Blood")

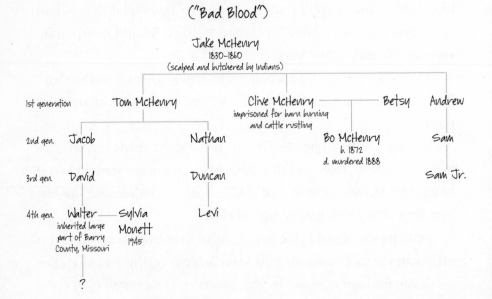

Jake McHenry
1830–1860
(scalped and butchered by Indians)

1st generation	Tom McHenry	Clive McHenry — Betsy	Andrew
		imprisoned for barn burning and cattle rustling	
2nd gen.	Jacob Nathan	Bo McHenry	Sam
		b. 1872	
		d. murdered 1888	
3rd gen.	David Duncan		Sam Jr.
4th gen.	Walter — Sylvia Levi		
	inherited large part of Barry County, Missouri	Monett 1945	
	?		

"The probate records show inheritances in Sylvia's generation by Walter, Sam Jr., and Levi," Briggie said, taking the pencil from behind her ear and pointing out the names on the chart. "The marriage records show a marriage between Sylvia Monett and Walter McHenry in 1947. He inherited a large part of Barry County, according to the deeds."

"Good work, gang. Now for the next generation." Alex clapped her head suddenly. "Miss Betty! Today is her bridge day!"

"Oh, glory," Briggie said. "How could I forget? But it's probably a luncheon thing. We'll have to wait a few hours."

"Speaking of lunch . . . ," Alex started.

"Who in tarnation is Miss Betty?" Richard asked. "Another one of these Keepers?"

Daniel was looking at Alex quizzically. "Where have you been?" he asked, ignoring his father.

Alex turned to Richard. "Miss Betty is the librarian in Trotter's Bridge, and she plays bridge with one of Kerry's mother's pals. She was going to try to find out about Sylvia McNee's child by her marriage to this Walter."

"Why do you care about that?" asked Daniel.

Briggie answered, "Kerry's mom is downright scared of something. The only thing we can figure is that it has to do with her first marriage. She doesn't want Alex and me doing Kerry's genealogy. On the outside chance that her fears have something to do with the Keeper's murder or Kerry's McHenry blood, we're just trying to cover the bases." She gathered her things. "They have some real good catfish at that restaurant across the street."

"But Kerry couldn't be descended from her own half-siblings! She must be descended from one of these other guys," Daniel objected.

"It never hurts to get all the facts," Briggie said composedly. "We know, for example, that since Walt died in an accident and left no will, Sylvia must own a large part of Barry County that her present husband doesn't own. That settles something that's been puzzling me. Why would the son of the mayor marry a McHenry widow? To get his hands on her property."

"Good thinking, Briggie," Alex said. "So if Kerry is descended from a McHenry, it's logical that it would be one of Walter's cousins?"

"Well, you never know about those genetic flukes, like her crooked finger. It could go back to old Jake himself, for all we know," Briggie said, her face troubled.

They walked across the street to Naomi's Diner. It was certainly a step up from the Blue Tail Cafe. The windows were hung with blue and white gingham, and the tables, decorated with daisies, were heavy oak with benches. They were greeted by a waitress with white hair in a net, wearing a gingham apron. "Briggie Poulson! I haven't seen you in a coon's age! Down here for the fishing?"

"Hello, Annette. We're fishing all right. Genealogy." Briggie introduced everyone. "I told them your catfish was the best in the county."

They were seated at a table with a nice view of the back garden and its blooming irises. After studying the menu, they all ordered catfish and hush puppies.

"I found out something startling on my little excursion today," Alex informed her business partner, who was studying the dessert menu displayed on a card by the salt and pepper.

"Good," Briggie said absently. "I wouldn't like to think you'd been wasting your time."

"Well, I've got a suspect for Miss Maddy's murder, I think. Who would have his ambitions ruined by the revelation that he had McHenry blood?"

Briggie looked up. "What do you mean?"

"Is this multiple choice, Alex?" Daniel asked sourly.

"For Pete's sake, Alex. You're not talking about that squirrelly little Mike Wentworth, are you?" Briggie exclaimed.

"Got it in one." Alex said.

"Who in the world is Mike Wentworth?" Richard asked.

His son answered. "The most unlikely suspect and therefore sure to be the guilty one. He's a nondescript person, a lawyer, by the way, who always seems to be around. No one really knows why. He's running for the state senate. Seems to be friends with Kerry and the mayor."

"Well done, Watson," Alex said. "He also has the McHenry curse of a crooked little finger."

"But he's from Overland Park," Daniel protested.

"What's he doing here, then?" Alex asked.

"If he had politics in mind, this is a good place to start," he remarked. "Not much competition."

"But no one would vote for him except the outlaws, if they knew he had McHenry blood," Briggie observed. "Fine work, Alex. I guess we need to go to Topeka for his birth certificate."

At that moment, steaming plates of deep-fried catfish, okra, and hush puppies were placed before them, along with four root beers.

"I have a perfectly capable granddaughter who can do that for us," Richard remarked. "All we have to do is give her the particulars."

"Marigny?" Daniel said. "Dad, she doesn't even do her homework."

"But this is different. This is grown-up stuff, and it's a mystery," Briggie said. "Boy, is this catfish good or what?"

Alex nodded. "You're forgetting something, Briggs. We don't know the year he was born."

"Another reason to use Marigny," Richard said triumphantly. "She can look him up in the high school yearbooks in the school library. That'll give her a ballpark age."

Daniel was shaking his head.

"She can do it, Daniel," Briggie said, spearing a hush puppy with her fork. "Just give her a chance. She's always complained that you treat her like a kid."

"She is a kid!"

"Sixteen," Briggie said. "Old enough to qualify as a part-time assistant to RootSearch, Inc. Tell her we'll pay her according to results. Twenty-five bucks."

"That might motivate her," Daniel said. "She's after me to buy her a ticket to some concert."

"Good. That's settled." Briggie finished her last morsel of catfish. "Now then, Naomi's pies are especially good. I'd suggest the rhubarb at this time of year."

On the way back to the courthouse, the same pickup Alex had noticed before cruised by just as they were about to cross the street. This time, Alex was on the driver's side. She saw a man who looked like a Texas movie star with blond hair and a crooked nose that she imagined had been broken in a bar fight. He stared her up and down insolently as he let the truck crawl by.

"A friend?" Daniel asked, amused.

"More like the enemy," Alex answered. "I'm almost sure those are McHenrys, checking me out.

"Well, I'm sure they like what they see."

Alex made a face. "When does Marigny get home?"

"School gets out at three o'clock. I'll start phoning her then."

Once they were ensconced at their table on the second floor of the courthouse, Briggie said, "Now then. We need to decide what to do next. As I see it, we have several problems facing us." She counted them on her fingers. "What is Sylvia afraid of? Who murdered Miss Maddy? Who shot Kerry? And lastly, our assignment: Does Kerry McNee have McHenry blood, and if so where does it come from?"

She pulled out the descendancy chart she and Alex had constructed from the information in the scrapbook. "There are a few other things we can check while we're here." Looking at the three of them, she said, "Let's try to put things in perspective."

Alex said, "We know Miss Maddy and Kerry are connected somehow, because that's what she told Kerry. So let's try to fill in the missing parts of the McGovern-Delacroix descendancy chart."

"Who are they?" Richard asked.

"Well, everything started with Claire, the first Keeper." Using her pencil, she pointed to Claire's name. "She raised Mary McGovern, the daughter of her sister, Patience. Then, according to the family Bible, Mary married Pierre Delacroix and had two daughters. Sarah and Nancy. We know that Nancy, Miss Maddy's ancestor, married William Colby, and we know from the county history that Sarah married Ernest McNee."

Richard nodded his white head.

Alex took up the tale. "Pierre Delacroix was the closest thing to nobility that the county had. He was a wealthy fur trapper. They even have his statue in the town square. His first daughter, Sarah, was born in 1868, but the Bible gave no further information about her. I can't help but think she quarreled with her sister about something. Briggie, what does the *Handybook* say about records for the county?"

Briggie consulted the genealogist's bible. "Should have birth and death records between 1883 and 1893. And all the marriage records are here."

"So, let's check and see what they have on the two sisters," Alex suggested. Richard wrote this on a yellow legal pad.

"We ought to look for William Colby's will, too," Briggie added. "He should have been quite wealthy, since his wife, Nancy, was a Delacroix. There may be descendants besides Miss Maddy. Obviously, she was named Madeleine or something like that."

Kerry's Genogram

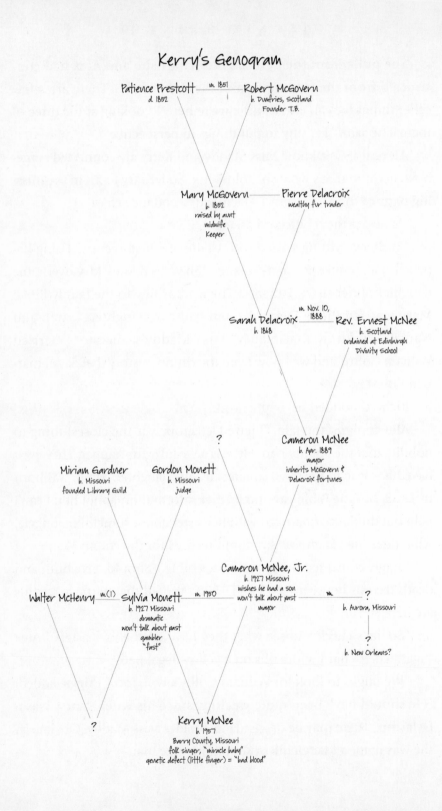

Patience Prestcott
d. 1852

m. 1851

Robert McGovern
b. Dumfries, Scotland
Founder T.B.

Mary McGovern
b. 1852
raised by aunt
midwife
Keeper

Pierre Delacroix
wealthy fur trader

Sarah Delacroix
b. 1868

m. Nov. 10, 1888

Rev. Ernest McNee
b. Scotland
ordained at Edinburgh
Divinity School

?

Cameron McNee
b. Apr. 1889
mayor
inherits McGovern &
Delacroix fortunes

Miriam Gardner
b. Missouri
founded Library Guild

Gordon Monett
b. Missouri
judge

Cameron McNee, Jr.
b. 1927 Missouri
wishes he had a son
won't talk about past
mayor

Walter McHenry

m(1)

Sylvia Monett
b. 1927 Missouri
dramatic
won't talk about past
gambler
"fast"

m 1950

m.

?
b. Aurora, Missouri

?
b. New Orleans?

?

Kerry McNee
b. 1957
Barry County, Missouri
folk singer, "miracle baby"
genetic defect (little finger) = "bad blood"

Alex twisted a ringlet around her finger. "While we're at it, we should ask Mike Wentworth if he knows if Miss Maddy had a lawyer. She was descended from the Delacroix family, too, so she probably had some property. It would be interesting to find her will. It's an outside possibility, but she might have been killed for her property."

Richard nodded. "That's a motive that should certainly never be discounted."

"Before we do anything else, let's try Miss Betty," Alex suggested. Maybe that will throw some light on this if we find out who Sylvia's child is."

The librarian was breathless when Alex reached Miss Betty on Richard's cell phone.

"Oh, my!" she said to Alex. "I've been waiting for you to call! Gladys didn't know everything, but she did know that Syl had twins! Can you imagine her just leaving them behind when she married the mayor? Maybe that's why her son Joe is the biggest devil in this county. He's handsome as all get out, I can tell you that. Drives a big red truck and seems to have plenty of money. But there's been rumors about him for years."

"What kind of rumors?"

"Well, I shouldn't repeat gossip, but they say that he's kind of the local crime lord. Nobody's really pinned anything on him. Someone else always takes the fall."

"What kind of crimes?"

"Everything from murder to selling narcotics. He's a bad 'un, as they say."

Alex thought this over. "Do you think Sylvia might be afraid of him?"

"I would be. She's a wealthy woman, and he and Cynthia stand to inherit."

"Cynthia is the other twin?"

"Yes. She must be married, but Gladys didn't know what had become of her."

"Well, thanks a lot, Miss Betty. You've given us a lot to think about."

"I'd be real careful, if I were you," Miss Betty cautioned as she hung up.

Alex repeated the conversation to her friends. While she was doing so, Charles walked into the courthouse, looking tired.

"How's the patient?" she asked, trying to make her voice light.

"You and I, Alex, need to have a little conversation."

Chapter Sixteen

Alex looked down. There was a note of sternness in Charles's voice she didn't like.

"I'm working now, Charles. I'm afraid it will have to wait."

"This is more important than your work. Come along. We'll go for a walk, and then you can get back to the drama queen's mystery."

His eyes were compelling, and without realizing she was even doing it, she stood. He took her hand and, turning it, raised it to his lips and kissed the palm. Alex's resistance melted. Following him down the stairs out into the spring afternoon, she scarcely noticed the black clouds that promised a squall coming from the south.

They walked down the cracked pavement, pink magnolia petals blown by the wind strewing their path. "I'm sorry, Charles. I overreacted when I saw you holding Kerry's hand . . ."

"Why do I have to constantly prove myself to you, Alex? Don't you believe I love you?"

The question was so much like Stewart's that it stabbed her in a tender spot.

"There's a lot you don't know about me, Charles. You're the first person I've ever opened my heart to, except Briggie. I'm trying to change, but I'm wondering if I ever will."

"What are you talking about?"

"The way I feel about you is so intense, it's making us both unhappy. I'm damaged goods, Charles."

"I've seen the tragedy in your eyes, Alex, but you never talk about it. Why?"

"You think I'm strong and brave, but the truth is, I'm not really. I'm not your Jeanne Moreau. You've romanticized me. I'm just plain, ordinary Alex Campbell with a messy past."

"When will you open up to me, Alex? When will you trust me?"

"You deserve someone better than a psych case."

"This whole conversation reeks of Dr. Daniel Grinnell. Has it occurred to you that he might have made up that entire scenario between Kerry and me?"

She stopped and looked at him. There was steel in his voice, and his gaze was sharp. "Daniel wouldn't lie," she said, hoping her words were true.

"He'll do anything he can to put you off me."

"He's never lied to me before," she said heatedly.

"Well, either Daniel was lying or Kerry was lying. Who had the most to gain? Didn't he tell you I was a player?"

Alex felt his anger like a lash. She shrank. He was hitting at another weakness. She had never fully recovered from her mother's drunken rages, and anger always put her middle in knots. And he was right. What did Kerry have to gain by telling Daniel that story?

She was silent. She couldn't bear to admit to another weakness by asking him to stop. Another sign that she was just too neurotic for a normal relationship.

"My feelings were never engaged with Kerry McNee. Nor with any other woman but Philippa—until you." He turned her to face him and looked directly into her eyes. "We are going to have to work this out somehow, Alex. I am working beastly hard to live worthy of the gospel, to prepare for my baptism. I want to be born again. I want all of that other life to disappear and be forgotten. You must learn somehow to trust me, darling. Do you think you can? Otherwise, our marriage will be a bust."

Alex kicked a stone into the street. "Maybe we got engaged too soon," she said. "There's still so much you don't know about me and what makes me tick. I know I'm not the person you think I am."

"You're pulling back, Alex. I can feel it. And it's all Grinnell's fault. He's a shrink. He knows just what buttons to push. He didn't have to call me today about Kerry. She would have survived without me. I don't even think she was expecting to see me."

"You want to blame Daniel," she said with sudden insight, "but the fact is, those buttons do exist. He's not the only one who can push them. I'm scared, Charles." She looked up at him, pleading for him to understand.

"How many times do I have to tell you?" he asked with some heat. "Love is soul to soul, heart to heart. To me, you are the most beautiful and desirable woman in the world because you are you. Alexandra Borden Campbell. The whole package. Not just the wrapping. I love your feistiness, your courage, your guilelessness. And I love that sunny little place in your heart that you sometimes show me is just for me. It thrills me on those rare occasions when you confess your love to me."

"They are rare for a reason, Charles. For me, it is a very rare thing for the sun to come out. I have given you everything I have to give, but I'm afraid it's not nearly enough. You'll have to give me time." She drew the ring off her finger. "In the meantime, you'd better have this back."

He frowned heavily, and his eyes showed incredulity. "I can't believe this."

"It's just that you're like a tidal wave in my life, Charles. And I've got a very fragile hold that's keeping me from being swept away."

"It's Grinnell, isn't it? You think he's safer than I am."

Alex was silent. Finally, she said, "Would you be getting baptized if it weren't for me?"

"Of course not. I wouldn't even know about the gospel."

The red pickup chose that moment to drive by again. The passenger gave a loud wolf whistle.

"You know that's not what I mean."

Pain showed clearly on his face. "If you can ask that, you were right to give me back the ring."

He turned and walked the other direction, into the coming storm.

Alex's entire spectrum of feelings was harrowed up—anger, love, fear, and despair.

Getting into the CRX, she completely forgot the search she was engaged in and began to drive south, her tears flowing freely. Why was she so confused? Why was she denying herself Charles's healing love?

Without realizing it, she was following the red pickup as the tears continued. She didn't know where she was headed, and she didn't care. She was ashamed to admit it, but it seemed that without Charles her life had no definition. All the meaning that had come into her life since Stewart's death seemed to have melted away—her business, her friendship with Briggie, even her faith. It was as though she had experienced another death.

With a crack of thunder, the storm broke overhead, and suddenly she could no longer see where she was going. Her wipers couldn't keep up. Even with her headlights on, she could barely see the taillights of the truck ahead of her. Following at a crawl, she realized vaguely that they were now in a thick oak forest. She didn't know how long she had traveled when the truck stopped.

The driver of the pickup got out and slogged through mud and rain to her window. He was the blond man she had seen earlier. His blue work shirt was open at his tanned neck and rain streamed down his face and hair, but he didn't seem to notice it. He was angry. Alex realized that they had pulled up to a long building, barely visible in the storm.

"So, lady, why you followin' me?" Then he noticed her tears. "Hey, did that dude spoil your day?"

Sniffing, she said, "Yeah, he did. Sorry, I didn't mean to follow you. I was just driving."

"Well, now that we're here, how 'bout a beer? See if we can make you feel better. Put that cocky little smile back on your face."

He reminded her of Matthew McConaughey with his crooked nose and Southern drawl.

"Thanks very much. I don't drink beer, I'm afraid."

"I should have known. You're probably one of those white wine ladies, aren't you?"

She just gave him a smile. "If I can back up in this mud, I'll just be on my way."

"Well, now, I'm afraid I can't let you do that. You so upset an' all. Plus your wheels are up to the hubcaps in mud. That puny little car will never get out on its own. I can tow you with my truck when the rain stops. Come on in."

"Is this where you live?"

Again that suspicious glint in his eye. "Naw, it's just where I keep my assets."

Assets?

She shrugged. "Okay. I'll come in. Just until the rain stops."

The man grinned, and she felt his animal magnetism. He must

have every woman in the county after him, whoever he was. She was suddenly glad he had the tobacco-spitting chum with him.

As soon as she entered the door, something came down on the back of her head. There was an explosion of pain, and then darkness.

*   *   *

Alex was on the Left Bank in Paris, sitting at a tiny, crooked table in Mimi's Café. Henrie Fouchet was reading a poem about maggots. Stewart's arm was draped across her shoulders, and she was dressed in black tights, a black mini-skirt, and black turtleneck. The coffee was strong and black. The air hung heavy with smoke, but it wasn't cigarette smoke. Why couldn't she open her eyes? Her head felt as if she had been slugged with a mallet. Slowly she grew more awake, and she remembered that Stewart was dead and she was nowhere near Paris.

She wondered why she could not see and became aware that she was lying on something hard. Trying to sit up, she felt a jolt of pain through her arms and realized with a shock that her hands were tied.

"She's come to," a husky voice said.

Genealogy had *never* gotten her into this kind of mess. Where in the world was she, and who were these people?

"Even with that blindfold, you can tell she's a looker," another man said, his voice thoughtful.

She croaked, "I need some water."

Husky Voice said, "I've got a little bitty bit left in my canteen."

Yuk! "No thanks. Who *are* you?"

"Let's just say we're representatives."

"Of what?"

"Now that would be tellin', and because the boss ain't decided what to do with you yet, we ain't gonna be tellin' you anything."

"What do you mean?"

"We'll see what Joe says, but my guess is that you're bound for Table Rock Lake. That's one of his favorite spots. Doesn't have no bottom."

The threat terrified her, and she began to shake. This wasn't about genealogy. Was it possible that she had just talked to Joe McHenry, king of crime in Barry County? What was this place? Obviously she had stumbled onto something she never should have.

"My friends," she said, trying to sound calm. "They'll find out. They're good at things like that."

Husky Voice responded, "Well, then, we'll just have to issue a little warnin' about the Cox children. You wouldn't want one of them in that lake with you, I don't imagine."

"I'm just a genealogist," she protested. "I'm not here to fight crime. I didn't even know there was any crime, except Miss Maddy's death."

"Well," the more thoughtful man said soothingly, "you can rest your mind about that. We didn't have no quarrel with Miss Maddy."

This information stumped Alex completely. "Then why do you want to kill me? I just want to find her murderer. Do you know who it was?"

"Oh, we got a good idea. But in this county we follow the golden rule. 'Do unto others' . . . and all that. And we sure don't like nosy strangers."

"Do you realize I'm acquainted with the sheriff?" she tried to bluff.

"Aw, that don't worry us none. You might say that us Marines stick together," her husky-voiced captor said with a laugh.

"Joe'll make the final decision what to do with you. But right now, he's a little busy."

Alex was silent. *What was going on here?* Charles, Daniel, Briggie, not to mention Richard, would scour the county for her, she was certain. But they didn't know the terrain at all. And how long would it be before they knew she was even missing? And the sheriff was part of the whole setup! What a blow.

Bound though she was, she must try to get some kind of clue. She thought she was lying on a cement floor, though with her hands tied in front of her, she couldn't actually feel it. Little light was filtering through her blindfold. But there was a smell.

Then she knew why she had thought she was in Paris. *Marijuana.* This place reeked of it. Her captors were enjoying a joint or two.

She took a stab in the dark. "You must be the McHenry boys I've heard so much about."

There was a throaty laugh. "Not much point in denyin' that."

How had she found herself in this den of snakes? Real cottonmouths, just as Sylvia had warned.

"Well, we'll just say good afternoon, ma'am. Depending on what Joe says, we'll see you later. Maybe tomorrow."

Alex's spirits sank even lower, but she didn't give them the satisfaction of saying anything. The door shut behind them.

For a while she lay there and prayed hard. "Heavenly Father, no one knows where I am, so I don't see how I'm going to get rescued, but please provide a way."

Then, impatiently she set to work on her bonds. It was difficult. Her captors were truly experts at knots. After no perceptible success, she finally decided to stand up.

That was a bad idea. Whatever had happened to her head made her dizzy. She sat down with a thump. Terribly thirsty, she wondered how long it would be before tomorrow. Would she live that long?

All the other times her life had been in danger, the attacks had been sudden. She had never been left to contemplate her fate. Was the man who had lured her the infamous Joe? Sylvia's son? The one who was the murderer? She had no doubt he would kill her, because the men had been perfectly open about their relationship with the sheriff. Joe wouldn't want that to be common knowledge.

What was this place? Some kind of enormous storage shed? As Sylvia had predicted, she was on a dangerous road. Obviously the woman knew what she was talking about. Did the mayor know? Was the whole county involved in one giant conspiracy?

Not so long ago, she wouldn't have minded dying at all. But now she had thought she had a future. Shivering uncontrollably, she thought about drowning. How long would she struggle before she accepted the inevitable? Should she just breathe the water and get it over with as soon as possible? No. She had always been a fighter. It was instinctive. Somehow, with the Lord's help, she'd get out of this. She *wasn't* going to die.

But as the hours went by, and she still couldn't free herself from her bonds, she began to wonder. Maybe it was her time to go. Briggie would see that her temple work was done. And Charles . . . he would find someone else to love.

She thought of the Cox children, running carelessly over their small farm. She remembered her fiancé with the smitten Abee. Why had she wasted even one minute being jealous? She could see the features of Charles's face clearly in her mind as he tucked the little girl beside him on the bench at church. What would he do when faced with "Joe's" warning? Surely, he wouldn't put the children in danger. She strove for some calm thought to comfort herself.

Charles's face. Concentrating hard, she relived that moment last winter, when he had first told her he loved her, his eyes aflame as he kissed the inside of her wrist. Then her mind visited Tiffany's the day they had chosen her ring—a sapphire surrounded by tiny diamonds. It had been a brilliant winter day just over a month ago. She had felt she had been given the world—a unique combination of Charles's existence and her own: summers with her mother, who was fighting multiple sclerosis on the North Shore of Chicago, fall and winter at Oxford while Charles tutored, and then spring with Briggie, touring wherever RootSearch, Inc. might take them.

Of course, she thought with a jolt, that was all before she had remembered Megan. Before she had discovered the deep longing within her for a child. Now, even if she decided she could go through with the marriage, the odds were very long that she would have the chance to settle somewhere and start a family for Charles to dote on, the way he doted on the Cox children.

How could she contemplate a future she might never have? That was no way out of this mess. She had been entirely too weak-kneed lately. Letting Charles go instead of fighting her insecurities. That was what he loved about her—that she was a fighter. How could she get out of here? Anxiety returned, churning in her stomach until she was ill with it. What was Joe up to? He clearly thought she knew more than she did.

She could tell even through her blindfold that it was getting dark. And cold. Never had she felt so completely helpless. She commenced praying again, with even more fervor this time. The many instances when the Lord's people had been delivered from bondage came to her mind. Her situation might *seem* impossible, but she had to believe that the Lord could do anything. She wanted to see Charles again with an ache that predominated over everything, even her fear. These couldn't be her final hours. It seemed she had just begun to live. She had been uncomfortable with strong feelings, but now they were an asset. She *wouldn't* give into despair.

Hours later, when the night was far advanced, she heard the dogs. At first their barking was faint. Was it her imagination or were they coming closer? It sounded as though there were a pack of them. She heard a man with a loud voice calling them back, but the dogs kept coming closer and closer, barking in deep, imperative tones.

Who was this? Who would be out with dogs in the middle of the night? The mysterious Joe? Soon the animals were scratching at the door of her prison, barking wildly.

"There ain't no coon in there, Dolly, you crazy pup. Dutch, I'm surprised at you. What d'you all want to get inside here for? This is McHenry territory. Best leave it alone."

Alex screamed with all her lung power. The dogs' barking crescendoed. Finally, she heard wood cracking and the door flew open.

She sensed the brightness of a flashlight through her blindfold.

"What have we here? You dogs ain't so dumb after all. Looks like some lady got on the wrong side o' the local business."

Alex smelled chewing tobacco on the breath of her angel of mercy as he untied her blindfold. He turned out to be a hirsute individual with little beady eyes, wearing the proverbial coonskin cap. She almost couldn't believe her eyes. Finding her voice, she said, "Thank you, sir. Could you please untie my hands? I've been here since this afternoon."

"Yore head ain't lookin' too purdy," the man judged. "How'd a little lady like you get on the wrong side of the McHenrys?"

"I've no idea, actually. It was raining and I couldn't see, so I followed a red pickup in front of me, and it led me here. I think it was someone called Joe."

"Joe? That don't sound good. We gotta get you outta here purdy quick then."

Alex tried to stand. Her legs wobbled, and her head pounded.

Her rescuer said, "Only one way t'do this. Mah truck's too far for you t'walk. Now, I'm going to swing you up and over mah shoulder. Don't mind if I smell o'coon. This here's a mighty old coat."

The dogs jumped up and licked her face as her head dangled over the coon hunter's shoulder. Once they were outdoors again, they ran on ahead through the thick, wet forest, barking gleefully. It was almost as though they realized they had done a good deed.

The jolting of her head was almost as unbearable as the scent of dead raccoon, but she wasn't complaining. They trudged by what appeared to be a small wood-framed house. Whatever it was, it reeked of something even stronger than the coon smell. Alex tried to identify it.

"What is that smell?" she asked.

"You don't wanna know, lady," her rescuer said. "You don't want to mess with them McHenrys. Partikarly that Joe. He's a real mean 'un. Folks say he were raised by bear."

If Joe was who she thought he was, that was an accurate description of Sylvia when she was threatened. Alex wished mightily she had never set foot inside this lawless county. Dr. Jon might find it unspoiled, but she never wanted to see another oak forest again.

"Now," the giant coon-hunter said, "this here's my truck. I hope yore not too particklar. I already bagged a coon t'night, and it's in the back. Problem is, he got sprayed by a skunk, so the odor ain't real pleasant."

Alex fought nausea as he put her in the front seat of the ancient, rusted-out truck. It was probably held together by baling wire.

"Now, young lady, where can I take ya?"

She needed to see Dr. Jon to get some medical attention. She would call Charles's cell phone from there. "Dr. Jon's, if you know where it is."

"Oh, yeah. He stitched up Dolly real fine when she got shot by one o' them McHenrys who thinks the whole forest b'longs t' them."

The dirt track out of the forest was bumpy, and Alex was certain she was going to be sick. But in her heart she was thanking the Lord over and over for her deliverance.

Susan must have heard the ancient truck, for she came running out of the house and greeted her with unbounded relief. "Oh, Alex! They're all out looking for you! You're hurt! Who's that with you?"

Alex turned to her rescuer. "I owe you my life, sir. Thank you. I'm Alex."

"Moe. Just call me Moe. And no need to mention this to anyone. Wouldn't want it to get around. Could cause some hard feelin's, if you know what I mean."

"No one that lives here will find out, except Dr. Jon," Alex told him. "And you can trust him. Thank you so much. And thank your dogs for me."

"Wait here," Susan instructed Moe. In a moment she returned with a white package. "Liver for your dogs," she said.

Moe tipped his coonskin hat. "Thank you, ma'am."

Chapter Seventeen

Susan's face was drawn with worry and exhaustion. "I'll just call Jon on his cell, and then you can call Charles. He's worried about you, and there was some kind of blowup with Daniel."

Alex, lying on the couch in the front room, could hear the relief in Jon's voice even though Susan was telephoning across the room.

"He's on his way," she said once she had disconnected. "I'm not sure where he was. The reception was bad."

Before Alex could call Charles, she needed to tell Susan about the threat.

"Those men who kidnapped me, Susan. They were doing something illegal. They threatened your kids. I can't stay here."

Susan's hand went to her throat. "We've got to call the sheriff. Do you have any idea who they were?"

"Just that they were McHenrys. Their leader is someone called Joe. I think he may be Sylvia McNee's son."

"Joe McHenry." Susan shivered. "I've heard that he's wanted for murder, but the sheriff can't lay his hands on him."

"The sheriff is in on it, they said. He's an old Marine buddy."

"The sheriff! Oh, good heavens! What are we going to do?" Susan's habitual calm had deserted her completely, and she was wringing her hands. Then, seeming to notice this futile behavior, she said, "Well, I'm no doctor, but I can at least get you cleaned up. You have some sort of head wound."

Leaving the room to get a basin of water and cloths, she said, "Don't forget to call Charles."

Alex dialed his cell phone.

"Darling!" he said. "Where are you? What happened to you?"

She told him, as concisely as possible, ending with, "I was rescued by a friendly raccoon hunter and his dogs. I'm at Jon's."

Susan re-entered the room and began to clean the back of Alex's head carefully with warm water.

"God answers prayers," Charles said. "I'll be with you as soon as I can. I'm down on Blue Creek. I'll call the sheriff and let him know you've been found."

"Don't," she said urgently. "The sheriff's in on it. I don't want him to know where I am or even that I've been rescued. They've threatened Jon and Susan's kids. As soon as I'm fixed up, we've got to get out of here."

"Good grief, this gets wilder and wilder. First Miss Maddy, then Kerry, now you. And no law enforcement we can trust."

"They claimed they weren't responsible for Miss Maddy." She heard the rumble of Jon's truck. "Charles, I've got to go. Jon's here. Can you get in touch with Briggie and Daniel?"

"I've got Richard's cell phone number. He and Briggie are together somewhere in the woods. Frankly, I don't care where Daniel is or how to get in touch with him. We had a rather heated disagreement when I called him a liar."

Alex was astounded. Cool, collected Charles? But at that moment, Jon burst through the front door.

"Hurry, Charles, please." She punched the End button.

She repeated her story to Jon as he took stock of her physical condition. "There's no one we can trust, Jon. And they've threatened your kids. We've got to get out of here as soon as you fix me up."

"We'll just see about that. You were kidnapped. That's a federal offense. We're calling the FBI. They can send agents down tomorrow if I call tonight and we'll get this whole county cleaned up." Jon's jaw was set, and his eyes hard. "It's an open secret that the biggest cash crop here is marijuana, but lately there's been something even worse. I've been seeing people in my practice who're definitely meth users."

"Meth?" Alex echoed. "You mean methamphetamines? You think they're making that here?"

"Missouri is becoming the biggest source for meth in the country, believe it or not. I've long suspected that that's what Joe and his gang are really up to in those woods. The sheriff always tells me he's looking into it. Occasionally, he'll arrest some small fry, but with your evidence that Joe's involved, I now have what I need to call the Feds. Particularly if the sheriff's crooked."

"But your children!"

"Susan can take them to her mother's in Rolla. I figure that's far enough away."

Rolla was on the main highway to St. Louis, at least three hours from Trotter's Bridge. Alex relaxed. "That's a good idea. There are so many of these McHenrys running around, I know the kids wouldn't be safe here. I'm so sorry to have caused all this trouble."

"This county is knee-deep in trouble and has been for a long time. Drugs, car theft, murder, you name it." He finished his examination. "Well, you've got a pretty bad concussion. How are you feeling?"

"Pretty rotten, to tell the truth. I've got one heck of a headache."

166

"I'm afraid I can't give you anything for the pain but extra-strength Tylenol because of the possibility of concussion. I need to take some stitches, but I can do that now. I'd say, on the whole, you're one lucky lady."

"They were going to drop me in Table Rock Lake," Alex shuddered. "I'll bless the smell of coon and skunk forever."

"I can have my boys make you up a sachet for your underwear drawer if you like," Jon said, grinning.

"Speaking of smells," Alex said thoughtfully. "On the way to the truck we passed this little wooden house. It really stank. Worse than coon. Moe told me not to ask questions about it."

"Did it smell like ammonia or strong urine?" the doctor asked.

"That's it! That's what it was."

"That was a meth lab."

"So, you were right! I really couldn't think of what I had done that was worth being tossed in the lake for. But that must be it." Then she saw that Jon had prepared an injection. "Good grief, Jon. Don't you think I've been through enough today?"

"Just a little local anesthetic, Alex. I need to stitch you up." After he had given her the shot and was stitching her head, he added, "I suspect this goes against the grain, Alex, but you've got to stay down for a couple of days with that head of yours. You should probably be in the hospital."

Alex groaned. She had been in the hospital before with a concussion. As tired as she was, as much as her head ached, she itched to be back at work. She had gotten nowhere with finding out who was responsible for the Keeper's death. Or Kerry's shooting. Were they both tied up with Joe McHenry, or did the genealogy have something to do with it?

Jon looked down at her, his eyes troubled. He scratched his fuzzy head. "I don't think they would have talked in front of you unless they intended to kill you. You're an important witness. Now we've brought the Feds down on them, Joe McHenry is *not* going to be happy. And *you* are not going to be safe until they are brought down."

"Well, I'm not happy, I can tell you that. I didn't get into this to tangle with some dope gang."

"Maybe that's why Sylvia warned you off." They were both silent for a moment, and then he said, "For now, I'm going to pack your head in ice. You must lie as still as you can. I want you to stay lying down."

"I'll stay here on this sofa," she said. "I don't want to be squirreled away from everything. And Charles is coming."

At last Charles strode swiftly into the room. It was the first time she had seen him less than perfect. His hair was tangled, his shoes and slacks muddy to the knee, and his sweater covered with tiny stickers. Most surprising of all, he had a swelling black eye. He put his arm around her and lifted her tenderly, holding her entire upper body against his chest. Alex could feel the racing of his heart.

Burying his face in the mass of ringlets her hair had become, he whispered, "Oh, Alex, I really thought I'd lost you."

"Careful," she cautioned him. "I smell like raccoon." Then she gave herself up to being cosseted, returning his kisses with the passion of one who was suddenly very glad to be alive and able to feel. All her doubts were in another part of her brain. Putting a hand up to his mussed hair, she smoothed it. "Oh, how I love you," she whispered when she was able. There were tears in her voice as well as her eyes.

Pulling back, she looked into his eyes and saw such tenderness there that it stole her breath. How could anyone love her so much?

"When I realized you'd disappeared, I was crazed," he responded. "You have no idea what the last hours have done to me. I have never prayed so hard that there was a God and that he would please help this old sinner. I thought it was my fault."

"I prayed, too." Then, to lighten the torment in his eyes, she said, "You should have seen my heroic deliverer! He had on a coonskin cap, just like the old fur trappers wore. He was called Moe, but I'm not supposed to tell anyone."

"I'm determined to buy one of those caps. I would cut a dashing figure in the Christ Church quad, don't you think?"

She kissed him again.

Moments later they were set upon by Briggie and Richard, who were suitably outraged by her tale. Briggie was toting her deer rifle, and Richard had last autumn's oak leaves in his hair.

"Meth!" her friend said scornfully. "Glory be, I thought they only used that stuff in Hollywood."

"I hope you didn't roust any McHenrys in your trek through the forest," Alex said. "I'm not ready to have my business partner arrested for homicide."

"Didn't see anything but an early patch of marijuana," Briggie said regretfully. "Richard identified it, of course. I wouldn't have known what I was looking at." She examined Alex's head. "You don't look too good, honey. You're lucky to be alive, you know. Richard and I have been praying all day and all night."

"The FBI are coming in tomorrow," Alex reassured her. "I just hope it's not Mulder and Scully."

Richard asked, "Who the devil are they?"

Briggie sighed and shook her head, "Don't you watch the *X Files?*"

Richard and Charles arranged to watch over Alex in shifts. Their clothing and personal items still at the cabin in Cassville, Susan gave them new toothbrushes and assured them there was an extra bed up under the eaves. Alex said good night to Susan, Briggie, and Jon, and fell asleep with her hand in Charles's. Beside him was Briggie's deer rifle.

The next morning, Alex was awakened by Zina, who stood looking at her somberly. "My daddy thaid thome bad guyth hurt you."

"Yes," Alex said sleepily. "Dashiell wasn't doing his job, Zina. I guess he needs to grow up a little more before he can protect me."

"We're going to Grandma Hanthen'th. Will you feed my cat for me? I didn't tell you before becauth we were jutht playing with the kittenth, but her name is Mary Poppinth, and Daddy doethn't get home before her bedtime. She needs lotth of milk for her kittenth."

"What do you feed her?"

"Mommy keepth the cat food in the mudroom on the shelf, tho I can reach it."

"I'll remember," Alex promised. "I hope you have fun at your Grandma Hansen's."

"She doesn't have kittenth," the little girl said sadly, "jutht puppieth. They get me all dirty. She has kennelth."

"Oh, does she sell her dogs?"

"Yeth, they're called Golden Retrieverth."

Alex, who was really more used to dogs, said, "Oh, Zina. They're beautiful dogs and so good-natured. Just put on some old clothes and wrestle with them."

Moving her head as little as possible, Alex was trying to eat oatmeal when Daniel stalked into the front room. Charles had gone upstairs to sleep at about four A.M. and Richard had left her, once the family was stirring, to borrow Jon's shaving gear. Except for the cacophony of voices coming from the kitchen, Alex was alone. Noting her pillow of ice, Daniel said, "I suppose no one thought to call me and tell me that you were safe? I haven't slept all night. I've been out with the sheriff."

Any feelings of remorse Alex might have had were dissolved by the observation that he, too had a black eye.

"The sheriff is crooked," she said. "I'll bet he took you on one heck of a wild goose chase."

Daniel ran a hand through his reddish hair and shook his head wearily. "I guess it shouldn't surprise me. He had me convinced that somehow you had ended up in Table Rock Lake. You know it is supposed to be bottomless? What a heartless son of a gun."

She shivered. "If he had had anything to do with it, that's probably where I'd be. Fortunately, I was only tied up in some crummy cabin in the woods, and a very gentlemanly coon hunter found me."

Daniel didn't even crack a smile. It dawned on her that he was trying very hard not to let her see his anger. "How do you know the sheriff's crooked?"

Alex told him about her conversation with her captors.

"What in the world are they up to?"

"Meth, marijuana, murder . . . you name it," Alex told him wearily.

"Good grief, Alex! What in the world have you gotten yourself into now? They must not have planned to let you live to tell that story, or haven't you realized that? With your usual recklessness, I suppose you plan to stay here and make yourself a target again?"

She was reminded by this speech of everything she most disliked about Daniel. "The FBI will be arriving this morning. Jon's determined to clean up the county, though how they can pull up every marijuana weed . . ."

"Meth is really dangerous, too. They have to wear moon suits to disassemble the labs. What a lovely place this has turned out to be. So why did they kidnap you? And what does all of this have to do with genealogy?"

"Well, I think my kidnapper was Kerry's half brother from her mother's first marriage. I don't know if he specifically has something against me or if it was just that I couldn't see in the rain and followed his pickup. He took me to a kind of warehouse in the woods. I guess that must be where they store the drugs." She paused and then asked with genuine curiosity, "Who scored the first blow?"

Daniel's face took on a grimness she had never seen there. "I did. That high and mighty Brit accused me of lying."

"Did you?"

Daniel looked down and away. "I may have embellished a bit."

"What about yesterday morning? Did Kerry really ask for Charles?"

This time he walked away and stood with his back to her, looking out the window. "No."

"I can't believe it, Daniel," she said, allowing her anger to surface. "What did you think you'd accomplish?"

"Kerry's wild about him. She staged one of her scenes," he said.

"And you thought you'd help the romance along a little bit?" She couldn't stifle her sarcasm.

"Well, she was in pain and feeling very sorry for herself. I'd had about all I could take. Kerry's not plucky like you are, Alex."

"That's no excuse. You know what a hard time I have with trust. I'll never be able to trust you again, Daniel. You realize that, don't you?"

He turned and looked down at her. "But you trust Charles? That's rich! I still think he's a good-for-nothing womanizer, no matter what he's managed to make you believe."

"Get lost," she said, as her head throbbed with anger.

"So Sir Lancelot can put another notch in his belt?"

Alex flushed. "You should know by now that I don't go in for affairs."

He had her at a disadvantage because she couldn't walk out.

"Just for curiosity's sake, how do you know Kerry wasn't telling the truth and your fiancé doing the lying?"

"I trust Charles, Daniel. I don't trust Kerry McNee for a second."

Chapter Eighteen

Susan and the children were piled into the Dodge van and sent off with hugs and kisses by ten A.M. Charles, Richard, Jon, and Briggie saw them off. Briggie returned to the house, chuckling. "Alex, you have a real rival in that little Alana. She's pestering Charles to wait for her and marry her when she's sixteen."

Alex grinned, picturing it. "What did Charles say?"

"He told her by that time he'd be a gray old man and she wouldn't want him anymore."

"Very tactful."

"Where's Daniel?" Briggie wanted to know.

"I sent him away. Briggie, he lied to me. Kerry never sent for Charles yesterday. And I think he made up a lurid tale about Kerry and Charles having an affair."

Briggie chuckled to herself. "They're both sporting shiners. I don't think the Barry County Courthouse has seen so much drama since the case of the cats and the copperheads."

"The cats and the copperheads?" Alex asked, momentarily diverted.

"Remind Jon to tell you sometime."

"Tell me now, Briggie. I could use a distraction."

There followed, in Briggie's inimitable style, a story of two parents, each struggling for custody of their child. The child's *guardian ad litem* told the court that the mother's trailer was filled with at least two dozen flea-infested cats. The judge ruled that she needed to get rid of the cats before she could have a prayer of gaining custody of her son.

"Then you know what that wacky woman said?" Briggie asked.

Alex shook her head and immediately wished she hadn't.

"She said the cats were the only way to keep the copperheads out of the trailer!"

Alex laughed, and the laughter did her good.

Briggie settled herself in the rocking chair, and the men soon joined them, seating themselves on the sofa across from the one Alex was lying on. Predictably, Briggie got out her descendancy chart. "We made some progress . . ."

There was a knock on the door, and Jon went to answer it. Briggie left her sentence dangling. Mike Wentworth stood on the doorstep.

"I went to visit Kerry, and she said Daniel told her Alex was kidnapped and that you've called in the FBI! Maybe we'll finally see some action around here."

"What exactly do you mean by that?" Alex asked.

"What do you think I mean? Justice in Barry County is crippled by the drug trade."

"If you know that," Charles said smoothly, "why haven't you called in the FBI before now?"

The lawyer looked uncomfortable. "Conflict of interest," he said shortly.

"You mean you're Sylvia's lawyer and it's her son who's running the show," Alex said.

"Something like that," he said grudgingly. "But I didn't know any of that when Sylvia came to me to draw up her will. I've done some title searches for Joe, so he's technically my client, too."

"That doesn't look good for your campaign," Alex remarked.

"What campaign?" Charles asked.

"Mike is running for the state senate."

Charles laughed. "Bad luck."

"When Joe is arrested, I can refuse to take his case," Mike said. "Alex, do you think he had anything to do with shooting Kerry?"

"I have no idea who that was," she said. "Or even if Kerry was the target. The shot came from the woods. It would be pretty hard to get a good aim from that far away."

"Well," he said, indicating her ice pack, "how badly are you hurt now?"

She smiled at his discomfiture. "I've been through worse. If the past is anything to go by, both my eyes will turn black shortly."

"I didn't know genealogy was such a hazardous occupation," Mike said.

Charles laughed again and kissed Alex's forehead. "It is when Briggie and Alex are involved."

It was mid-morning when the FBI agents came to take Alex's statement. Agent Stone had a bull neck, and despite his head of white hair, his face was surprisingly unlined. He looked as if he worked out at the gym several hours a day. His smile was broad and comforting as he shook her hand. His partner, Agent Donovan, was a sturdy woman who wore her platinum hair in short spikes and had blue-gray eyes that reminded Alex of Scottish skies. She also had a tattoo of a butterfly on her ankle. They weren't the least like Mulder and Scully.

Stone was dressed in a well-fitting navy blue suit, but his partner was dressed like no FBI agent Alex had ever imagined. Her suit was turquoise, and her blouse was tropical orange. They didn't look as thought they were prepared to scour the woods.

Jon brought kitchen chairs into the living room for the interview. Charles and Briggie sat on the sofa across from Alex. There was anxiety in Charles's eyes, and Alex was sorry she had put it there.

Agent Donovan began by saying, "So you stumbled right into a drug op, Alex. How did that happen?"

Alex told her story once more, describing her assailant in detail but apologizing for not knowing where in the forest the warehouse was. "It wasn't a very long way from Cassville. It's hard to guess because I was just creeping along in the rainstorm, but I think the turnoff onto the dirt road was only five miles south of the courthouse, at the most. But we were in the forest for at least twenty minutes on some kind of road before we stopped at this long warehouse-type building."

Grinning, Agent Stone said, "The copters will sight it. We anticipate quite a haul. Meth, the doctor says."

"Tell us what your captors said about the sheriff," the blonde Agent Donovan asked.

Alex repeated what she had heard. "Apparently Joe, if that's who my attacker was, had some other urgent business. Otherwise, I'd probably be at the bottom of the lake right now."

"Dr. Cox told us he suspects the operation was run by one particular family." Agent Donovan consulted her notes. "The McHenrys."

"Yes," Alex said. "They've been the local troublemakers for about four generations now."

"Like the Mafia, or something?" Agent Stone asked, pulling at his tie.

"Sort of, I suppose. It all started with a lynching in the middle of the last century," Alex told them. "Ever since then, they've been a law unto themselves."

"You sound like you've made a study of them," the female agent said, looking at her with interest.

"I'm a genealogist. I came down here from Kansas City with my business partner to do some genealogy for a client. We were warned off right away by our client's mother, who also happens to be the mother of the man who is rumored to be the drug lord. We don't know a whole lot about the present generation, but I gather they're very dangerous. I don't think you'll find many locals ready to help you identify them."

Stone spoke up. "We're going to comb every inch of forest in this county with our operatives. They'll be armed with automatic rifles, and they'll have the drug dogs with them."

"We'll get the drugs, but our real concern is the perps," Donovan said earnestly. She recrossed her legs, showing off her tattoo. "Rumor isn't enough."

Alex immediately thought of Moe. He wouldn't thank her for getting him involved. But if he had witness protection . . ."There may be someone who can help you, but I have no idea of how to find him."

Charles interceded. "I think there might be an easier way, Alex."

She looked at him. The expression on his face was grim. "I only hope we're not too late," he added.

"What do you mean, Charles?"

"Kerry's mother."

Alex's hands flew to her face. "Oh, my gosh. If her son's as bad as they say, and she knows . . ."

Donovan tapped her gold cross pen impatiently on her pad. "Just who are you talking about?"

"Well," Alex said after a deep breath, "I told you our client's mother warned us off. She has a son by her first husband, who was a

McHenry. Joe McHenry. I'm not positive but I think he's the one who kidnapped me. From what my captors said, it appears that he's the boss of the operation. His mother probably knows all the McHenrys and just what they're up to. She threatened us when we first came to town. Shortly afterwards, a local historian was murdered and all her records burned."

"Hmm," Donovan said. "The name of McHenry's mother?"

"Sylvia McNee. She lives in the retirement home. I hope you can get to her before her son does."

The agents left quickly.

"Now, Alex," Charles said. "I don't want to be overbearing or put a crimp in your style, but the good doctor did tell you to stay on that couch. So what are your plans for the day?"

"Well, I hate to admit it, but this meth thing scares me. I've never been involved with organized crime before, so I think I'm just going to leave it to the feds and get on with my own little business. Where are Briggie and Richard?"

"Briggie's making bread, and Richard's gone down to Cassville to retrieve our things."

"She's not usually so tactful. Can you ask her to come in? If I have to lie on this couch, I might as well get something done. Did anyone ever call Marigny?"

"I'll have Briggie come in."

"Yes, I phoned Marigny myself yesterday, after she got home from school," Briggie told Alex. "She was tickled to death by the assignment. She's driving over to Topeka after classes are over today."

"Good," Alex said. "Did you ever find out anything about Sarah?"

"I can't imagine why it wasn't written in the family Bible, but she married Ernest McNee, the minister from Scotland, just like it said in the county history. Perfectly respectable. The only odd thing is that she was twenty-three and he was fifty-four."

Alex inspected the chart Briggie handed her. "So that's how Miss Maddy and Kerry are connected, then," Alex said, looking at the chart. "They are both descended from Mary and Pierre Delacroix."

"Yes. That agrees with the county history we read, but don't you think it's kind of weird that she married someone so much older? It almost looks like an arranged marriage or something."

A pounding sounded from the front door. Charles got up to answer it. It was the FBI again.

They entered the room. "Sylvia McNee's missing," Agent Donovan reported.

"She might be at her husband's house—I forgot to tell you, he's the mayor," Alex said.

"That's what the little redhead at the retirement home told us. We telephoned. He says he hasn't seen her for a couple of days. He was actually quite worried. Apparently, they missed some big charity do last night in Springfield that she had really been looking forward to."

Alex thought of Table Rock Lake. She had never seen it, but the thought of cold, bottomless waters made her shiver.

"Apparently Joe McHenry is in the habit of disposing of his victims in a bottomless lake down by Cassville. I'm sure that's what they were planning for me."

Donovan said briskly, "If that's the case, then there's no possibility of dragging for the body."

Alex thought for a few seconds. "Have the helicopters started their search yet?"

"No," said Stone. "I'll call it off for the time being. We don't want to tip anyone off."

Pulling the radio from his belt, he walked away from them, speaking curt commands.

"Maybe she got a little scared," Briggie said. "A couple of days ago, her daughter was shot."

"What's this?" Donovan said. "For a quiet little town, you sure do have a lot going on."

"We're not sure they meant to hit Kerry," Alex said. "The two of us were standing quite close together on the back porch of this house when a shot came from the woods. It could have been meant for either of us."

"Why?"

"I've got it!" Briggie crowed. "Alex *was* the target. Mike Wentworth shot at her to stop our investigation! He doesn't want anyone to know he's a McHenry because he's running for state senator."

"Who in the world is Mike Wentworth?" Stone asked as he came back into the room, tugging at his tight collar."

"We're not really certain," Alex said. "He's around the McNees a lot, but we don't know if he's a relative. We should have his birth certificate today."

The agents took a moment to digest this. "Why do you think he's a McHenry? And why would he shoot you?"

"Genetics," Briggie said. "He's got the McHenry crooked finger. And he's running for office, so I'm sure he wouldn't want anyone to know he's a McHenry."

"Well, I'll be . . . First time I ever had genetics come up in a drug case," Stone said.

"Actually, the drugs are really secondary to our investigation," Alex said with a grin. "I know they're dangerous and almost got me killed, but we're going to leave them up to you and concentrate on our little genealogy problem and the murder of Miss Maddy."

"Honey," said Donovan, "you may be concentrating on your genealogy problem, but family trees are the last thing on Joe McHenry's mind, I can assure you. Without you, we have no case against him or the sheriff. You're our star witness. We don't want anything to happen to you, believe me."

Charles stood and came over to stand by Alex's makeshift bed. "I'm taking good care of her. We all are."

"Maybe these McHenrys and Mrs. McNee have all taken off, now that they know you've escaped," Donovan speculated.

"That'd be about half the county," Jon objected. "And while all the ones I know of have some sort of criminal thing going, I can't believe all of them would be involved in the marijuana and meth."

"You know," Donovan said, "I'm actually a profiler, and I'm getting a very unusual picture here."

"I know," Alex said. "We came down here to find the bad blood in our client's genealogy. This is almost enough to make you wonder if there is such a thing."

"Yes . . . not bad blood, but some kind of genetic problem, maybe. You say it all started with a lynching a hundred and fifty years ago?"

"Well, it could have been going on before. That's just the first record we have."

"There weren't whites here too long before that time. This was Indian land. Osage," Jon said. "There is a legend that they used to mine for silver somewhere around here."

"I think it might be a good idea for us to visit the local police and see if we can get hold of the records for all the McHenry perps," Stone said.

"The police are scared of the McHenrys," Jon told him. "Reprisals."

"So this lawless community just runs around in the woods? That is very strange, Dr. Cox," Agent Donovan remarked. "Like something you'd find in a horror story."

"We're trying to turn things around, my brother and I. He teaches at the school, but he says that even as first and second graders these McHenrys are troublemakers. I try to help the older ones with their drug and alcohol addictions, but I haven't had much success. It's almost like there's something in the water," Jon said sadly.

"I wish I could do a genogram on the lot of them," Briggie said, obviously disturbed. "That really bothers me about the little kids. Usually little kids of that age are pretty sweet, even if they are mistreated."

"Then there's Kerry and Mike," Alex said. "It seems they both have McHenry blood, though we haven't been able to find it yet. Mike appears to be a model citizen—unless he really did take a shot at me to keep me from ruining his political career—and Kerry is a very successful folk singer. But neither of them was raised in the clan." She paused. "You know, you might have some success talking to the mayor. Ask him about Joe McHenry. He must know about him. He might be willing to talk, now that his wife has gone missing."

"I think that's indicated," Stone said. "We'll go over there now."

"Richard and I will go down to the library and read the papers for the last few years. Maybe the McHenry crimes were at least reported in the paper. That will give us some names to start with."

"Are your agents looking for the warehouse and the meth lab?" Alex asked Agent Stone.

"Yes. But they're trying to be covert about it. They don't want to scare anyone away."

Alex gave them her cell phone number. "Could you keep me informed? As long as Joe McHenry is on the loose . . ."

Agent Donovan smiled a grim little smile. "We'll let you know what we uncover. Your friend's idea of a genogram is not a bad idea. If we can get these people into families and trace their past—"

"We might be able to get a better picture of what's going on," Briggie concluded.

"I can help with medical records, and my brother Will can help with school records," Jon said.

"Sounds good," Agent Stone stood up. "It must be hard raising a family here."

"Everyone isn't like the McHenrys. There are some really good people here, too, and they need a doctor. But I sure will be glad if we can get this mess cleaned up."

Chapter Nineteen

Soon, everyone had gone except Charles, who insisted on staying with Alex. He had brought Dashiell in from the barn for her to cuddle. She kept him in the crook of her arm, where he curled up and snoozed peacefully.

"This is driving me crazy," she said. "I wish I could be with them when they talk to the mayor."

"For you, genealogy is a full contact sport," Charles told her.

"Something *is* teasing at my brain. Everyone's forgotten Miss Maddy in all this meth business. But Miss Maddy was murdered to keep her from telling something about Kerry's genealogy. Where did Kerry's McHenry blood come from? The only hole in her genogram is her grandmother McNee. I wonder if she was a McHenry. Briggie said there was no marriage record for them in Barry County, though. And if her grandmother were a McHenry, surely Kerry would know."

"Seems kind of weird that that one woman married someone more than twice her age," Charles said. "Leaving you with that to chew on, I'll go make you some real food."

Chew on it Alex did, as she stroked Dashiell. There was some reason Nancy hadn't put Sarah in the family Bible. Had they fallen out? What would cause them to do that? Didn't Nancy like the minister? Or had they fallen out earlier? Maybe Sarah had had an earlier marriage.

Charles had left Kerry's genogram where Alex could reach it. She studied it carefully. Maybe because she had fresh eyes, one thing leapt out at her immediately. Why hadn't Briggie picked up on it? Cameron McNee was born in April of 1889, during the ten-year period for which Barry County had birth records. Supposedly he was born to Sarah and the Reverend McNee, but their marriage had taken place only the November before! Sarah had been pregnant by someone else, Alex was sure. And that someone else could have been a McHenry.

Charles brought her some of Briggie's whole wheat bread fresh out of the oven and a bowl of vegetable soup.

"You look energized. What have you discovered?"

"You were right about that marriage. It was fishy. Sarah was already pregnant. And, if I'm right, it was by a McHenry, and that's where that bloodline comes from."

"So, she wasn't such a paragon?"

"I don't think an upright minister from Scotland would have married a woman who was pregnant out of wedlock. She may have married someone else first, who died before the baby was born. That's the only other explanation. Remember, her father was Pierre Delacroix, so if she married a McHenry it would have been a disgrace. She would probably have run away with him to be married."

"Darling, you do have the most fertile imagination."

"It helps a lot in this job," Alex assured him, as she took a bite of Briggie's bread. It was heavier than Susan's but otherwise good. "I sure wish I weren't stuck on this couch. I want to visit the neighboring counties to see if they have a marriage record."

"Alex, for heaven's sake. Can't you ring them up?"

She looked at his handsome face. "I knew I didn't love you just for your looks," she said. "Can you bring me Jon's cordless phone?"

"Eat up your soup first."

"Did I ever mention that I don't like bossy people?"

"Well, it's good I have my looks, then. They compensate for so many character flaws, don't you find?"

Rolling her eyes, Alex allowed him to feed her soup by the spoonful. When she had finished, she asked him to bring her Briggie's *Handybook,* which he would undoubtedly find by her bed.

Once he returned, she opened the book to the map section. "I'll bet Sarah went to one of the surrounding counties. Or maybe Joplin or Springfield."

She spent the next hour phoning all the surrounding counties with no luck.

"How about Arkansas?" Charles suggested. "It looks like Barry County is on the state border."

"Yeah, it is. It also borders Kansas and Oklahoma."

"You're looking worn out, Alex. And I hate to tell you, but you now have two black eyes. Not that you don't still look charming."

Alex hit her ex-fiancé playfully. "I am awfully tired. But I hate to bail on you."

"Jon has a book on the Osage Indians I've been itching to read. Indians were a childhood fantasy—the Wild West and all of that."

* * *

Alex's dreams were confused. She was at Miss Maddy's stone cottage, which was filled with people in white who were climbing out of all her books. Luminescent and graceful, they were ministering to the woman who lay injured in her recliner. Then Alex was deep down a silver mine with Indians dressed in loincloths tying her up. But Charles came striding in, dressed as a buccaneer with a tricornered hat and holding a lantern. Just as he was about to rescue her, an angry thumping on the front door disturbed her slumbers.

She woke to hear the mayor roaring, "What did you mean by sending the FBI to my home?" Then he stopped dead in his tracks. "What the devil happened to you, Alex?"

Coming up from a deep sleep, she stared at the man swaying before her. He was obviously three sheets to the wind. "Your stepson, Joe, bashed me on the head," she said finally.

"Stepson! I have absolutely nothing to do with Joe McHenry and all his dirty little businesses, or any of the rest of the McHenry scum, and so I told the FBI."

"But you married a McHenry widow," Alex said.

"Only on the condition that she give her children up for adoption. She has absolutely nothing to do with them."

"Then why has she disappeared?" Charles asked.

"Maybe they've taken her. Has that occurred to you?" Cameron McNee asked.

"As a matter of fact, it has," Alex answered. "That's why the FBI agents are so anxious to find her."

That seemed to give the mayor pause. "Word has it that Joe lives down by Cassville somewhere. In the forest."

"Did you tell the agents that?" Charles asked.

"No. I thought they were accusing me of doing away with Sylvia or something."

Alex asked, "Are you sure Sylvia has nothing to do with him anymore?"

"Well . . . Syl has her own life. Always has. She's a lot like Kerry. Wrapped up in dreams and fantasies."

Alex remembered the soap operas. They seemed harmless enough. Then she remembered something else. "What about her daughter Cynthia? What has become of her?"

The mayor sank into a chair. "Cynthia? Well, from what I gather, which isn't much, she's a nasty piece of work. Some kind of self-proclaimed witch. Syl is scared to death of her."

Alex rolled her eyes as Dashiell sprang awake and began stretching himself. "That's absolutely all we need in this mix is a witch."

"I don't suppose she really is. A witch, I mean. She's just a real nasty character. Keeps house for Joe."

Alex was realizing that the mayor knew a lot more about his stepchildren than he had let on. She hoped she could keep him talking. "So she's never married?"

"She never found anyone as smart as she is, Syl says. I think she never found anyone as wicked as she is, except Joe."

"Why do you think the McHenrys are so wicked?" Alex asked, trying to get Dashiell to lie down again. He was scampering along her legs and batting at her naked toes.

Cameron McNee felt for his pipe in his pocket and stuck it in his mouth unlit. It suddenly occurred to Alex, noting his slack mouth, that he was very drunk. "You know, it's real strange. Except for Cynthia, the women and girls aren't at all wicked. It's just the men. They're born mean."

Alex took a deep breath, emboldened by her success, and plunged into her next observation. "Mike isn't mean."

Cameron McNee stared at her, seeming to come out of his fog. "I thought we were talking about the McHenrys. Michael's a Wentworth."

As the mayor's information seemed in danger of drying up, Alex quickly changed the subject. "Charles has been reading about the Osage Indians."

"Eeeyup," the man said, "They lived on the Ozark Plateau for a long time. Tradition says they used to mine silver around here. They say Barry County's riddled with Indian mines, but there's none on my property." He took his pipe out of his mouth and studied it absently. "I was always exploring when I was a kid. Down by the river there's caves. Mother never would let me play there. She was scared to death of lead."

"Lead?" Charles asked.

"Yeah, her daddy was a mine owner in Carthage, up by Joplin. They've got huge lead mines. Those poor old lead miners. They suffered all kind of effects. It was criminal, really. They got sick, and the mine owners got wealthy. Mother always felt guilty about that. She was glad to be down here away from it. She never wanted anyone to know her daddy's name."

Alex smothered a yawn. She was suddenly exhausted, but she knew what Kerry's father was telling her was important for the genogram. "Why don't you tell me about your mother? She's the only one on Kerry's genogram I don't know much about. What was her maiden name?"

"Alice Gordon. She grew up in one of those Carthage mansions. A real lady. She brought culture to Barry County. Fine woman, fine woman."

"How did your parents meet?" Alex asked idly.

"Well, Carthage used to be a real fancy place. They gave balls with real orchestras. Some of those old houses have ballrooms. Did you know my father was also the mayor here?"

Alex nodded.

He continued, "My father had just been elected mayor, so he was considered gentry, I guess. He got lots of invitations. Used to travel up there in his horse and buggy. He'd stay several days. My dad always said Mother was the prettiest little thing he'd ever seen. Kerry has the look of her exactly."

After a few more minutes, during which he was scanning the room, possibly for a whiskey decanter, the mayor left.

Alex resumed her telephoning. She was still at it, having covered all the bordering counties in Arkansas, when her cell phone rang.

"Alex, this is Agent Donovan."

"Oh, hello. Any news?"

"Nothing much from the mayor. I just wanted to let you know that there's no sign of a McHenry high or low. We've found several houses, including Joe McHenry's, and they are all empty. It looks like they've gone to ground somewhere. So you're still in plenty of danger."

"That's kind of what I expected," she said. "I got a bit more out of the mayor than you did. He came steaming in here, a little drunk, I think. But the only really interesting thing he said was that the McHenry women weren't criminals, just the men. That sort of does away with the idea that it's genetic, if that was even possible."

"Maybe there's some male rite of passage or something," the agent speculated.

"That takes place before they even start school?"

"No. I guess that doesn't work."

Alex asked, "Have your agents cleaned out the meth lab yet?"

"Yeah. And they've found enough marijuana for the entire population of Missouri, I think. In addition to what was drying in the warehouse, the stuff practically grows wild in the forest. Oh, and Mrs. McNee is back home. We left a voicemail, and she answered it. We're on our way over there now."

Alex felt a surge of relief. Her guilt would have doubled if Sylvia had been dropped in the lake because of her. "Thank heavens nothing's happened to her!"

"We'll be in touch," Donovan said.

"Thanks."

Charles insisted she take another nap while he did what he could to scrape together a passable dinner. He gave her a couple of Tylenol and took Dashiell outside so he wouldn't have an accident on the couch.

Alex dreamed of Miss Maddy again. This time the woman was flying through the cemetery, lingering at each grave and weeping as she clutched her scrapbook. Then there were Indians again, and she woke up with a scream in her throat as they were about to scalp her.

The pain in her head confused her for a moment. It *had* been a dream. She hadn't been scalped! Then she heard Briggie and Richard in the kitchen with Charles. Slowly, her situation came back to her. She called, "Briggie, any luck?"

Briggie entered the room, followed by Richard. Both of them were beaming with accomplishment. She showed Alex a number of family groups she had gleaned from the newspaper accounts of crimes that had been committed in Trotter's Bridge. Beside each of the names she had listed the crimes committed. Most of them were robbery with assault or just plain assault. There weren't any murder charges or anything to do with drugs.

"Boy, are they ever a lawless bunch!" Briggie said. "And despite the fear of reprisals, a lot of these McHenrys got sent to prison."

"Yes," agreed Alex, "but you'll notice none up them got sent up for very long, and none of these crimes is terribly serious. Not like murder or drugs."

Richard's cell phone rang. "This must be Marigny," he said.

"Hi, there, Ginger! What've you got?" Pause. "Okay, great. Can you read the whole thing to me in a second? I've got to get something to write with."

He walked into the kitchen.

"I wonder how the FBI is doing with Sylvia," Alex said.

"I hope a whole lot better than we did," responded Briggie. "How's your head, kiddo?"

"I just had a nap, so it's better, I think. I've got to get up tomorrow." She explained her theory about Sarah's first marriage.

"Hmm. I can't believe I missed that. But if phoning is working for you, why not go that route?"

"I guess I just like to be 'hands on.'"

"Where have you called?"

"All the surrounding counties in Missouri, including Greene and Jasper, where Joplin and Springfield are. And all the bordering counties in Arkansas."

"Well," Briggie said, "in their day, the big resort town was Eureka Springs down in Arkansas. I wouldn't be a bit surprised if that's where they went. But are you sure she was married? She could have just gotten pregnant."

"I don't think it'd be in character," Alex said. "But you may be right. What county is Eureka Springs in?"

"Let me see that map," her friend said.

Alex proffered the *Handybook*.

"It looks like it's in Carroll County. What year are we talking about?

"1888."

"Good. They've got records from that year. I'll just make a quick call if you hand me that phone."

Alex lay back, exhausted again. Before Briggie was off the phone, Richard came back into the room, a puzzled look on his face.

"What is it, Richard?"

"Well, this doesn't make any sense," he told Alex. "According to the birth certificate, Wentworth's parents are Jerome Wentworth and Laurel McCain Wentworth. But the birth date is two years earlier than the date the birth certificate was issued!"

"Adoption!" Alex said, her mind racing. "Mike Wentworth was adopted when he was two. Too young to remember. His old birth certificate will have been filed away somewhere under lock and key, if it's even still around."

Briggie gave them an annoyed glance and walked into the kitchen, clutching the cordless phone to her ear.

"What are the chances of his having that crooked finger if he doesn't have McHenry blood, I wonder?" Richard tapped the piece of paper against his lips.

"He's always at the McNees'. Why?" Alex demanded.

"I think we need to find the answer to that question. According to this certificate, he's forty years old. Do you suppose he's in love with Kerry?"

"I think it more likely that he's her half brother, though I don't know how we'll ever prove it, unless either Cameron or he admits it. The good old mayor spun us a story of getting a girl pregnant in high school. He said she went to New Orleans. I'll bet she was a McHenry and went to Kansas City, had the baby, and was living with this Wentworth or something. Maybe she died. We ought to check death records in Johnson County, Kansas, for a female McHenry."

"Do you buy Brighamina's story that Wentworth tried to shoot you because he didn't want the truth to come out?"

"It could be," Alex said. "It very well could be. Dang! I hate being stuck here on this couch!"

Briggie came back into the room, exuding triumph. "I was right. Sarah Delacroix and Bo McHenry were married in Eureka Springs in June 1888."

McHenry Descendancy Chart
("Bad Blood")

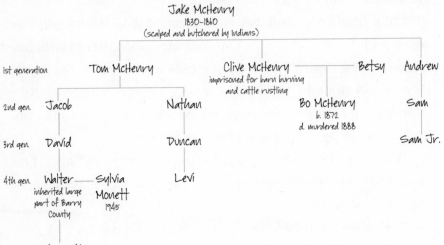

Jake McHenry
1830–1860
(scalped and butchered by Indians)

1st generation — Tom McHenry — Clive McHenry — Betsy — Andrew
imprisoned for barn burning
and cattle rustling

2nd gen. — Jacob — Nathan — Bo McHenry
b. 1872
d. murdered 1888 — Sam

3rd gen. — David — Duncan — Sam Jr.

4th gen. — Walter — Sylvia — Levi
inherited large   Monett
part of Barry   1945
County

Joe & Cynthia

"Bo McHenry!" Alex exclaimed. "Get your McHenry descendancy chart, Briggie! That name is really familiar for some reason."

Her friend dug through her denim briefcase until she came up with what she was looking for.

"Yes! He was Jake McHenry's grandson, through his son Clive. Alex, he's the one who was murdered when he was sixteen. In 1888. Charles found his tombstone in the cemetery."

"Oh, good grief," Alex said. "My head is positively bursting! Sarah Delacroix was the daughter of Pierre Delacroix, practically the patron saint of Trotter's Bridge. And his daughter of twenty runs off with a sixteen-year-old McHenry. Briggie, do you realize the marriage wouldn't even have been legal? Bo was underage!"

"Who do you suppose murdered him?"

"If only we had Miss Maddy's scrapbooks!" Alex moaned.

"All her articles were from the big-town newspapers. I guess we'll just have to check them," Briggie said. "But at least we've found Kerry's McHenry blood." Pausing, she appeared to be thinking. "Glory! Do you realize that both mayors, not to mention Kerry, should be named McHenry? They weren't descended from the Reverend Ernest McNee but from Bo McHenry. I doubt they even know!"

"This is an enormous amount to take in, Briggie. Do you understand the broader implications? Both mayors have been stellar citizens, as far as we know. They were raised outside the McHenry family system. Whatever taint the McHenry males have seems to have passed them by."

Alex looked at her incomplete genogram of Kerry's family. Borrowing a pencil from Briggie, she filled it in with the new information.

At the bottom she put several big questions.

Who murdered Bo McHenry?
Does Mayor McNee know he's a McHenry?
Why don't the "McNee McHenrys" have the McHenry taint?
Did Cameron McNee sire Michael Wentworth?
If so, does Michael know?
What is the cause of the McHenry taint?
Who shot Kerry?
And who the heck murdered Miss Maddy?

Kerry's Genogram

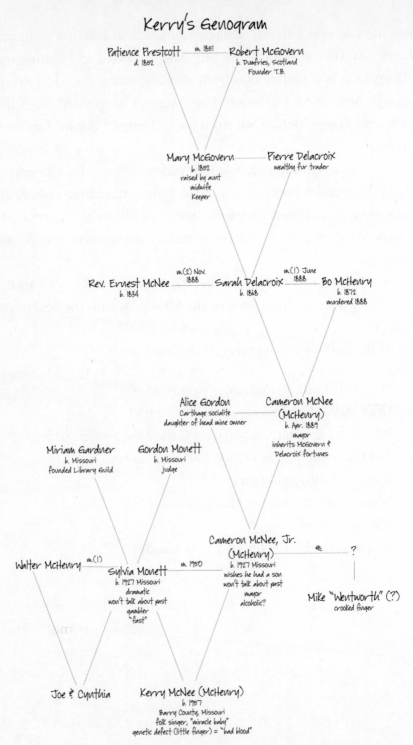

Patience Prestcott
d. 1852

m. 1851

Robert McGovern
b. Dumfries, Scotland
Founder T.B.

Mary McGovern
b. 1852
raised by aunt
midwife
Keeper

Pierre Delacroix
wealthy fur trader

Rev. Ernest McNee
b. 1834

m.(2) Nov. 1888

Sarah Delacroix
b. 1868

m.(1) June 1888

Bo McHenry
b. 1872
murdered 1888

Alice Gordon
Carthage socialite
daughter of head mine owner

Cameron McNee
(McHenry)
b. Apr. 1889
mayor
inherits McGovern &
Delacroix fortunes

Miriam Gardner
b. Missouri
founded Library Guild

Gordon Monett
b. Missouri
judge

Cameron McNee, Jr.
(McHenry)
b. 1927 Missouri
wishes he had a son
won't talk about past
mayor
alcoholic?

?

Walter McHenry

m.(1)

Sylvia Monett
b. 1927 Missouri
dramatic
won't talk about past
gambler
"fast"

m. 1950

Mike "Wentworth" (?)
crooked finger

Joe & Cynthia

Kerry McNee (McHenry)
b. 1957
Barry County, Missouri
folk singer, "miracle baby"
genetic defect (little finger) = "bad blood"

Chapter Twenty

Just as Charles put his French onion soup on the table, Sylvia arrived. Alex braced herself for fireworks, but the woman looked pitiful as Jon took her through to the kitchen. Listening to the conversation, she admired his adroitness.

"Jon?" she asked plaintively, her face ashen. "Why are the FBI here? They were asking me all about Joe. I don't even know how they knew he was my son. He was adopted by his uncle when I married Cameron."

"Come, Syl, and join us for dinner," said Jon. "We're just about to eat. You look like a strong wind would blow you over."

The woman doubled over, clutching her middle. "I couldn't. I'm too upset. Do you have any idea what it's like to be grilled by the FBI? I went on a shopping trip to Kansas City and stayed overnight. They seem to think I was committing a crime."

"Well, your husband was worried about you. He said you missed a big engagement in Springfield last night," the doctor replied.

"Oh, my land, I completely forgot about it! That's what happens when you get to be my age. What happened to that woman on the couch in there?"

"Alex was attacked and kidnapped by Joe. She has a concussion. The FBI has found a meth lab and truckloads of marijuana in the forest. I'm sure you and the mayor will be glad to get that out of the community."

"Are they trying to pin that on Joe?" Sylvia asked in a small voice.

"What do you know about Joe's activities, Sylvia?"

The woman suddenly resembled a clam.

"He's a little reckless, but he's always been a good son. Not likely to get mixed up in anything like that. Who says he is?"

Sylvia's voice had turned sharp and suspicious. To Alex's relief, Jon dropped the matter.

"Well, then, it's just hearsay, and that's not admissible in court," the woman said. Alex could hear the stubbornness in her voice and winced.

"You forget, he knocked Alex out and kidnapped her. What do you have to say about that?"

Sylvia was silent. Then she said, "That's terrible about the drugs, but I don't think Joe would do anything like that."

"Well, he's disappeared, so maybe we'll never know," Jon finished. "Now, please sit down, Sylvia, and try to calm yourself."

"I'll just be going. The FBI were so evasive. They didn't really tell me anything. And, of course, I couldn't tell them anything. Joe was adopted by his uncle when he was three."

"So you don't have any contact with him?" Jon asked. Alex, listening from the living room, knew it was a trick question, because the mayor had already spilled a few beans.

"No, I'm afraid not. That wouldn't have made Cameron at all happy. In his position, he can't really afford to have anything to do with the McHenrys."

The pathetic note Sylvia infused into her voice would have convinced Alex if she hadn't known better. What an actress she was!

Sylvia left shortly thereafter. Alex was still wondering why she had come when Charles came in and sat on the edge of the couch. "What did you make of that?" he asked, kissing her forehead.

"She's an excellent liar. She must have been testing the waters to see what we knew."

"I'd say she's a nasty bit of work," Charles added. "I wonder if the FBI is having her followed."

"Probably not," Alex guessed. "If her husband hadn't talked to us, we might have swallowed her pitiful little act. And the mayor didn't give the FBI the time of day."

"I'm half tempted to stake out the retirement home tonight. I'm sure she knows where Joe is, and she'll want to give him a report on the FBI."

"There are such things as cell phones. She's probably talking to him right now."

"Yes," Charles agreed with a little sigh. "You're probably right. What do you think we should do?"

Alex showed him her list of questions. "Those are the things I'm wondering. Of course, the last question is the most important. I think Mike Wentworth is the obvious candidate for Miss Maddy's killer. Sylvia could have called the mayor, and he could have told Mike about our project to do Kerry's genealogy."

"So how can we find out if he really does have McHenry blood?"

"The only thing I can think of is trying to find a death certificate for his mother. Either she gave him up for adoption when he was two, which doesn't seem very likely, or the Wentworths adopted him after she died."

Charles stroked Alex's hair back from her head and planted a kiss at her hairline. "I love it when you're so earnest. Even when you have black eyes. What is it Pooh-Bah said in *The Mikado?* They 'give verisimilitude to an otherwise bald and unconvincing narrative.' "

"That's true. If Joe hadn't attacked me, we'd be missing a huge part of the McHenry story. Well," Alex said, sitting up a bit as she forgot her condition for a moment. "I guess we can't put it off any longer. We need to call Kerry and tell her we know about her bad blood."

"I have a feeling we should tell her to keep it to herself. I don't think her father is going to be the least bit pleased," Charles remarked as he handed her the telephone.

*　　*　　*

Alex should have been prepared for it, but she wasn't. Daniel appeared with Kerry at the Coxes' house, and the two sat together on the couch across from Alex. Daniel's arm was wrapped protectively around his client, who wore a blue sling.

"How's your shoulder?" Alex asked.

"Dr. Jon gave me some antibiotics, and now I'm doing much better," she said. "Don't hold me in suspense. Tell me what you've found."

Alex assessed Kerry for a moment. Tonight she wasn't dressed as a femme fatale. She actually wore blue jeans and a navy blue turtleneck. The effect of these colors was to wash her out. She wore no makeup. Alex guessed that Kerry was playing poor little orphan girl. "Well, you do have McHenry blood, Kerry. Miss Maddy was right. But before I tell you about that, I just want to say something." Wishing she could sit up and face her client properly, and wondering vaguely what Briggie and Richard were up to in the kitchen, she continued, "There is no such thing as bad blood, in terms of good and evil. You and some other members of your family all have McHenry blood, and you are all sane and perfectly law-abiding. So, apparently, are the female McHenrys. We are trying to figure out what makes the males so wild."

Kerry took a deep breath and let it out slowly. "So who's been lying about my family tree?"

"I don't know that anyone living even knows about it, Kerry. I think Miss Maddy was the last one who did. Let me show you your genogram."

Charles moved one of the kitchen chairs that remained in the front room next to Alex's couch, and Kerry moved over to it. Daniel followed, looking over her shoulder. Alex reflected briefly how odd it was to have Daniel on the other side of a case. In the past he had helped her make her discoveries.

"This is you," Alex pointed. "Let's do your mother's side first. She married Walt McHenry in 1945 and had twins by him: Joe and Cynthia." She indicated her own black eyes. "Joe gave me these when I got a little too close to his drug operation. The FBI are on a manhunt for him right now."

"That's hardly cheering," Kerry said. "Drugs! Good grief! My father must be having seven kinds of fits." Then she reflected. "So I have a half brother and a half sister?"

"I warned you in Kansas City that you might not like what you found out," Alex told her. "Your grandparents were very respectable. They were the upper crust of Mount Vernon society. Your grandfather was a judge, and your grandmother was known for her charitable works. Your mother seems to have gotten a taste of the wide world when she worked in Washington, D.C., towards the end of the war. She came home, acted out wildly, and ended up getting pregnant and marrying Walt McHenry. I don't have many details about him, except that he owned a lot of property and died drunk in a car wreck."

Kerry's Genogram

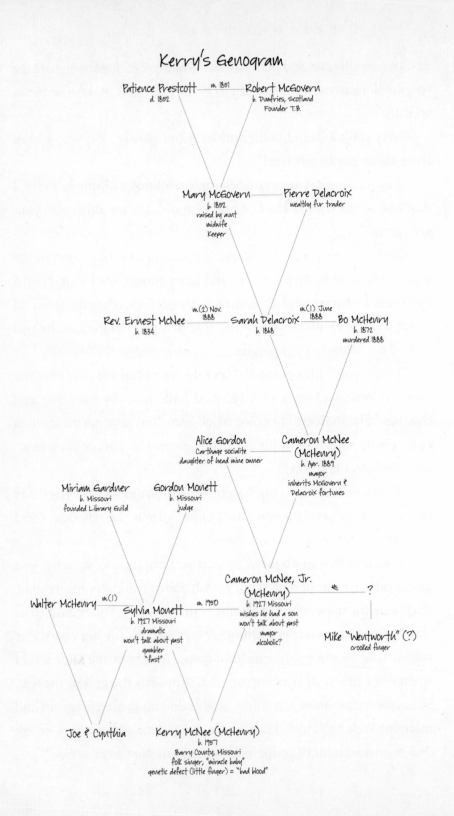

Patience Prestcott
d. 1852

m. 1851

Robert McGovern
b. Dumfries, Scotland
Founder T.B.

Mary McGovern
b. 1852
raised by aunt
midwife
Keeper

Pierre Delacroix
wealthy fur trader

Rev. Ernest McNee
b. 1834

m.(2) Nov.
1888

Sarah Delacroix
b. 1868

m.(1) June
1888

Bo McHenry
b. 1872
murdered 1888

Alice Gordon
Carthage socialite
daughter of head mine owner

Cameron McNee
(McHenry)
b. Apr. 1889
mayor
inherits McGovern &
Delacroix fortunes

Miriam Gardner
b. Missouri
founded Library Guild

Gordon Monett
b. Missouri
judge

Cameron McNee, Jr.
(McHenry)
b. 1927 Missouri
wishes he had a son
won't talk about past
mayor
alcoholic?

m.

?

Walter McHenry

m.(1)

Sylvia Monett
b. 1927 Missouri
dramatic
won't talk about past
gambler
"fast"

m. 1950

Mike "Wentworth" (?)
crooked finger

Joe & Cynthia

Kerry McNee (McHenry)
b. 1957
Barry County, Missouri
folk singer, "miracle baby"
genetic defect (little finger) = "bad blood"

"But that's nothing to do with me, because he couldn't possibly have been my father," Kerry protested.

"Right. Your mother and father married when they were both thirty. As a condition of the marriage, your father made your mother give up her twins for adoption."

"How horrid of him! I've always wanted a sister."

"Her name is Cynthia, but apparently she is the exception that proves the rule about McHenry women being normal. She is supposedly plenty mean and keeps house for her brother."

"Well, that doesn't sound promising. Go on," Kerry said, now the brave little soldier with her chin in the air.

"Okay. Now on to your father's side. Presumably you know all about him. We have some speculations we are checking into about that high school episode he mentioned, but nothing firm as yet."

"You mean I might have some more half siblings?" Kerry said, her voice sharp.

"Yes. You heard your father's story. We're still checking it out. Now, it appears that your paternal grandparents were good, normal people. In fact, your grandmother was a society girl—the daughter of a mine owner in Carthage. According to your dad, your grandfather had just been elected mayor and was invited up there to a ball where he met your grandmother, who apparently looked quite a bit like you. Her name was Alice Gordon."

"Okay." Kerry set her chin again.

"Now, it's the next generation back where the problem lies. We're still missing a few facts. But we know that Minister Ernest McNee was not the father of Cameron McNee Sr. He married your great-grandmother, Sarah Delacroix, when she was pregnant with your grandfather by her first husband, a man called Bo McHenry."

Kerry drew in her breath, her eyes round. "I've seen his grave! We used to go snooping around the graveyard when we were kids. He was murdered!"

"Yes, and your great-grandmother was then married off to Reverend McNee, who was more than twice her age."

Kerry was covering her mouth with her hand and looking at Alex as if her head had sprouted snakes. "My last name should be McHenry! I'm a true McHenry! Oh, no. I can never tell Daddy. He'd have a heart attack on the spot."

"I see no reason why you should tell him. It's really ancient history, you know."

Kerry considered. "I think I'll lie to him and tell him you didn't find anything."

"And *you'll* have to decide what you want to tell your children," Alex said.

"Does anybody know who killed Bo McHenry?"

"I don't know if we'll ever know. I imagine if we could get one of the clan to talk, there's some kind of oral history. The logical candidate would be Sarah's father—the illustrious and patriarchal Pierre Delacroix, who would have been horrified by her runaway marriage to a McHenry. They were married in Eureka Springs, by the way. However, knowing how murderous the McHenrys are, his murderer could have been one of his own family."

Alex was worn out and terribly thirsty. She could feel every beat of her heart in the painful pulse at her temple.

"Go on," Kerry insisted. "My great-great-grandfather was Pierre Delacroix, the one in the town square?"

"Yes," Alex said. "He married Mary McGovern, whose father was another prominent founder of the town. Your father inherited his spread. Mary's father, Robert McGovern, was married to Patience Prestcott. That's as far back as the Keeper's records go."

"Whew!" said Daniel. "That's quick work, Alex. Where is Briggie, by the way?"

"Last I knew, she was in the kitchen with Richard, but it seems awful quiet."

Daniel hastened into the kitchen as though pursued by furies. "They're gone, Alex!" he called. "Oh criminy! What can they be up to? There's a note here from Jon, saying he's gone off to his hospital rounds, but nothing from Dad or Briggie."

Alex looked at Charles, who shook his head.

"Why in the world are you so upset, Daniel?" Kerry asked. "I'm the one who just had twenty shocks administered. Your father is presumably able to take care of himself."

"Not when he's with Briggie. As a combination, they're dangerous!" He pointed to the rifle beside Charles. "They didn't even take Briggie's deer rifle."

"That's actually a good sign," Charles said. "She's more worried about Alex's safety than she is her own. So maybe she's not doing anything too dangerous."

"She thinks she's invincible," Alex said, wondering where on earth they could have gone. Then she relaxed against the arm of the couch onto her ice pack. Cell phones. They were marvelous inventions. "Call your dad's cell phone, Daniel."

Relieved at this suggestion, Daniel pulled out his own cell and punched in the number. He listened. "It goes right to voice mail," he reported wearily. "He's out of power or out of range, or he turned it off."

Alex looked up Jon's number on her own cell phone and dialed. The doctor answered on the first ring. "Dr. Cox."

"Hello, Jon, it's Alex. Have you any idea where Briggie and Richard have gone? Were they here when you left?"

"No. They left right before. They were kind of funny about it.

Almost sneaky. Didn't even finish their soup. They went out the door through the mudroom."

"When was it in relation to when Sylvia left?" Dread made Alex's stomach leaden.

"Right after she left," Jon said. "Oh gosh, you don't think they followed her, do you?"

"That's exactly what I think," Alex said. "What on earth are we going to do, Jon? They could be in all sorts of danger."

"I'll swing by the retirement home and the McNee residence on my way home. They may be on a stakeout."

"Well, if they are, tell them to come home and quit playing Nick and Nora. They're too old for it, and Briggie doesn't drink martinis." Punching her phone off, she said to those assembled, "They've done it again. They went off following Sylvia."

"Mother?" Kerry said. "Why?"

"Because your mother lied to us about Joe. She said she hadn't kept up with him, didn't know anything about him, but we know from your father that she did. And Joe's missing. The FBI are hunting him down. Briggie and Richard must think your mother will lead them to him."

"My mother in with the McHenrys on this drug operation? You've got to have a screw loose, Alex. She doesn't have the brains. She lives inside the covers of a Harlequin romance."

"Even Harlequin romance readers can take care of their children," Alex remarked. "She told us she couldn't believe Joe would ever be involved with drugs. He's probably pulled the wool over her eyes, and she thinks he's being persecuted by the FBI. I'll bet he has some childhood hiding place she knows about."

Kerry leaned back in her chair, and Alex knew she was genuinely befuddled, no longer playing a role. "I can't tell you how hard this is to take in."

"Alex understands," Daniel soothed her. "When she started in on her genealogy, her father was murdered."

Charles looked at Alex in surprise. As with most of her past, she had kept that fact under wraps. She regarded Daniel with annoyance.

He seemed not to notice. "They had a family secret that was so bad it sent her mother into alcoholism, and they packed Alex off to Paris when she was eighteen with no explanation."

"What was it?" Kerry asked.

"I don't discuss it," Alex said, looking daggers at Daniel. Charles didn't know about those things, either. "Daniel, don't say another word. You are violating my confidence."

"Well, it's just that as you can probably tell, my father is an alcoholic," Kerry said. "Maybe he has a secret, too. About that woman and his baby. It's too weird that both my parents gave away their children. No wonder they spoiled me rotten."

Kerry, as usual, was unaware of anyone but herself. Alex was breathing hard in unexpressed fury, Charles was looking at her with questioning eyes, and Daniel stared at Charles as innocent as a cherub.

Chapter Twenty-One

Kerry was sagging like a bag of flour, her eyes glazing over as she tried to take in all that Alex had told her. Daniel, in his concern for his father and Briggie, didn't seem to notice that Alex had closed her eyes and was praying silently when Charles said firmly, "We must try not to panic. I think right now would be a good time for us to say a prayer."

Alex open her eyes and looked at him with amazement and gratitude. "Thank you, Charles. That's a wonderful idea. I'm going to kneel."

Getting off the couch gingerly, she made it to her knees and supported her body with her elbows on the couch. Charles knelt beside her, taking her hand. Kerry and Daniel stayed where they were.

"Heavenly Father," Charles said in his wonderful mellow voice, "Thank you for the gospel, which brings such comfort and light into our lives. At the moment, we are truly concerned for our friends, Richard and Briggie. Please bless them that they may come to no harm. Bless us that we may know what to do to help them. In the name of Jesus Christ, amen."

"Amen," echoed Alex. Warmth spread through her, a combination of the Spirit and Charles's offering the prayer. She had never heard him pray before.

He helped her stand and get back onto the couch.

Kerry chose that moment to say, "I see you're no longer wearing your engagement ring, Alex. Does that mean you're not marrying Charles?"

"Oh, for heaven's sake, Kerry, can't you see this is not the time for that?" Daniel said, irritated.

Alex ignored Kerry's question. "While we're waiting for Jon to come home, maybe we should call Marigny about getting a death certificate for a female McHenry who died in Johnson County when Michael was two." Looking at the information Richard had scribbled down about Mike's birth certificate, she said, "That would be 1954."

"What are you talking about now?" asked Kerry. "What has Mike got to do with this?"

"Marigny won't be able to manage that!" Daniel exclaimed.

"She's been a great help, so far," Alex told him. "She got the goods from Topeka today. This should be a piece of cake." Dialing the cordless phone, she waited for Marigny to answer.

Finally, the girl picked up. Alex could hear the eerie music of the *X Files* opening credits in the background as Marigny said breathlessly, "Hello?"

Alex congratulated her on her good work that day and asked if she could please do them another favor. Marigny responded enthusiastically. Explaining the problem, Alex was encouraged by the girl's enthusiasm, assured her she would be paid, and then hung up.

"You don't have the right touch, Daniel," Alex said with a grin. "You've got to start treating her like a grown-up."

"Will someone please tell me what you're looking for?" Kerry asked.

Alex considered and then glanced at Charles, who gave a minimal shake of his head. "All in good time. Don't you think you've had enough surprises for one day, Kerry?" he said.

"I want to go home, Daniel," the singer said fretfully. Alex reflected that no one would know her as the elegant, confident superstar she was if they could see her now.

Daniel said, "Kerry, I'm sorry. Maybe you can lie down on this other couch for a while. I'm not going anywhere until I find out what my insane father is up to. He may have gotten himself into a real pickle. You don't know Dad when he's with Briggie."

"Is he in love with her or something? He's so overbearingly proper, and I've never seen her in anything but sweats."

Daniel shook his head. "They started out as blood enemies, but somehow over the last year things have changed. He thinks she's the most amazing woman he's ever known. He pretends he's got the upper hand, but Briggie's got him running in circles."

Alex agreed. "It would be funny if I weren't so worried about them. Briggie told me her first husband looked like Clark Gable, only taller."

"Clark Gable?" Kerry echoed. "What did he see in her?"

Alex grinned. "Plenty. They had nine children." She thought of her friend with a sudden wave of fondness. Briggie never did anything halfway. *That's the reason I love her.*

At that moment her cell phone rang.

"Honey," Briggie said, "I think we've struck gold. We've been following Sylvia. She's headed down by the river, and I don't think it's to do night fishing. I think she knows where Joe is."

"Briggie, that dang Suburban of Richard's is so big, she'll be sure to spot you."

"We're being real careful," her friend said. "There's another car between us."

"Well, for heaven's sake, keep in touch. I've been worried sick."

"Will do. Over and out." The phone went dead.

"They're following Sylvia down by the river," Alex reported.

"What in the world is my mother doing down there at this time of the evening?" Kerry asked.

"I have no idea," Alex responded.

At that moment, Jon walked in. "They weren't at either place," he said.

"We just heard from them. They're following Sylvia. She's headed down to the river."

"The caves!" Jon said. "I should have thought! Those McHenrys are holed up in the caves down by the river! Some of them are enormous, with corridors spreading for at least a mile. This whole plateau is limestone."

Alex's heart quickened. "If Briggie and Richard stumble onto them, they're going to end up in Table Rock Lake! We've got to call Agent Stone!"

Charles pulled the agent's card out of his pocket and handed it to Alex. She dialed the number.

"Agent Stone."

"Agent Stone, this is Alex Campbell. My business partner and Richard Grinnell have tracked Sylvia McNee down to the river. Jon seems to think she's headed for some caves down there. I'm worried about my friends. I'm afraid if they run into that bunch of McHenrys hiding out there, they'll end up in Table Rock Lake."

"We're on our way," Stone told her. "What're they driving?"

"A black Suburban. Can you keep us informed?"

"Will do. You just nurse that head of yours."

211

"Well, what do we do now?" Kerry asked, her voice querulous. "Play Hearts?"

Alex's irritation with the singer had finally reached the boiling point. "Look, Kerry, it's because of you my friends are in danger. So put a sock in it, will you?"

Kerry looked astonished, Jon was somber, Charles didn't even try to mask his own irritation, and Daniel paced the room, running his hand through his hair.

The time passed somehow, but they heard nothing. Daniel tried phoning his father, but once again the call went immediately to voicemail.

It was nearly 9:30 when Alex smacked her forehead unthinkingly with her hand. "Kerry! Does your mother have a cell phone?"

"Well, yes," the singer said. "Do you want me to call her?"

Alex restrained herself. "Would you? Whatever you do, don't tell her you're with us, though. Can you make up some excuse to find out where she is?"

"I can try," Kerry said. She had sobered at Alex's accusation that she was to blame. Alex handed her Jon's cordless phone. Kerry dialed, her face thoughtful.

"Hi, Mother!" she said brightly into the phone. "I have something really exciting to tell you, but I tried the home and your house and couldn't reach you. Where are you?" Silence. "Springfield? What're you doing there?" Another silence. "Oh, how fun! I didn't know they were in town. Is Dad with you? No? Well, maybe he's passed out and didn't hear the phone." Silence again. "Oh, I'll wait to tell you in person." Pause. "Yes, my shoulder's fine. As a matter of fact, Dr. Jon's checked me over." Silence. "Okay, bye."

Kerry pressed Off and shook her head. "I never knew my mother could lie so convincingly. She says she's gone to an Oak Ridge Boys' concert. She loves them, but as far as I know, they're down in Branson."

"I'm really worried, Charles," Alex said. Her head was banging, and her stomach rebelling against the French onion soup. "Can you call Agent Stone again?"

This time, they failed to reach the FBI agent. Their call went to voicemail.

"That does it!" Alex said. "Kerry, do you know the way to Table Rock Lake?"

"Sure," she said, gulping. "Do you really think they're drowning Briggie and Richard? It's a huge lake."

"Just take us to the dock you're most familiar with that's closest to the river," Alex said. "Charles, be sure to take Briggie's rifle. We may need it."

Daniel started a feeble protest about Kerry's shoulder and Alex's head, but Charles cut him off. "Look here, Grinnell, this is pretty desperate. Pull yourself together."

Jon said, "I've got an automatic. I'll come, too."

They squeezed into Charles's Lexus, Charles driving and the lanky Jon beside him, cradling the revolver. Alex sat in the back with the deer rifle, reminding herself that it had a hair trigger. Daniel sat between her and Kerry.

No one spoke except for Kerry, giving terse directions.

How in the world could she bear losing Briggie? Alex thought of her staunch friend, who had rescued her from her bottomless grief and abandonment in Scotland. Stewart's Scottish relatives had been so stoic and phlegmatic that Alex couldn't pour out her grief to them. The cold village kirk had offered no comfort. There hadn't been a body to mourn, or even a memorial service. After she lost the baby, Alex had begun to waste away, not caring whether she lived or died. One day Briggie had appeared at her bedside, and in her gruff

American accent had told her she was related to Stewart. Briggie invited her to get out of her bed and try to help her prove it. Since then, she had issued one challenge after another. *Come home to the States where you belong. Come live with me in my house, and we'll start a genealogy business together. Go to my friend, Dr. Brace, and get some help for your depression. Listen to the missionaries—they have a message that will give meaning to your life. Go see your parents and make peace with them . . .*

Briggie was too tough to die! And too good. But the lake was bottomless and huge.

Alex's head felt like it was under a thousand pounds of pressure. Formerly rigid with anxiety, she now slumped as fear overtook her. Daniel must have felt it.

"Dad won't let anything happen to Briggie, Alex. He's very protective of her, actually, though she hates it."

"They're both old, Daniel. And Joe McHenry is young and strong."

"Don't give in to your fear, darling," Charles said over his shoulder. "Remember the counsel Briggie's always giving you about fear and faith."

Fear and faith cannot exist in the same heart at the same time.

Alex sat up straighter.

They were close to the lake now, Kerry told them. Alex struggled to peer into the darkness.

It was difficult to see, but she could tell there was a black vehicle in front of them. "Is that the Suburban up ahead?"

Charles switched to high beams.

"Yes," he said. "But as far as I can tell there's only one person. The driver."

"Briggie and Richard may be tied up already, lying in the back. Doesn't this car have more power than the Suburban, Charles?"

214

"They're probably about equal."

"Try passing!" she said fiercely.

Charles jerked the Lexus into the oncoming lane and punched the accelerator. The Suburban put on a sudden burst of speed and pulled away from them.

"Stay on their tail!" Alex commanded.

"Alex, I really do know what I'm doing. Pipe down, darling."

For a few moments, Alex sat with her teeth clenched and her arms around herself, squeezing hard. Briggie's rifle fell to the floor. The rifle!

"Jon! The rifle! Can you shoot at the tires?"

"Pass it up here," the doctor said tersely.

"It has a hair trigger, so watch it," Alex warned as she passed the rifle between the two front seats.

Jon rolled down the window, stuck the rifle out and took aim at the tires. The Suburban swerved violently but was unscathed. Now it was weaving across the road in front of them. The lake was dead ahead.

"Pray, guys," Jon said as he took aim again.

This time the back rear tire exploded, the suburban spun out, teetered on two wheels, and then righted itself. It limped slowly toward the shore. Charles laid on the speed until they were right behind it. "Jump out, Cox. Your automatic!"

Jon didn't need telling. Wrenching open the door, he ran with his long-legged stride until he was even with the Suburban. He took his first shot. The driver ducked and braked inches from the dock. He hopped out and, using the Suburban for cover, fired back at Jon. He missed. The doctor fired through the windows, but the man dodged the shot and let off one of his own. Alex saw Jon wince, reposition himself, and fire several shots before he fell to the ground.

One of his shots must have wounded the driver, for he dropped his pistol to clutch his chest.

Without thinking, Alex threw open her door and ran around the back of the two vehicles to where the doctor lay. *Who do you find to doctor the doctor?* She examined the big man. He was bleeding from a shot in his side but was conscious.

"See to Briggie and Richard, Alex. I'll be fine," he muttered and then passed out.

"Charles!" she called out. "He's hit! I don't know how bad it is."

He was beside her in a moment. "Grinnell," he yelled. "Leave Kerry to her hysterics, and look for your father and Briggie, man!"

Charles tore away Jon's shirt. "The blood's not spurting," he assured Alex. "But the bullet's in there somewhere. He needs a hospital."

Alex went to where Kerry was sitting in the Lexus sobbing convulsively. Alex slapped her soundly. "Kerry, we need your help! Is there a hospital in Cassville?"

"Y-yes. It's just a small one."

Daniel cried out, "Dad and Briggie are in the back! They're tied up and gagged."

"Well, do something about it, for heaven's sake," Alex called back. "Jon's hurt. We need to get him to the hospital." Leaving Kerry, she ran to the Suburban, heedless of the sharp pain behind her eyes.

Wrenching the keys out of the ignition, she pressed all the little buttons on the automatic opener until the rear of the Suburban popped open, revealing the limp bodies of Briggie and Richard. Her heart stopped. Were they already dead?

"Briggie! Richard!" she cried, crawling inside the car. They were trussed hand and foot. Surely, if they were dead, that wouldn't have been necessary, would it?

216

She felt beneath Briggie's ear for a pulse. *Yes! She was alive.* Daniel had crawled in beside her and was doing the same with his father.

"Dad's okay. How about Briggie?" he asked.

"Alive," Alex said. "They must have been knocked out with drugs or who knows what. They need the hospital, too."

Scrambling out of the car, she dug in her pocket for her cell phone and dialed 911. When the dispatcher replied, she asked her to hold and passed the phone to Kerry, "Tell them where we are and ask for three ambulances," she said. Then, trembling with shock, fear, and pain, she collapsed.

Chapter Twenty-Two

When Alex woke, she seemed to be on a gurney behind a screen of closed drapes. Her head was floating somewhere, unattached to the rest of her. She felt the sense of well-being that comes with strong painkillers. The important thing was that Charles was holding her hand. She brought it to her lips and kissed it, laid it by her cheek, and drifted off to sleep.

Morning sun shone on Alex's face through a foreign window. Where was she? She glimpsed a disheveled Charles sitting in an uncomfortable chair, dead asleep. The events of the night returned to her—Briggie! Richard! Jon! Were they all right? She didn't want to wake Charles, so she got out of bed quietly. He jerked awake.

"Where in Hades do you think you're going, woman? Lie back down this instant."

Alex obeyed meekly. "I just wanted to find out about the others."

"Briggie and Richard seem to have been drugged with an overdose of something. It's been touch and go. They've been given a strong stimulant and a couple of big orderlies are trying to get them

218

to walk around, as we speak. We got there just in time, Alex. That devil was going to jump out just before the car went in the lake! I don't know how we managed to be in the right place."

"Your prayer, Charles," Alex reminded him. "It worked."

He put his head in his hands. "Thank God."

"How is Jon?"

"They got the bullet out. It was lodged in his spleen. They had to remove that, too."

"And I got by with only a headache!" Alex said.

"You're to stay in bed today, the doctor said. You started bleeding internally again."

"Oh, drat! Charles, you must get some rest. Can't you rent one of those little cottages outside Cassville? What's happened to Daniel and Kerry?"

"Daniel's with his father and Briggie, trying to revive them. The FBI agents are there, too, hoping they're going to get a lead. I have no interest in where Kerry has got to. I'm not leaving you for an instant, my love, so you can forget about that. Joe McHenry is much too close and too desperate."

"Has anyone phoned Susan?"

"Jon was able to talk to her after he recovered from surgery. Apparently, it was all he could do to keep her from coming down from her mother's. He doesn't want her in danger, too. Now, let's get you some breakfast, and then we're going to have a little talk. The one you've been avoiding for the past nine months."

"Oh, Charles! Not with Briggie still so touch and go!"

But he picked up the phone to order her breakfast and tell the nurse she was awake.

A cheerful brunette with freckles turned up almost immediately. Her name tag said she was Anna. "I'm so glad you're awake! Charles has been telling me that you've had a rough couple of days. I'd say that was an understatement. We'll get you back on your feet. Here, let me just take your vitals."

Once she had done that, she asked what Alex wanted for breakfast. "Just toast. And do you by any chance have cocoa?"

"You're on my watch, and I'm not going to let you waste away. Oatmeal is good for the soul as well as the body. Toast isn't."

Alex agreed reluctantly.

"Okay, darling," Charles said, as he moved his chair next to her bed. "Begin. I assume your search at Oxford and in France to find your grandfather was part of the family scandal."

"Oh, Charles. Do we have to go into this now? I'm feeling so vulnerable."

"You accused me of not knowing anything about you, Alex. That's a pretty grave accusation. You ended our engagement."

Alex looked down at the waffle-woven blue blanket on her bed. Could she risk it? Charles thought she was strong. Could she tell him the truth?

"Charles, I'm afraid of destroying your image of me. I've tried to be strong, like you think I am. I'm really afraid you'll want nothing to do with me when you find out the truth."

"Alex, you saved me from a life in prison. That wasn't done by a shrinking violet. Just a couple of months ago you confronted and bested a murderer. Then there was last night. We all have our vulnerabilities. It's part of what makes us lovable. Don't you think you can trust my love for you?"

"Frankly, no."

Charles stood and paced. "Look, you said Grinnell knows all your weaknesses and still loves you. Are you going to marry him, then? I thought you loved me."

Taking a deep breath, Alex kept looking down, unable to meet his eyes. She loved him now more than ever. She had no choice but to trust in his feelings for her. "Okay, then. My parents had received threatening letters. It is too much to go into, but they thought a huge scandal was going to break out, accusing my grandfather of murder and stripping them of their fortune. It all surfaced when I was about fourteen, as close as I can figure. They kept it all a secret from me. But that's when my father became a workaholic, never getting home until eight or nine at night. He used to be my best friend. We played tennis together all the time. But all that stopped. He was literally never home. The worst part was that my mother became an abusive alcoholic. I know you can't imagine it, knowing her now. But she was really, really scary, Charles. I was terrified of her."

"Did she physically abuse you?"

"She tried to kill both of us twice—once in the car and once by leaving on the gas on the stove. I had to grow up fast. There was no one I could trust, no one I could turn to. She listened in on all my phone conversations. I could never bring any of my friends home because of her. And if I went anywhere, she came positively unglued. She was so afraid I would tell someone the truth of what she was like that she would scream at me and slap my face. It was a day-to-day survival course." Alex paused. Charles, now by her side, smoothed back her hair from her face with great tenderness.

"Go on, darling, get it all out."

"She overdosed on a pretty regular basis, and I had to get her into the hospital. It was hard to tell when she had just passed out and when she had taken something. I almost lost her a couple of times. Then I began to wish she would die."

"It sounds like a living hell," Charles said.

"Because of all that, I can't stand anger or for people to yell at me. It's hard to explain, but there is still a place inside me that is that abused person. I get panic attacks, Charles. I go catatonic. I can't move or speak. My body tries to play dead so it won't get hurt."

"Even now that your mother is better?"

"Yes. I don't know if they'll ever go away. So now you see that I'm really not brave at all."

"You'll never sell me on that, Alex. I've seen you in action. Just last night, for example. And when I lose my temper, I generally shut down. Last night I was ready to strangle Grinnell. That's the angriest I've ever been, I think. I did yell at him."

"Well, I don't get angry, either, which is actually a problem. I turn inward, and the anger becomes depression. I get very quiet and start having flashbacks. Like when Miss Maddy was killed. Instead of being angry with the killer, I blamed myself and then had that flashback to when Megan was born dead because I hadn't taken care of myself." She breathed deeply and clutched the sheet. "And if anything really bad happens, I always flash back to Stewart's death, when the universe seemed out of control. Generally Briggie brings me out of it, but you see what a mess I am."

Charles's eyes were gentle as he put a hand up to her face and cupped her chin. "Darling, you're amazing to have come through everything you have. You are truly a survivor, which only makes me love you more."

"Charles, it was my fault that my father was killed. I'll have to live with that the rest of my life, and it's a horrible thing. He invited his murderer into our house, because I demanded that he tell me the truth about what made everything change."

"You can't blame yourself because someone wicked murdered your father. That was the murderer's fault, not yours."

"My therapist and Briggie have been telling me that for the past year, but it won't wash. And though she doesn't mention it now, my mother blames me. I just have to live with it. Like I have to live with causing Philippa's death, and Gladys's last winter. And now poor Miss Maddy."

"I don't blame you for Philippa's death, Alex. I know what really happened."

"I'm a living, breathing catalyst," she said somberly. "Everywhere I go, people get murdered."

"Alex, you and I both know that family secrets cause massive harm and dysfunction. They're like rot. Each generation, they get worse. The rot has to be cut out, so the family can become healthy again."

"Can you think of any possible way that the McHenry family can become healthy?"

"I'm convinced there's something that's causing their behavior. Something you'll discover."

"Nevertheless, Miss Maddy's dead, Briggie and Richard came within a hair's breadth of being dead, and poor Dr. Jon has to live without a spleen."

"But look at Holly Weston. Now that all her family secrets have been disclosed, she's working through the trauma. Already she's a happy, normal girl. And your mother! She's a positive delight now."

"I have to admit that with my mother, I still keep waiting for the other shoe to drop."

"That's only natural."

"But I haven't told you the worst. The thing that would make me almost impossible to be married to."

Charles leaned closer and squeezed her hand. "Out with it, and we'll see."

Alex stared straight ahead, noticing for the first time a huge bouquet of sweet peas, her favorite. "Where did you ever find the time to get me flowers?"

"I found a very accommodating florist in town. I rang them up."

"Thank you." Alex looked into his eyes and wondered how in the world she could tell him her worst problem. "Before I go on with this self-flagellation, do you think you could check on Richard, Briggie, and Jon? I'll try to sustain my courage."

"So far, darling, you haven't scared me off."

He left the room. As he left, Anna came in. "Shall we get you a quick shower while he is gone? He's absolutely scrumptious, by the way. We need to get you fixed up, although I don't know what I can do about those black eyes. I'll comb out your hair, too. Then you can have your breakfast."

When Charles returned, Alex was dutifully eating her oatmeal.

"Briggie is definitely better. She's spitting nails and demanding to see Agent Stone, who's on his way. Richard is still a bit foggy but on the mend. Jon is resting. They had to give him a sedative because he kept wanting to get up."

"Briggie should save her strength. They will know something is wrong when their driver doesn't return and they find the Suburban. They'll have switched caves by now."

"Agent Stone is pulling all his people off the drug search for the moment, and they're going through the caves with assault rifles."

Alex shuddered, trying to imagine it.

"Now quit stalling and let me know the worst, darling."

"Well," Alex took a deep breath. "I suppose it all started when my father left me alone with my mother so much. Remember, I was only fourteen, which is a rotten age, anyway, and I had great difficulty coping with a crazy woman. At first I was scared, and then I was angry. Gradually, I just became helpless and hopeless, which Daniel tells me are the hallmarks of depression. All I know is, I felt completely abandoned by anyone who had ever loved me."

She looked at the sweet peas, trying to convince herself of their meaning. How could Charles put up with her neurosis in the long run?

"I can see how you would feel that way," Charles encouraged her. "Go on."

"When I was eighteen, they just bundled me off to Paris to live with the daughter of friends. They sent me a monthly check. That was it." As so often happened when she thought about that period of her life, she could feel the dampness of her one-room flat and smell the garlic from the floors below.

"My roommate was a fly-by-night who was heavily into drugs. Our apartment was on the Left Bank, and most people were experimenting with some drug or another. I don't know why I never did. I think I felt I was on the edge of the world and if I did anything to upset my mental balance, I would fall off and be lost forever."

"Thank goodness you were spared that," Charles said, moving her tray table away, and taking her hand once more.

"Then I met Stewart. As you know, he was a photographer. He wouldn't have anything to do with drugs because he needed to be really clear-headed to do his job. He was determined to be world class."

"And he was, wasn't he?"

"Eventually, but that came later. When I met him, he was still struggling. I started out as his unpaid sidekick. He knew he could depend upon me. I helped with the light meter and all that sort of thing. We took a few trips together—Greece, the Dalmatian Coast, Sicily. I don't know exactly when, but at some point he stopped treating me like an assistant . . ."

"Spare me the details, darling. It's enough to know that you eventually got married."

"Yes, after about a year. In Scotland, where his ancestors were from. Inverary."

"And?"

"Well, I couldn't ever believe he loved me. I had encased myself

225

in these walls, you see. No matter what he said or did, he couldn't convince me. It drove him crazy. It was much easier for me to pretend I was still just his assistant. I think that's why he wanted a child. He thought that would finally break through my walls if I could feel love for another human being."

"Don't tell me. Then the crash came."

"Yes." Alex pleated her stiff white hospital sheet. "The ultimate abandonment. Losing the baby must have been more than I could bear, because I never grieved over it until that day I talked to you on the telephone."

"Are you telling me, Alex, that you can't feel love for me, either?" Charles's voice was gentle but sad.

"No. I'm not telling you that. Everything changed when I was able to forgive my mother last winter. The Savior healed me. It was an incredible experience, Charles. I gave all my fear and resentment to him, and he showed me who my mother really was." She remembered that moment, when she had been riding with her mother in the ambulance, looking at her worn, sad face. "I guess that's what finally enabled me to let down my walls. Before I could blink I was head over heels in love with you."

Reaching over, he kissed her cheek. "I'm so relieved to hear you say that."

"But there's still all this history inside me, Charles. You're so good-looking, you don't know the effect it has on people. There will always be Kerrys. I don't want to go through life being jealous, being afraid I'll lose you."

"Don't you think I've learned over the years to discount my looks?" he asked. "To know when people's feelings for me are real and when they're sincere? I've been very lonely, too, Alex. Except for Philippa, whom I couldn't marry, I knew no woman ever loved me for myself. Until you."

"But I'm terribly afraid of these feelings, Charles. I've never felt this way."

"We'll take it slowly. It's all new to me, as well. I don't want you marrying me until you're sure of me."

"And you don't care that I'm really not Jeanne Moreau?"

"Believe me, now that I know your story, she can't hold a candle to you. She was an actress. You're real."

At that moment, Daniel came through the door, a bouquet of white roses in his hands. "Alex? You're awake!"

"Yes. I just finished my breakfast, as a matter of fact."

Charles stood. "I'll go check on the others." He left the room, and Alex automatically put up her defenses so Daniel couldn't see inside her head.

"How's Kerry?" she asked.

"Having a pretty rough time. She simply can't take it on board that her mother led Briggie and Dad into that trap and almost got them killed."

"I warned her she might find out things she didn't want to know."

"But she's not strong like you, Alex. All her life, everything's always gone her way. This is something neither fame nor fortune can fix."

"Maybe she should go back to Kansas City. There are a lot of questions to answer, and she may not like the answers at all. Someone shot her. Someone killed Miss Maddy. I may be mistaken, but I think before this is over, she's going to need serious therapy, Dr. Grinnell."

"*You* seem remarkably chipper. I don't detect any of the vestiges of the usual mea culpa you go through in your cases."

She put her head to one side and looked him in the eye. "Charles and I have just been talking about it."

Daniel looked down at his shoes. "He doesn't think too much of me, I'm afraid."

"Why do you think that?"

"Here's this gun battle going on, Jon gets hit, Charles goes to him, and what do I do? Do I run to see how Briggie and Dad are? No. I put my arms around Kerry and let her have hysterics on my shoulder."

"You must care about her very much," Alex said.

"That's the thing that's so ridiculous. I don't care. Not at all. I did once. But now, especially compared to you, she's almost intolerable. There you were, in spite of your injury, running around, taking care of everyone."

"That doesn't necessarily mean I'm more worthwhile than Kerry. You have to remember, Daniel, she's dealing with a lot right now. Not only did someone shoot her, but she's just found out she's a McHenry, and her mother led Briggie and Richard into a murderous trap."

"You don't have to tell me that. I'm her therapist, for crying out loud. But you know what really gets my goat?"

"What?"

"The thing she cares about more than any of it is that Charles is obviously in love with you. She can't understand it. It really doesn't compute."

"Maybe it's time you taught Kerry to look beyond appearances."

"What about you, Alex? Can you look beyond appearances? I love you. I always have. But you've never trusted me. You've always held me at a distance. How can you love a GQ model, for heaven's sake? How can you trust someone you know every woman he meets is lusting after?"

As usual, Daniel had put his finger unerringly on the right point.

"It's going to be very difficult, Daniel. I won't lie to you. And I'm not sure I'm up to it. But there's a lot more to Charles than his looks.

I'm sorry that I've hurt you. But you've lied to me, Daniel. You lied to get your own way, to put me off Charles. That's a trick worthy of an adolescent."

He hung his head. "I was desperately afraid you were making a mistake. I still am. You're so fragile sometimes, Alex. I couldn't bear to see you hurt."

She pounded her fists on the bed. "I'm *not* fragile! I've had some tough challenges that have made me justifiably wary, but I'm a survivor, Daniel Grinnell. You don't need to spend your life protecting me. That would drive me crazier than I already am!"

"You *won't* see, will you, Alex? You're a challenge. Once he has you, he'll discard you. Just like he did Kerry."

"Maybe you're describing yourself, Daniel. Have you ever thought of that? I think you're in love with the idea of taking care of me. I think if I were completely mentally healthy, I'd lose all appeal for you. You see yourself as my knight in shining armor, ready to pick up the pieces. Well, I don't need anyone to pick up the pieces, Dr. Grinnell. The Lord and I are managing just fine."

He gazed at her with a shocked look on his face, still clutching his bouquet of roses. She could tell her words hit home.

She asked more gently, "Who broke up the affair between you and Kerry?"

"I did, as a matter of fact."

"Why?"

"I'd had enough psychology by then to see that she was a spoiled, narcissistic drama queen."

"Well, she's had a few nasty shocks," Alex said. "And I predict more in the near future. They may knock her off the pedestal she's placed herself on."

"I'm not interested in Kerry. Narcissists don't change. Not at her time of life. Her troubles will make her more of a drama queen than ever. She'll work them into her act."

Alex didn't know what else to say.

"You never met Caroline, Marigny's mother. I married her because she convinced me that she needed me desperately. What she needed was unadulterated worship. When I couldn't give it to her anymore, she left me for someone who could. My worst nightmare is that Marigny might grow up to be just like her."

"Get Briggie to take her in hand," Alex advised. "I promise she would never let that happen. She's really good with kids after raising nine of them. Did you know that one of them is a millionaire who chooses to live in Brazil and teach entrepreneurship at some university there?"

"Yeah, Briggie would never let anyone take himself too seriously."

"No. That's why she is such a help to me. More help than any therapist ever was, I'm sorry to tell you. One of our Church leaders once said that the study of the gospel will change behavior faster than a study of behavior will change behavior."

Daniel looked doubtful. "Briggie says Charles is going to be baptized."

"That's what he tells us."

"I suppose it's occurred to you that it's all on your account?"

"Yes, it has. But I don't believe that any longer."

Daniel looked at her ringless finger but apparently thought better of asking any more questions. "Well, I guess I'd better go check on Dad."

Charles came in a few moments later. "Did he manage it?"

"What?"

"To turn you against me?"

"He voiced all my fears, but I just told him I was working on them."

"Your mentor is frothing at the mouth to tell you all she knows. May I let her in?"

"Briggie? Oh, yes! As soon as possible!"

Chapter Twenty-Three

Alex, honey, I'm afraid I've been a foolish old woman. I understand it's you I have to thank for getting the rescue operation underway."

"You were almost fish food, Briggs," Alex said severely. "Don't you ever do anything like that again. I couldn't bear it if anything happened to you."

Her friend and mentor embraced her with unusual gentleness. "Well, at least we found McHenry headquarters, Alex. All these people were living in a gigantic cave. One of those caves you see on the Discovery channel, with tons of corridors and stalactites and stalagmites and the whole bit. They had it set up like a house. When Agent Stone gets here, I'm going to show him exactly where it is."

"The McHenrys'll be gone, Briggie. There are other caves, you know. But Charles tells me that Stone's agents are examining all the caves they can find, and they're carrying automatic weapons."

"You know what absolutely blew me away? Guess who everyone takes their orders from. Guess who's head of that drug operation!"

"I assumed it was Joe McHenry . . ."

"No! It's Sylvia!"

"Sylvia? Good grief, I never thought she'd have the brains!"

"All that's an act. She's the real boss—hard as flint. Everyone takes orders from her. She's the one who decided we had to disappear into the lake."

"Was Joe there?"

Briggie's little brown eyes glistened. "You bet. And I gave him an earful about what he did to you. He wanted to know how you escaped, but I just told him you should never underestimate a genealogist. Just think what he must think now!"

At that moment, Agent Stone entered her room, followed by Agent Donovan, who now wore a raspberry suit with a black blouse. "Are you ready to take us to this stronghold, Mrs. Poulson? Are you certain you feel up to it?" asked Stone.

"Never better!" Briggie assured him.

"That was some good work last night, Alex," Donovan told her.

Nurse Anna interrupted their conference. She looked Stone up and down and evidently decided she liked what she saw. "So you're what an FBI agent looks like!"

Stone actually winked at her. "Have you come to chase us away?"

"Yes. Alex has had entirely too much company and not enough time to rest. Besides, I need to change her ice pack."

Alex wished them well on their expedition, sorry that she couldn't accompany them. Briggie should be dead tired after the night she had spent, but as usual, her friend was on the chase and wasn't going to let anything stop her.

But Sylvia! Alex marveled at this new information. How had she gotten involved in running a drug operation of all things? The woman was in her sixties! Then her thoughts went to Kerry. What a terrible thing for her to have to cope with. When they caught Sylvia, she would undoubtedly be imprisoned for the rest of her life.

Then it struck her. Sylvia was not a McHenry by birth. Had she gotten the "taint" somehow from her first husband? *What was it that made the McHenrys so wild?* Something was teasing her mind. She had an idea that she possessed a clue. Maybe if she had the genogram, she could figure it out. But it was back at Jon's.

On that thought, she fell asleep for a couple of hours. She awoke when Nurse Anna came in to take her vital signs. Charles was reading the paper.

"How are Richard and Jon?" she asked.

"They're both awake," Charles replied, kissing her lightly. "Oh darling, how I wish I had a camera. I could blackmail you forever."

"No chance. I'm not the least bit vain. Too many years of living with Briggie."

"How do you feel?"

"A little tired but frustrated. I know I have some kind of clue about this McHenry taint, if only I could remember."

"Would it help if we went over the case?" Charles asked.

Nurse Anna interrupted. "One thing I can tell you. I've gathered from Mrs. Poulson that those McHenrys were holed up in a cave. We were raised never to go near them. They're full of lead. Lead poisoning has terrible side effects."

"Lead! Oh, glory! as Briggie would say. That's it!" She turned to Anna. "Could I just go for a short visit to see Dr. Cox? I'll go in a wheelchair, if you like, and Charles will hold the ice pack on my head. Won't you, Charles?"

Nurse Anna stood with both hands on her hips. "Is this likely to score me points with the big guy?"

"What big guy?"

"That FBI agent with the gorgeous chest and arms."

Alex laughed. "Yes, it will definitely score you points!"

Jon was reading the paper with obvious boredom. He looked up as Charles wheeled Alex in.

"Good afternoon," Alex said. "Or is it still morning?"

Jon looked at his watch. "It's 11:30. They'll be bringing something repulsive for dinner soon."

"Well, at least it won't contain lead," Alex said.

"What are you talking about? Lead?"

"Nurse Anna just told me those caves where the McHenrys were hiding out are full of lead! I remember a documentary I saw once about lead poisoning. Doesn't it do something to your brain?"

Jon laid the paper on his lap and looked at her. She could almost see the wheels turning in his head.

"I should have thought of that! There are lead deposits all over this plateau. And one of the side effects of lead poisoning is criminal activity, even murder. They've done all kinds of studies on lead paint victims. Oh, my great-aunt Fanny, Alex! You've hit on it! I'll bet the little McHenry boys have had a hideout in the caves for generations. As close as those caves are to the river, they probably have streams inside them that are part of the underground water around there. I'll bet they all drank enough lead to turn them into serial killers. I need to order a blood sample from that fellow I shot last night."

"Is there any cure?" Alex asked.

"As I recall, there is a therapy involving chelation. And the British developed something."

"How can we find out for sure there's lead there?"

"I'll put a call into the Missouri Department of Natural Resources. They'll send out an assay team."

Charles said, "So much for the curse down to the fourth generation. It looks like we've the means to end it."

"Oh, it would be wonderful if all those people could get help! Especially the children!" Alex said.

"It will certainly be a mitigating circumstance in the McHenrys' trials, I would think," Charles said.

"Miracles never cease," Jon said. "You don't know how long I've been praying about how in the world I could make a difference in this county."

"I wish I had Agent Donovan's number. She'll be real interested to hear this."

Charles handed her a card. "I haven't changed clothes since yesterday. It was in my shirt pocket." He wheeled Alex over to the hospital telephone next to Jon's bed.

When the agent answered, she sounded curt and impatient.

"I'm sorry to disturb you, Agent Donovan, but this is Alex Campbell. I have some important input for your profiles of these McHenrys."

"What is it?"

"We think that that cave where they were hiding contains lead. Dr. Cox is going to call the DNR and also get a blood sample from the man who was trying to kill Briggie and Richard. Dr. Cox says lead poisoning contributes to severe criminal behavior."

"Yes, yes, of course!" the agent said. "I've heard it blamed for the fall of the Roman Empire, even. Well, by gum, if this doesn't change everything."

"I know they're all dangerous, hardened criminals," Alex said, "but there is a cure, Dr. Cox says. We're especially anxious about the children."

"When we get the perps, we'll arrange to take everyone away in vans to the state mental health facility where they can be on lock-down."

"Except Sylvia McNee," Alex told her. "Briggie told me she is the

236

head of the whole drug operation. She spent her pampered child-hood in Mount Vernon, not scrambling around in caves."

"Mrs. Poulson can give us a deposition. A simple blood test should let us know about Sylvia. Now, I've got to get back to the boss and tell him. Thanks for the information, Alex."

Alex looked triumphantly up at Charles, who kissed her. "I'm not going to relax until they've picked up Joe and his mother," he told her. "Now, back to bed."

That afternoon, when word came from Agent Stone that the band of outlaws had been cornered in another cave, along with their wives and children, he added, "Unfortunately, Sylvia McNee and her two children were nowhere to be found."

Alex said to Charles, "You need some fresh air and a change of scene. There's no reason why we should both be cooped up. I'll be safe enough in the hospital. Why don't you go back to Jon's for a shower and a change of clothes?"

Charles agreed reluctantly. Briggie, who had returned and was nodding in the uncomfortable hospital chair, promised to keep an eye on Alex.

"You know," Briggie said after Charles had left, "I sure wish Miss Maddy could have lived to see this day. What do you think she would have done?"

"She said she was a steward for the Lord. I think she would have decided it was time to share the contents of Elder Call's pamphlet."

"Well, we can sure do that for her," Alex said. "Perhaps her funeral would be a good time. I'll talk to Jon about it. Now, Briggie, we've got to concentrate. We're not finished."

"No," her friend agreed. "There's still Miss Maddy's murder, Kerry's shooting, and Mike Wentworth . . . Good grief, poor Marigny will be trying to get through to us on your cell phone, and it's at Jon's."

Nurse Anna told them they could purchase long distance calling cards from the front desk. While Briggie went to do this, Alex laid back with her eyes closed. She hated to admit it, but she was really bushwhacked. Her head was splitting and spinning with all the developments . . . Sylvia the leader of the McHenry dope gang, lead poisoning the answer to the mystery of the wild McHenrys. Just on the edge of sleep, her mind grasped one more thought, *who killed Bo?*

Alex woke to feel a shot puncturing her arm. Startled, she looked up, straight into the surgical-masked face of Joe McHenry. Then she was out.

She was in the Highlands with Stewart. He was dressed in full Scottish kit from the lace at his throat to the dagger thrust into his knee-high hose. It was the summer solstice, and he was throwing the javelin in the summer games. But something was wrong. His face was badly marred. One eye was in the middle of his forehead, and the other on the side of his face. The teeth in his mouth were all on top of one another. He wanted to kiss her, but she shrank and ran. She ran so fast it was as though she were sailing. Then suddenly, she was in a blender, whirling round and round. First her feet were cut off and then her legs. She started to scream, and the sound was so loud in her ears, she screamed louder.

She was very tiny. But the sound had stopped. Like a fairy presence she was drifting over the Chicago lakeshore until she found herself in her house. Her mother was scuttling from room to room, looking for where she had hidden her liquor. Alex was trying to hide behind the couch, but she kept popping up. Her mother turned to her and began screaming, her face distorted like a witch's mask, all her hair standing on end. She kept reaching for Alex, trying to capture her, but Alex flew away, this time to Paris.

She was at the Opera in a box overlooking the stage. Charles, in tights, was singing the part of Don Giovanni, seducing an innocent

Kerry, who was simpering across the stage towards her boudoir . . .
Then Alex was at Megan's snow-covered grave. She was bleeding red
all over the snow. Stewart's dog, Providence, took her for a ride on
his back, over the icy heather, up and up and up until they reached
the moon . . .

Someone was holding her close, the room was spinning, she was
struggling, but whoever it was, held her tight. A pinch on her arm,
and then everything slowed down. Until it stopped.

Chapter Twenty-Four

Alex was being dragged across the room. "Walk! Walk! Walk, Alex! Wake up, Alex!" Charles was commanding. "I love you, Alex, wake up! Think of our children! I insist that we have a daughter called Zina and another called Alana! Walk, Alex! Walk! We must have a son called Jonathan as well! What do you think of the name Brighamina?"

Alex was wretchedly sick on the floor. Charles dragged her somewhere else. It hurt to be dragged by her armpits. She took a tentative step and then another. Then she collapsed, and Charles held her up again. "Alex, you're to live! Do you understand me? I positively cannot go on living in this crazy world without you! I want to be sealed to you. Walk, Alex, walk!"

Why was he goading her? All she wanted was to sleep. She was so tired and lethargic.

"Walk, Alex, walk!"

Someone else took her right arm and slid a shoulder into her armpit. "Alex! You didn't let me die!" Briggie shouted. "I'm not going

240

to let you die! We have to finish this case! Do you hear me, Alex! You are not to die! Don't go back to sleep! It's fatal! You've been given an overdose of morphine! You've got to fight! They gave you some drug starting with an L. But you have to fight, too. They gave you as much of the antidote as they safely could!"

Then she heard Nurse Anna, "You can make it, Alex! We're all pulling for you."

Richard chimed in, "Alex Campbell, I've never known you to be such a wimp! For heaven's sake, wake up! You've got to help Brighamina and me solve this case. You know we always make a mess of things if we're left on our own."

Perhaps that last plea finally did it. She started placing one foot in front of the other. Opening her eyes, she felt the light pierce them and shut them quickly. Her head was pounding. "If you seduce Kerry, I'll kill you," she murmured to Charles.

"Not much chance of that. I'm a little busy right now," Charles told her.

It was a long time before she could walk with weight on her feet. Then Nurse Anna gave her another shot. "Caffeine," she said.

Alex's head finally began to clear. "Charles," she murmured. "I don't think I'm going to die now."

The sun had set. Agents Donovan and Stone were in her hospital room when they finally allowed her to sit in a chair. She felt her head droop, and Briggie pulled it back up unceremoniously by her hair.

"Who was it, Alex?" Donovan probed sternly.

"Joe," she said with a sigh. "Joe McHenry."

"It must have been pure revenge," the agent said. "He hates you like poison."

"We've got a watch on the airports," Stone said. "They must have enough money to leave the country and set up in the Carribean or somewhere like that. Sylvia's passport's gone."

When the agents left, Alex started shaking all over. She felt cold and sick. As though reading her mind, Charles wrapped her in a blanket, picked her up and settled in the chair with her in his lap, holding her close. "My sweet love," he whispered in her ear. "I almost lost you that time, but you're going to be fine. I'll take care of you. Always."

"Mmmm," she said. She was feeling more awake all the time, but she didn't want Charles to stop holding her. It had been years since anyone had held her, and even then something inside her had been stiff and unyielding. Now, it was as though she were melting, and she could feel his love seep into her like the spring rains revitalizing the winter landscape. Her heart warmed, and she cuddled her head under his chin. "I love you, Charles. Was it you who rescued me?"

"Yes," he said, squeezing her to him. "When I came back, you were so deeply asleep and so pale, I was worried you'd overdone it. Then you screamed. But you were still asleep. I called Nurse Anna. She was just going off her shift, but she took your pulse. It was hardly there. Then she noticed you were scarcely breathing. She called in the doctor, who examined you and said you were nearly comatose. He was at a loss to account for it."

He squeezed her again and kissed her hair. "The Spirit must have been with me, Alex. I noticed the puncture on your arm. I raised Cain at that point and started interrogating the staff, thinking one of them had done it. Meanwhile, Nurse Anna thought to check the drug supply. Enough morphine was missing to put you under for good."

Alex looked into his face. It was haunted and gray. The only time she had ever seen him look like that was when Philippa had died. "Fortunately, they had Levallorphan in stock. The antidote. He didn't know if it would work, you were so far gone. But Briggie and I weren't about to let you go. Do you realize what the odds are that a little hospital like this would have the antidote for morphine overdose?"

"They see a lot of drug addicts," Alex said.

After a while, Alex was able to eat some of her dinner. Charles had another bed brought into the little room. He lay down on it, and they held hands across the space between the beds. "That was too close, Alex."

"Yes," she agreed. She fell asleep with no dreams to taunt her.

*   *   *

The following morning, Briggie came calling with the results of her talk with Marigny.

"There was a Jeanne McHenry, who died of breast cancer when Michael Wentworth was two. Her occupation was listed as housekeeper. I'll bet you anything she was the Wentworth's housekeeper, and they adopted him when she died," Briggie told her.

"I wonder if Mike even knows he's adopted," Alex said. Aside from what felt like a giant hangover, she was feeling more herself. Charles had left her in Briggie's care to go the cottage he had checked into the day before. There he could shave and dress.

"There's not really an easy way to find out," Briggie said. "But he did come down here to live, and he does spend a lot of time at the mayor's house."

"I think he's the mayor's protégé. It might be better if we brought it up with him," Alex mused.

"Or with Kerry," Briggie said. "She's coming down this morning with Daniel to see how you are. They spoke to Nurse Anna to see if you could have visitors."

Alex agreed that that would be the best approach. Then she said, "If they don't catch Sylvia and her kids before they leave the country, we may never know who killed Miss Maddy."

"You think it was Sylvia?"

"Miss Maddy may have known about the whole drug op and that

243

Sylvia was the head of it. That's a pretty strong motive for murder," Alex said. "But it could have been Mike. He certainly wouldn't want it to get out that he was an illegitimate member of the McHenry clan when he was running for the state senate."

"I think I can see Sylvia calling Joe and getting him to do the dirty work."

"That may have been true of the fire," Alex said. "But what about the actual murder—the one that came off? Miss Maddy would never have called Joe McHenry to come and pick her up at Jon's," Alex objected.

"You're right," Briggie said with a sigh. "It's just that Mike is always so peppy and full of enthusiasm for life. I hate to think his ambition would drive him to murder an old woman by hitting her over the head with a rock."

They were still musing on this difficult point when Daniel and Kerry came in. Kerry surprised Alex with an enormous bouquet of white gladioli and a kiss on the cheek. "I'm so sorry you almost died, Alex. It's all my fault. If I hadn't gotten you involved with my rotten family, this never would have happened."

Alex managed a smile. "Didn't anyone tell you about the lead poisoning? It really isn't completely your brother's fault that he is the way he is."

"Yes. Daniel told me, but that still doesn't excuse my mother. You know, it's weird, but I've always been a little afraid of her. She treated me like her dress-up doll, like a toy. And she was extremely manipulative. I was always a daddy's girl."

Daniel moved to Alex's bedside and, without thinking, moved a curl off Alex's face behind her ear. The move was a tender one, and as though realizing it, he quickly drew back his hand. "This time your mate wasn't a lot of help, Alex."

She smiled at him. "No. It wasn't, was it?"

"I'm so relieved you're okay."

"Me, too. Those hallucinations were the closest I hope to get to hell."

"Are we going to find out who murdered my great-grandfather?" Kerry asked.

"That secret may have died with Miss Maddy," Briggie said. "Have you told your father that he's a McHenry?"

"I wouldn't dare! I think it would give him a stroke on the spot. And he's not the type that would find a little thing like lead poisoning any kind of excuse."

"Uh, Kerry, I have something a little delicate to discuss with you," Alex said.

The singer's eyebrows went up. "More problems with my family?" Her tone was incredulous. "What could be worse than having a mother run a drug operation and attempt two murders, not to mention a half brother who *is* a murderer?"

"How about another half brother? A nice one, this time?"

"Who on earth . . ."

"Have you ever noticed Mike's little finger?"

"Yeah, as a matter of fact. Just the other day. Are you telling me he's another McHenry?"

"Just in the same sense that you are. Remember your father's account of his adolescent indiscretion?"

"The one with the girl from Aurora?"

"We believe it was actually with a woman called Jeanne McHenry, who moved to Kansas City. She died of breast cancer. Mike was adopted by the Wentworths in Kansas City. We believe he was Jeanne McHenry's son by your father."

Stunned, Kerry tried to put the pieces together. "My father has no idea, I'm positive. He's always wanted a son. That's why I've tried so hard to be a success, so I could make it up to him."

"Hmm," said Briggie. "Do you think he'll be happy to find out?"

"Ecstatic!" Kerry said. "And I won't feel like I have to stay here and take care of him. He is so full of shame right now because of my mother that he doesn't feel like he can ever go out of his home again. And I feel like I've brought some deadly disease on my house."

"Do you think Mike knows the truth?" Briggie asked.

The singer considered this. "You know, he just might. He sort of turned up out of the blue one day, Daddy says. Mike said this was such a beautiful part of the state that he had decided to set up a law practice here, and he wanted to introduce himself to my father, the mayor. He's always treated me exactly like a brother, never the least bit of romantic interest."

Alex hid a smile. How that must have galled Kerry!

The hospital phone rang. Answering, Alex hoped it was the FBI. It was.

"Well," Agent Stone reported, "they were smarter than we gave them credit for. It seems they split up. Our agents have detained Joe and Cynthia in Kansas City, but Sylvia has slipped through our net. We're widening it now to include all international airports. But at least your would-be murderer is cuffed and behind bars."

"Thanks for calling, Agent Stone," Alex said. "That's a tremendous relief. And good luck finding Sylvia."

Alex reported to the group assembled in her room. Then she ked Briggie, "Do you want to call Jon and tell him he can bring his 'ren and wife home?"

'od idea."

't moment, Charles walked in, freshly shaved and wearing turtleneck that made his eyes like lapis lazuli. Everything 'n Alex's mind. He came straight over to her and kissed 'n an unusually demonstrative fashion. His British dissolving.

Then Nurse Anna entered and shooed everyone but Charles out of the room. Examining Alex's head, she commented, "Well the sheriff was arrested this morning. Seems all those McHenrys are squealing on one another, except there's someone no one seems to know."

"How did you find that out?"

"I've got me a reporter friend. The big guy just gave a press briefing in front of the courthouse."

"And what did Agent Stone say about this mysterious person?"

"He invited the public to tell what they know. He said they'd be given federal protection."

Alex turned to Charles. "Do you suppose he was talking about Sylvia?"

He shook his head. "After her performance with Briggie and Richard, I think everyone in that blighted family must know about her involvement."

"Well, honey, I'm going to miss you," the nurse said, "but the doctor says you can go. You're just to take it easy. Don't leap right back into that crazy life of yours with both feet."

"I'll see that she behaves," Charles said.

"Thanks for your wonderful care, Anna, and good luck with the big guy."

The nurse blushed. "I've got me a date for Saturday night, if the case is wrapped up by then."

Even with Charles holding on to her by the elbow, Alex felt as weak as a kitten on the way to the car. Thinking of kittens reminded her of her promise to Zina. "Oh, good grief! Zina's cat must be starving. I completely forgot I'd said I'd feed her!"

"You've been a bit preoccupied, darling. Jon and I have managed just fine."

"Thank you." She leaned her head back on the headrest. "Oh, Charles, all I want to do is tie up all the loose ends and get back to

Kansas City." She thought for a moment. "Oh, criminy! My car is still stuck in the mud somewhere in the woods."

"All in good time, my dear. We'll get everything taken care of. Now, how about coming to Chicago for my baptism?"

Alex had a sudden idea. "Wouldn't it be wonderful if you could be baptized here in Jon's pond? He could do it, and all the children could be present, plus Briggie and Richard and Daniel."

"Why do you want Daniel there?"

"It's hard to explain, Charles, but he's just part of my family. Like Briggie and Richard. I'm annoyed at him right now, and I certainly don't want to marry him, but he'll always be part of my life. He helped me sort it out. You see, he was with me when my father was murdered."

"I guess I can understand that. But all I've got to say on the subject is that the looks he gives you aren't brotherly."

"Do you mind if we stop in at Mike's office? Briggie says it's above that department store downtown. I want to feel him out about this McHenry thing."

"I know better than to argue. But if he's a murderer, it might be dangerous, and we don't have Briggie's deer rifle."

"What's happened to it, anyway?"

"Its rightful owner has reclaimed it. If there's a drug lord loose somewhere, we may need it yet."

"What did you think about that?"

"To tell you the truth, darling, Nurse Anna got her facts garbled. I think Agent Stone was referring to Sylvia still being at large."

"Probably. Well, here we are." They pulled up in front of a not-so-prosperous-looking department store with mannequins from the fifties in the window, their wigs dressed in pageboy hairstyles.

The stairs to Mike's office above were linoleum, and the stairwell musty. They found the lawyer chatting amiably with his secretary as he sat on the edge of her desk.

"Alex! Charles! What in the world are you doing out of the hospital, Alex? You're pale as a sheet. Weren't you shocked about Sylvia? I'm still trying to get my mind around it. The mayor's very upset. He's afraid to show his face."

"Yes," Alex agreed. "It was a shock. There are still a few loose ends we need to tie up. Could we have a word in your office?"

"I can't imagine what you would want with me, but since you've obviously made the effort, follow me."

Mike's office was paneled in phony walnut, his chairs were Naugahyde, and the drapes on his windows resembled burlap. But he had a state-of-the-art computer on his desk.

"What can I do for you?" he asked.

"Well," Alex began, "it's a little delicate." She took a fleeting glance at Charles, who nodded for her to proceed. "As part of our investigation, we looked into your parentage. Because of your little finger."

"My little finger?"

"Did you know that's a McHenry trait?"

Mike stared at his finger as though it had betrayed him.

"But Kerry has a crooked finger, and she's not a McHenry."

"You do know you were adopted," Alex continued carefully.

"Yes. My parents told me when I left for college. My birth mother was their housekeeper, and she died of cancer. The adoption was actually arranged before she died."

"Wasn't her name Jeanne McHenry?"

Mike blushed. "Yes. How did you find out?"

"I'm a genealogist. Now, tell me, does your birth father know who you are?"

"My birth father being . . ."

"Mayor McNee."

Agitated, Mike stood and started pacing the small office. "I don't know how you found out when it was so hard for me, but no, he positively does not know who I am. He sent my mother away pregnant and gave her money. She was from the bad side of town. He never had any intention of marrying her." The bitterness in Mike's voice was shocking to Alex.

"I thought you liked the man. Why did you come down here to practice if you didn't want to be near him?"

"I wanted to unmask him. To show what a hypocrite he is. I was actually glad about Sylvia. Though how you figured it out when you've only been in town a couple of days is more than I can fathom. I've been trying for the past year to come up with some irregularity in their lives. Now I just want to get elected so I can get out of here and up to Jeff City. I loathe Trotter's Bridge."

"So I guess you didn't kill Miss Maddy to keep her from broadcasting the fact that you were a McHenry?"

He stopped dead and he looked at her in shock. "Miss Maddy? That old woman in the woods? I didn't even know her. And I'm absolutely sure she didn't know about me."

"There's your little finger, Mike," Alex said. "She would have seen it as a sign of bad blood, like Kerry's."

Mike scratched his head, trying to figure things out. "If my crooked finger comes from my mother, where does Kerry's come from?"

"You can have your revenge, Mike," Alex said somberly. "I doubt if he even knows it, but Cameron McNee Jr. is actually a McHenry himself."

"What?"

"His grandmother was secretly married to Bo McHenry, who was murdered before Cameron Sr. was born. She married Reverend McNee, and Cameron took his name."

Mike grinned a large grin that was just short of outright glee. "Hallelujah! God's in his heaven, and all's right with the world. Let's go tell the old geezer! Right now! I can't wait to see his face."

Chapter Twenty-Five

Maybe it was because Alex had almost died, but the scenery driving out to the McNee home seemed particularly breathtaking. The oaks had begun to leaf out, and a mist of spring yellow-green blanketed the forest. It was hard to believe it had sheltered so much evil for so many years and that now the evil was gone. Wild purple iris grew in the ditches beside the road, and there were still a few late daffodils.

The trees arched like a canopy over the long driveway to the McNee home. Alex was glad to see Daniel's BMW parked in front of the imposing brick, white-columned home. No telling how Cameron McNee would react to their news.

The mayor greeted them at the door, and the odor of liquor surrounded him like a fog. He had his familiar unlit pipe in his hand. "Alex? Charles? Mike? Have they found Sylvia, then?"

"No," Mike said, "but we have a few little details Alex and Charles have uncovered that might be interesting to you. Family things."

The mayor looked somewhat startled but invited them in. Kerry and Daniel were watching *Out of Africa* on the big screen TV; however, Daniel turned it off with the remote when he recognized the visitors.

"Alex, are you feeling okay? It's good to see you up and moving."

"Have they found Mother yet?" Kerry asked.

"No," Charles replied. "They've got a watch on all the international airports."

"So, you just came to visit?" Daniel asked. "Alex should be resting."

Alex felt Charles tense at this solicitous comment. Then Mike stepped forward and held his hand out to the mayor. "I'd like to introduce myself. I'm the son you threw away."

"Son?" the man was clearly uncomprehending. "Threw away? I don't understand . . ."

"No, you don't even remember my mother, do you? Jeanne McHenry. You paid her a couple thousand dollars and told her to get out of town. You thought she was a piece of trash you could dispose of."

The mayor staggered visibly. "You're . . . my . . . son? I've always wanted a son! Kerry! This is your brother! Soon to become a state senator! My very own boy! Tell me about your mother. Is she still alive? Did she marry a Wentworth?"

"My mother died a miserable death from breast cancer when I was two. I don't remember her. She was housekeeper for a couple called Wentworth. They are not only wealthy but kind and generous. They adopted me. They sent me to Princeton."

"My son! A Princeton grad! That just goes to show you can't keep a McNee down!"

"A McHenry, sir," Mike said sharply.

"Well, your mother was a McHenry, but you're a McNee!"

"You'd better sit down, sir," Mike said in an ominous voice. "I'm afraid I've got some bad news for you."

The man moved away from Mike and sat down on his recliner, dazed.

"Kerry's and my great-grandfather Bo McHenry was secretly married to Sarah Delacroix, our great-grandmother. Your father, Cameron Sr., was their son, not the Reverend McNee's."

As the mayor listened to this, his face grew purple, morphing into a mask of rage. "Where did you ever get that idea? Was it these crazy genealogists?"

"The record of their marriage is in the Carroll County, Arkansas, courthouse," Alex said quietly. "Kerry and Mike both have the McHenry birth defect. A crooked little finger."

Cameron McNee roared and drew a pistol from the side pocket of his recliner. Aiming it at Alex, he fired and missed, shattering the glass of his wife's china cabinet. Mike stepped in front of her. "Are you going to kill your only son?" he asked, his voice like silk.

Alex said, "You killed Miss Maddy, didn't you? She told you a long time ago that you were a McHenry, that you had bad blood. You didn't want us talking to her. When Sylvia called you, you went out and set fire to her place."

"That was Joe . . ."

"But it was you Miss Maddy called for a ride out to her place when she was staying at Jon's, wasn't it? You liked to keep her sweet, I imagine, so she wouldn't let your secret out," Alex continued. "You probably pretended to be a friend to the poor woman, didn't you?"

Charles was holding her tightly around the waist. Mike stood in front of them like a basketball guard, holding his arms out to each side. The mayor was growing steadily more rabid.

"One thing I don't understand," Alex said, adrenaline keeping her strong and upright. "Who tried to kill Kerry?"

"That was Cynthia, Sylvia's brat. She hates Kerry like poison. She couldn't stand that she was famous and wealthy and beautiful and her mother's favorite." He still held the gun, though it wavered in his hand. He was clearly very drunk. Suddenly, he took aim at Charles's head, which was not protected by Mike's shorter stature.

Mike said tersely, "Don't you dare."

Cameron McNee shot. Charles threw himself and Alex on the ground. Daniel pulled out his cell phone and dialed. The mayor turned the gun on him. "Put that down, or I'll shoot you through the head."

Frantic to distract the man, Alex asked from the ground, "What did Miss Maddy tell you about Bo McHenry? Did she know who murdered him?"

Cameron laughed the laugh of the very drunk. "The sainted Pierre Delacroix strangled Bo with his own hands. And no one but Pierre's wife ever knew. Unfortunately for him, she was a Keeper, so she passed the information down. But Joe took care of it. Now no one knows . . ."

"Except all of us," said Kerry. "Are you going to shoot your children?"

"I've got plans. You've just accelerated them a little bit."

Alex slapped the floor as a new idea struck her. "You're the real head of the drug scheme in this county, aren't you? Sylvia ran the day-to-day stuff with Joe, but I'll bet you were the one who got it out of the county into the mainstream. You were very careful no one ever knew."

The mayor let off another shot, this one into the ceiling. "You all are going into the tornado shelter. Right now. And I'm going to join my dear wife." He stood, brandishing his gun. "Up!"

Alex and Charles stood. Kerry and Daniel looked at one another and got off the couch.

"Now! Back to the kitchen door!"

Alex signaled to Charles that she wanted to be last in line. She was depending on the fact that because he was drunk, Kerry's father's reflexes would be slow.

As they walked down the hall to the kitchen, the mayor following, Alex prayed with all her might. She hated small, dark places and had ever since her mother had locked her in the closet. And in a cellar it was doubtful that Daniel's cell phone would work. It was up to her.

They walked through the kitchen door into the garden. It was awash with purple, white, yellow, rust, and blue iris. The sun was bright and hurt her eyes. Would she be able to do it? Could she bring it off in her weakened state?

The mayor shot the padlock off the tornado cellar doors. He motioned Mike to open them. Creaking, the open doors exposed a black hole in the ground. *She would rather be shot than go down there.* Then Alex heard something scrambling inside. Rats!

Instinctively, she screamed and screamed. Their captor whirled to face her and her sanity returned. She would *not* be imprisoned with rats! Adrenaline infused her weakened body and primitive survival hormones rushed through her. In a flash she administered a powerful roundhouse kick into the mayor's solar plexus. Losing his balance, he fell straight into the cellar as his gun flew sideways. Still empowered, Alex shut the doors and stood on top of them, trapping Cameron McNee with her weight. "Someone call the FBI," she said.

Chapter Twenty-Six

Miss Maddy's funeral was held in the city park beneath a canopy of blooming magnolias. It was in the early evening, so that most of the town could attend. The drug bust and subsequent arrest of the McHenry clan, not to mention the arrest of the town's mayor on charges of murder, was enough to bring out even the most timid of Trotter's Bridge souls to meet Alex, Briggie, and Charles. There was an ad hoc receiving line by Miss Maddy's casket as people pressed forward to greet them and thank them.

"We never did think this town would be safe again."

"Thanks for getting rid of that drunken bum of a mayor."

"To think this county had a meth lab!"

Jon finally signaled for everyone to be seated on the folding chairs they'd transported from the VFW hall. He stood behind the makeshift pulpit he'd brought from the opera hall.

"I'd like to begin these services with a hymn, 'Amazing Grace.' As we sing, think carefully of the words. It was written by a man who had a great sin on his conscience but who repented and changed his ways."

The words calmed the crowd. Without accompaniment they sang the much-loved hymn. Alex sat next to Charles with Zina on her lap. On Charles's other side, Abee was tucked under his arm.

After the hymn, Matthew, Jon's twelve-year-old son gave a solemn invocation. Then Jon took the pulpit, his voice mellow, rich, and soothing.

"A lot of you are probably wondering what your doctor is doing conducting these services for Miss Maddy. The fact is, I am the leader of the local branch of The Church of Jesus Christ of Latter-day Saints. Now, you probably know that although Miss Maddy was a devout Christian, she didn't go to any particular church.

"There was a reason for that. Long ago, her great-great-aunt was converted to our church by a missionary, Elder Call. His companion, Elder Samuels, was lynched by Jake McHenry on a tree in the cemetery. Elder Call left, promising Claire Prestcott, whom he had baptized and fallen in love with, that he would return for her when it was safe. He went west to Colorado and worked in the gold mines, where he was killed in a cave-in the next year. But Claire, the first Keeper, cherished the only things of his she had left: a booklet of her beliefs, missing its cover, and a white handkerchief.

"Miss Maddy kept these things, and although she never knew what church Claire belonged to, she believed it would return when the curse against the McHenrys had gone down four generations. She felt herself to be a steward for the Lord, guarding her beliefs until that time had come.

"Now I don't know if it's just coincidence, but these good people," Jon indicated Briggie and Alex, "came down here to do a bit of family history research. In the course of that business, they discovered something very important. I want you to listen to this carefully and to remember the hymn we just sang. *The McHenrys did not have a curse on them. They were not born evil.* They were suffering from acute lead poisoning contracted in the cave where they all played as children. The Department of Natural Resources is in the process of imploding that cave, so no one else will unwittingly be poisoned. Some of the side effects of lead poisoning are criminal behavior and loss of IQ. The McHenrys accused of criminal acts are now in the state hospital, where they are being treated.

"Is this fair that these people should get away with their many crimes? Was it fair that Jesus Christ, the most loving and sinless man that ever lived was crucified? Of course not. But one of the reasons he allowed that to happen was to enable people to be forgiven who had sinned ignorantly or because of a handicap that they might not even have been aware of. He died for all of us. For you and for me and for all of the McHenrys. If we wish to claim the blessings of his Atonement in our lives, we must forgive the McHenrys. We must go forward, with no talk of bad blood or curses. We must close this chapter in the history of Trotter's Bridge and Barry County. That is what Miss Maddy would want as her memorial.

"I say these things, together with my witness that our Savior lives. In his name, amen."

The crowd sat still, stunned. "Now Miss Betty will give the eulogy."

The little rosy-cheeked librarian stood and gave a short summary of Miss Maddy's life, emphasizing her loyalty and discretion.

"For our closing hymn, we will sing 'How Great Thou Art,'" Jon concluded. "The benediction will be given by Alexandra Campbell, the woman who made the discovery that has forever changed our town."

Charles put his free arm around Alex's shoulders and gave her an encouraging squeeze. She had never prayed in public before and felt a great desire, for Miss Maddy's sake, to make the prayer just what the Keeper would have wanted. After the heartfelt singing of the hymn, she walked to the podium, feeling all the weakness caused by her recent experiences.

As she began, her voice quavered but eventually steadied as the Spirit infused her with strength. "Our Heavenly Father, we come before thee on this lovely evening to say farewell to one of thy great daughters, Madeleine Colby. She led a lonely life, Father, and we pray that now she is reunited with her ancestors, she may feel peace and love. We pray that she may learn the tenets of the gospel of Jesus Christ and that she may move on to become exalted in thy kingdom. In the name of our Redeemer, Jesus Christ, Amen."

Epilogue

The day after Miss Maddy's funeral, family and friends gathered around the biggest pond on Jon Cox's farm. Alex looked at Charles, dressed in Jon's brother's white shirt and pants. His face glowed with a serenity that warmed its Michelangelo perfection. With perfect trust, he walked out into the pond, followed by Jon.

Alex fingered the ring that was once again on her finger. Her heart swelled, and her eyes filled as Jon immersed Charles in the waters of baptism.

Everything was new. She hadn't believed her life contained the ingredients for happiness. But she had reckoned without her Savior. She wouldn't travel alone on this earth any longer. Soon she would have an eternal companion to share the adventure of eternity.

Zina squeezed her hand. "Why are you crying? Are you thad?"

"No, darling. So far, this is the happiest day of my life."

About the Author

G. G. Vandagriff, a passionate genealogist and mystery lover, is the author of three previous novels in her Alex and Briggie series: *Cankered Roots*, *Of Deadly Descent*, and *Tangled Roots*. She is also the author of *The Arthurian Omen* and a regular columnist for *Meridian Magazine*.

A graduate of Stanford University, G. G. obtained her master's degree from George Washington University. She and her husband, David, are the parents of three children and the grandparents of one. They reside in Provo, Utah.

G. G. would love for you to visit her at ggvandagriff.com